EVELYN, AFTER

EVELYN, AFTER

A Novel

Victoria Helen Stone

LAKE UNION
PUBLISHING

Published by Lake Union Publishing, Seattle

www.apub.com

ISBN-13: 9781503938717
ISBN-10: 1503938719

Cover design by Danielle Christopher

Printed in the United States of America

This story is for Tara, because I would never have written it if you hadn't asked. Thank you.

CHAPTER 1

Today was the end. It had to be. Evelyn couldn't go on like this.

She squinted against the morning sun, trying to get a better view of the man walking toward her. He stepped into the street a half block ahead of her parked car.

Phone pressed to her ear, Evelyn craned her neck to see past the rearview mirror. "I told you," she murmured into the phone, "I still have the flu."

"That doesn't explain why you keep ignoring my emails!" Jackie Arthur squawked over the line.

The man definitely seemed to be heading toward the gallery as he pulled a key ring out of his pocket and twirled it around one finger. He had light-brown hair like the man in the pictures she'd seen, but sunglasses blocked too much of his face from view. She wished he'd take them off so she could be sure.

The voice on the phone kept whining into Evelyn's ear. "The book fair starts today, and only half the boxes have been unpacked."

Evelyn shook her head. She couldn't concentrate on what she was doing and listen to Jackie's complaints at the same time.

But Jackie continued. "As the volunteer organizer, you're the only one who—"

"What do you suggest I do?" Evelyn interrupted. "Spread the stomach flu through the whole high school? Does that seem like a good idea?" This woman was interfering with something far more important than a stupid book fair.

"I . . ." That one sharp syllable faded into a moment of silence before Jackie's voice turned snide. "You've had this stomach bug for two weeks. Frankly, I'm surprised you haven't been hospitalized by now. You sound remarkably strong."

Strong? That was funny.

The man drew even with the windows of the art gallery and slowed. Yes. It had to be him. He stopped to slip a key into the door and seemed to unlock the adrenaline in Evelyn's body. It surged into her blood, and she went rigid. The edges of the phone bit into her palm as she strangled it.

"I have to go," she whispered. "I'm going to be sick." She didn't care if Jackie suspected Evelyn was playing hooky. Somehow the world would keep turning even if Evelyn Tester didn't show up for her volunteer work at her son's high school. And the kids walking by the book sale with their eyes on their phones wouldn't care one bit if the shelves were organized correctly or not. Why should Evelyn care? Why had she ever cared?

She tucked the phone into her purse and opened the car door.

Last month, she would have noticed the beautiful morning. The crisp breeze. The spring leaves of the tree she'd parked beneath dancing with green light above her head.

But the bits of old Evelyn still tucked deep inside noticed only enough of the scene to know that new Evelyn did not give a damn. She shut the car door and kept her gaze on the small building across the road.

The gallery was a neat, pale square of white paint and glossy windows among the colorful shops of the street. The glare of the sun kept her from seeing anything of the art on display behind the glass, but the work listed on the website was nicely curated. A couple of local artists mixed in with more expensive pieces.

It was a place she might have visited in the past, a night spent sipping wine with her husband among other upper-middle-class couples. She would have enjoyed it so much, she'd have kept her arm looped happily through Gary's, even when he started to get bored. She would have teased him out of his normal distraction. It was exactly the kind of place she loved.

But now? Now her stomach turned at the sight of the sign above the door: "The Whitman Gallery."

Objectively, she knew the name was tasteful and elegant, perfect for a boutique shop, but she wanted to throw bricks at the neat black script. She wanted to write *WHORE* in red paint above it, then break the windows and rend her garments, screaming out her betrayal and grief to anyone who would listen.

It wouldn't be fair, of course. The gallery belonged to Noah Whitman, not his wife. But if life were anything close to fair, Evelyn wouldn't be here right now, trying to learn more about the woman who'd been sleeping with her husband.

Juliette. *Juliette.* A name so sweet and lovely, just like the woman herself, as far as the community was concerned. A perfect blond second-grade teacher with two perfect little children and a perfect husband and a perfect life. And still it hadn't been enough for her. Still, she'd wanted Evelyn's husband too.

Evelyn clenched her hand until the deep bite of her fingernails snapped her out of her anger.

She knew this wasn't right. She was going to give it up. It wasn't healthy. Tracking down every detail she could find on Juliette. Driving past her house. Sitting outside her school. And now this . . . spying on the woman's husband. He, at least, was innocent in all this, or innocent of everything except loving that woman.

But he was like Evelyn, wasn't he? She couldn't blame Noah Whitman for loving his wife. Evelyn had loved Gary for twenty years, and what he'd done wasn't her fault, was it?

She slipped on her sunglasses and crossed the quiet street, too aware of the sharp click of her heels on the road. She couldn't remember the last time she'd worn heels before today. Then again, she couldn't remember the last time she'd shaved her legs either. But she'd gone all out this morning. Showered and shaved and styled her long hair. She'd put on makeup and a touch of perfume and a sleek black skirt.

Her appetite had vanished, and she was conscious of how flat her stomach was now. From a size fourteen to a ten in just two and a half weeks, and she couldn't even be happy about that, because Juliette Whitman was a size four at most. She must've looked amazing naked.

Forcing the scowl from her face, Evelyn smoothed her hand over her disappointingly brown hair and glanced down to be sure the buttons of her red blouse weren't gaping. She had bigger breasts than Juliette, at least. One stupid, sexist triumph to hold on to. A point for her in a sexuality competition. She was ashamed that she even cared to compete, mostly because she knew she'd never win.

But something about this long scavenger hunt into Juliette Whitman's life *felt* like winning. Evelyn couldn't pin down what it was. If she could just ferret out all the woman's secrets, somehow Evelyn would win *something* back. Dignity. Self-respect. Superiority. Sanity.

If she couldn't quite connect the dots between meeting Noah Whitman and restoring happiness to her life, well . . . it didn't matter. Evelyn was going to take her sister's advice and concentrate on rebuilding her marriage. She just needed to see this other person Juliette had betrayed first. Then she could move on.

When she reached the door, her hands were so sweaty that her fingers slipped right off the metal pull. Wincing, she scrubbed her hand on her skirt and tried again, hoping he wasn't watching from inside.

Cool silence greeted her. If music was normally piped in, it hadn't been turned on yet. She took two steps inside and waited in the quiet, cringing a little at the loudness of the door whooshing shut behind her.

The space was outfitted in normal gallery style, nothing original in the plain walls and white display stands. Evelyn had seen this room in dozens of other art galleries, but this was the first time her hands had itched to deface the whiteness. She wiped her palms on her skirt again, eyes darting around to be sure the man wasn't hiding in a corner.

But no, she was alone for the moment, likely the earliest visitor to show up in months. Careful of the click of her black heels, she turned to take in the displays, wondering if Juliette's hand was here.

Her first impression was so unwelcome that her face crumpled into a frown: as a whole, she liked the art.

She could see immediately that the gallery was arranged by artist, each visible wall a different medium or style, but the overall tonality was beautiful. Harmonious. It worked, and it worked *well.*

She'd wanted so badly for it to be ugly. Clumsy. She'd wanted to smirk at the knowledge that Juliette's husband must have terrible taste. Why else would he be so unable to see past the easy prettiness of that woman he'd married? At least Evelyn could comfort herself that her cheating spouse was a psychiatrist, trained in manipulating thought.

But no, there was no smirking on Evelyn's part. She stepped closer to the first piece. An artist she'd never heard of, someone a little too fond of the impasto technique, but he wasn't bad. The whorls of thick paint complemented the emotion of the sky.

"Good morning."

Her heart scrabbled to climb up her throat as Evelyn spun toward the voice.

It was him. Noah Whitman. Juliette's Facebook page had dozens of pictures of her two blond children, but only a few of Noah, and he was more handsome than Evelyn had thought. Taller too, his body framed in the dim rectangle of a hallway door.

"I didn't mean to startle you," he said, a surprisingly boyish smile appearing on the hard planes of his face as he stepped into the room.

"No, I . . ." Her throat was too busy swallowing her panic, and she could barely speak. She pressed a scolding hand to her heart and tried again. "I wasn't sure there was anyone here."

"Neither was I," he said, gesturing toward her with a coffee mug. "I normally have a couple of hours before the lunch crowd arrives."

She nodded, studying his face. The nose that looked too large in photos was actually a perfect foil for his square chin. Why was Juliette so dissatisfied with him? He seemed perfectly nice at first glance.

"That was a joke," he offered.

She flashed an obliging smile, and his own smile widened in response. The pulse she'd nearly managed to tame sped up again, and she felt so sorry for him in that moment that she almost turned and left. She didn't have any business invading this man's life.

"Can I get you a cup?"

"A cup?" she asked, before realizing he'd lifted his mug again.

"It's just plain old drip coffee, I'm afraid. I have an espresso machine, obviously—it's an art gallery. But that thing is a pain in the ass to use."

She nodded, and he set his coffee on a white block that held a bright-blue sculpture of a wave. Evelyn got stuck on the mug for a moment, wondering if it was going to leave a coffee ring, but common sense snapped her out of the thought. She wasn't a housewife here, responsible for keeping things tidy. She wasn't anything to him at all.

He seemed so normal. Had she expected a downtrodden sap? Maybe someone wearing a pair of cuckold's horns that caught a light only Evelyn could see?

Despite the evidence she'd gathered on Juliette, Evelyn didn't know how old Noah was. There was a Facebook page for his gallery, but not one for him. Juliette, on the other hand, took on the modern burden of social media with pride. She was thirty-six. Five years younger than Evelyn. Her husband looked a bit closer to forty, but who could tell with men? They didn't worry enough about others to age appropriately.

Reappearing with another mug, he showed her the tiny packet caught in his fingers. "Sugar?"

When she nodded, he said, "I thought so," and Evelyn wondered if it was the width of her ass that had clued him in. Her curves were probably startling after years of looking at Juliette's boyish figure.

Her brain conjured up an image of Gary's elegant fingers clutched around pale, thin hips, his wedding band glinting in flickering light. Even she knew this figment of her imagination was over the top, as if they'd had sex on a bearskin rug in front of a crackling fire.

She wiped the vision from her mind as she took the coffee and emptied only half the sugar packet in. Noah waited as she stirred it, then took the trash to a can by a bare desk, picking up his coffee on the way. Evelyn forced herself not to walk over and swipe at the surface with her sleeve.

"Is there something in particular you're interested in?" he asked.

"No, I just . . ." She'd worked out a cover story, but it felt far away now. "I passed by last week and saw the piece in the window. That's all."

"The Franklin? It's one of my favorites."

He led the way to the far wall, and Evelyn followed, hands clutched around the mug as if her palms weren't still slick with sweat. The heat was painful, but she didn't shift her fingers.

Noah stopped in front of a large painting. "Have you heard of him?"

"No."

"He lives in Oregon. Amazing contemporary landscapes."

She forced herself to look at the wall of paintings. The one they'd approached was a rising hill of black-and-green pine trees topped by stylized clouds in the distance. "He reminds me of Emily Carr," she said.

When he didn't respond, Evelyn felt a stab of anxiety. Art had been her greatest passion once, and she'd always taken pride in her knowledge, but it had been nearly twenty years since her last class. She darted a look at Noah and found that he'd turned his head to stare at her. Heat rushed to her cheeks.

"Emily Carr," he repeated. "Not just a window-shopper, are you?"

"Pardon?"

"He's always reminded me of Emily Carr, but you're the first person who's said that. I wasn't sure if I was projecting my affection for her onto his work, since they're both from the Pacific Northwest."

She could feel his study, his assessment, and her ego woke from a long nap and stretched hard beneath her skin. Yes. She knew her art, and he could see that. The first person to see it in a very long time.

"No," she finally said. "It's something in the lines."

"Yes, that's just it."

Satisfaction raised goose bumps on her skin. The only thing she'd been good at in the past decade was raising money for the school. Any school. Whichever one her son was attending at that moment. A passion that made other people cringe when they saw her coming. *Oh God, here comes Evelyn to request more money or volunteer hours.*

No wonder her husband had wanted someone else. She'd been such a *wife*. The dull, boring mother of his child.

Noah moved on to the next painting. She followed but stepped back a little. Shoulder to shoulder, she'd have to look at the paintings instead of him, but from here she could let her eyes measure his shoulders and his back and thighs, because there was a mystery in his body parts and she needed to solve it.

He seemed so normal. Approachable and warm. A man satisfied with his work and his life. Seeing him in person created more questions than answers. Did Juliette hate him? Or did she love him but still wanted other men?

He wasn't as trim and fit as Gary—the blue chambray button-down Noah wore couldn't quite hide the slight softness of his belly—but he was still an attractive man. Confident. At ease.

Despite Gary's six-pack, earned in his daily sixty-minute workout in their home gym, there was a stiffness in his body that didn't project as much strength as Noah Whitman's solidness. So what had Juliette seen in Evelyn's husband? Had she just wanted something different? Some manicured perfection to contrast with Noah's hairier forearms?

Evelyn stared at his arms, at the golden hair and the thick wrists and the fingers that didn't so much taper as simply end. She suddenly wondered if the rest of him was like that. Thick and blunt.

The silence hit her at the same moment as that shocking thought. She jerked her gaze from his fingers and found him watching her, lips parted as if he'd just stopped speaking, brown eyes still warm with a question he'd asked and she hadn't answered.

She wanted to stammer out an excuse for why she'd been staring at him instead of the painting, but there was no excuse. And maybe he didn't need one, because he turned, putting his back to his beloved paintings and facing her instead. "Are you an artist?" he asked.

"No!" The word jumped from her lips, sounding like alarm. "I mean, I used to paint, but I was just an art history major, really. A useless degree." She realized she'd tossed an insult in his face and waved a shaking hand in denial. "I mean, unless you want to run a gallery, of course. Then it's extremely useful. Clearly."

Luckily he laughed, and the sound was as rich and sturdy as the rest of him. "I have a degree in geology. You don't have to explain."

"Geology?" She meant to gesture toward the painting, but her nerves made her muscles dumb. Coffee sloshed over the rim of her mug onto her shirt. She gasped at the heat of it but shook her head at his murmur of concern.

"It's fine," she said, but he'd already taken her elbow to rush her toward the desk. He pulled open a drawer and grabbed a box of Kleenex.

"There's a bathroom in the back," he said as he shoved tissues into her hand. "If you're burned—"

"I'm not," she said, though her skin stung. "I'm only clumsy."

The dark stain marred two inches of her shirt just below her right breast. She pressed the tissue to the fabric, and now she was aware that she'd emphasized her breast, the outline a stark curve above her hand. She jerked the tissue away and crumpled it.

"No one's ever reacted to my geology degree with horror before."

She glanced up to find him smiling at her, and he looked so kind. She wondered then if she'd come here to tell him the truth. Not just about his marriage, but the darker, more dangerous truth about what his monstrous wife had done. Why else had she been so determined to visit his gallery? Why else had it felt like the last piece of the puzzle?

The shirt clung to her skin, the fabric cold and awful now, a wet stain against her warm body. A mark.

"Are you sure you're good?" he asked.

And maybe she was good, because Evelyn couldn't tell this happy man what she knew. Maybe she was better than she'd thought.

"I'm sorry," she bit out as tears welled suddenly in her eyes.

"Hey," he said, but if he added anything else, she couldn't hear it over her heels as she rushed toward the door, away from him, away from the bomb she'd thought to drop in his lovely life.

What the hell was she doing here?

She ran to her car and fumbled with the door, glancing over her shoulder to be sure he hadn't followed. He hadn't, but he stood in front of the gallery, watching. A tissue was still clutched in the hand he'd raised to his forehead to shield the sun, and his mouth had gone tense with concern.

She'd been mad to come here, but when she met his gaze, the dark jolt of emotion that hit her body wasn't regret. It was recognition. They were connected, she and Noah, connected by her husband and his wife and linked forever by one awful, irrevocable night.

And Evelyn could never tell him anything about it.

CHAPTER 2
BEFORE

Evelyn was dreaming of birds when he called. A flock of blackbirds bursting up from a field. An ominous sight, but beautiful, and then the birds scattered like leaves when the phone screamed.

She had the impression that it had been ringing for a long time, but that couldn't be right. The machine would have picked up.

Her hand found the cordless phone in the dark. She expected it to be heavy for some reason and knocked it too hard into her temple when she answered. "Hello?"

"I need you to drive the Range Rover out to Old Highway 23."

Evelyn frowned, her ears buzzing from the sleeping pill. "What? Gary?"

"Wake up, Evelyn!" The snap of his words cut through the hum.

She tried to sit up, but gravity felt odd. "What time is it?"

"It's almost eleven. Get dressed and get out here. Please." His voice was tight and low, and the words bent strangely through her drugged mind.

"To Highway 23?"

"*Old* Highway 23," he corrected. "Take White Oak to get here."

Her mind began to work, lurching forward in sluggish inches. She rubbed her eyes. "Is something wrong?"

"Yes, I've had a . . . minor mishap. I think the car is fine. I just need you to get out here and get me out of this ditch. Quickly. Please."

"Oh, God." Fear finally dissipated most of the haze, and she swung her legs to the side and sat up. "Okay. Just stay right there. I'll be there in fifteen minutes. Are you all right?"

"I'm fine. Remember, White Oak Road, then take a right. Hurry."

He hung up, and Evelyn sat on the bed for a moment, staring at the slashes of moonlight that crept past the blinds.

Hurry. She tried to get the urgency in her brain to reach her limbs. Gary had prescribed this new sleeping pill only two months before, and she hadn't realized until now just how strong it was. But no time for a coffee. He might be hurt.

"He isn't hurt," she said, the words disturbingly far from her ears. If he'd been hurt, he would've called an ambulance. He just needed help out of a ditch.

She managed to stand and shuffle toward the closet. She pulled off her nightgown and struggled into the yoga pants and sweatshirt she'd been wearing earlier. By the time she made it to the kitchen for her purse, she was feeling alert enough to drive. Almost.

At the door to the garage, she stopped and spun back toward the kitchen to grab a bottle of water from the fridge. A delay, yes, but the right decision. The icy water perked her up, and she hurried to the Range Rover and backed out of the garage.

As she swung around the curve of the drive, her headlights illuminated the garage door that hid her son's car. Maybe she should have told Cameron where she was going. But no. He'd get in touch if he noticed she was gone. She pulled away.

Ten minutes into the drive, she turned onto White Oak and relaxed her death grip on the steering wheel. The houses were on five-acre lots here, and there wasn't much traffic. She could worry less about passing a cop in her impaired state and more about what she'd find ahead.

If the BMW was damaged, Gary would be in a foul mood for days, and today was Thursday, which meant he'd be grumpy all weekend. Great.

Maybe she could get him to go golfing at that new course the next county over so she could have the house to herself for most of Sunday. Well, to herself except for Cameron, but at seventeen it wasn't as if he spent a lot of time in her space. He had his own car. His own life. She hadn't quite gotten used to that yet, but she was trying her best. He'd be off to MIT in a few short months, and that would be a much more brutal adjustment.

The streetlights tapered off until White Oak was a black ribbon in the night, and Evelyn's brain finally pushed an important question to the forefront: Why had Gary been driving on Old Highway 23? His office was miles past it, and this far north, Old 23 was nothing but a two-lane road tunneling through patches of forest and wetland until it hit the next suburb ten miles away.

She reached the deserted intersection and took a right as instructed. Two minutes later, her headlights flashed off something reflective on the left side of the road. Evelyn slowed and watched a silhouette walk out onto the blacktop. When the headlights caught him, she breathed a sigh of relief. Gary looked fine. A little rumpled, but not even limping. She pulled up next to him.

"Gary," she gasped as she lowered the window and reached for his hand. "What happened?"

"A deer." He gave her fingers only a brief squeeze before he pulled his hand away and scrubbed it over his face.

"Did you hit it?"

"No, but I probably should have. Turn around and pull past the car. I've got a rope in the emergency kit."

Of course he had rope. He was always meticulously prepared. Never caught by surprise. Except by that damn deer. She bit back a random smile and made a very careful three-point turn, aware of the soft shoulder and the ditch beyond. A cool green swamp smell drifted up from the wet woods past her headlights. Shivering in the cold, she wished now that she'd grabbed a jacket instead of water. In fact, she wished she were still under her down duvet, sleeping right through the ringing phone. He could have called a tow truck.

The interior lights clicked on around her when Gary opened the back hatch. Evelyn blinked stupidly before she climbed out to help. Her legs were thick and clumsy as she rounded the SUV.

"Get back in the car," Gary ordered. "We need to do this quickly."

"Why?" she asked.

He snatched the rope from the hidden well where the jack was stored. His voice went harsh. *"Why?"*

She glanced toward the BMW sitting pale and lifeless in the ditch as if it were hiding. "Have you been drinking?"

"Christiansen and I had a couple of Scotches. Just get back in the car."

"Why are you being so rude?"

He blew air through his teeth and crouched down to tie a knot around the hitch. "I'm sorry. I'm a little freaked out about the accident."

Jaw clenched in irritation, she stared at him until he looked up.

"Maybe you could be understanding. I thought I was dead there for a minute."

Fine. She tipped her chin in acknowledgment and climbed back behind the wheel. She'd probably be snappy too if she were worried about a DUI arrest.

Then again, she should be worrying about a DUI for herself, shouldn't she? Anytime she stopped concentrating, the world went a little fuzzy at the edges. She'd never had to function after taking one of the new pills. They were strong. She wanted to go back to sleep right here.

But at least now she understood why he'd called her and not a tow truck or the police. Dr. Gary Tester could not be arrested for drunk driving. That would be quite a black mark on his prestigious psychiatry practice. She watched in the side mirror as he dragged the rope down the steep ditch toward the BMW.

Though it would add to his grumpiness, she felt a deep burn of satisfaction that he was likely ruining a pair of four-hundred-dollar shoes in the mud and water. He'd become persnickety in middle age. He liked being better than everyone else. She hoped his loafers stank of swamp now.

Not a very generous thought when she should be thankful he hadn't been hurt or killed. If she remembered this in the morning, she'd blame it on the pills.

A few seconds later a car door closed, and the headlights of the BMW came on. "All right!" he shouted. "Easy!"

Evelyn put the SUV in gear and crept forward. She felt the resistance of the rope pulling taut, then nothing. The Range Rover didn't move at all. She hit the gas, and the engine roared.

"Try a lower gear!"

Right. Evelyn shifted down and tried again. The SUV roared and the BMW's engine hit a high pitch, and both vehicles began to move.

"Thank God," she muttered, getting a little more confident with the gas. The BMW lurched up the side of the ditch and crawled onto the road. She saw him wave, and stopped.

Gary walked between the two vehicles and quickly untied the knots. "Okay," he said as he lifted the hatch and shoved the rope inside. "Get going. I'll be home in a few minutes."

"You're welcome," she answered.

His eyes rose to meet hers in the rearview mirror. "Thank you." She held his gaze for a second longer before a blur of motion behind him made her jump. Gary straightened, and there was a ghost at his side. A pretty ghost dressed in gauzy white, her pale hair floating around her shoulders.

He closed the rear door and reached to steady the ghost's shoulders, but the figure jerked back, her arms flying up to fend off his touch, and she wasn't a ghost at all. She was a blond woman in a white sweater, and she shoved at Gary's hands and barked, "Don't touch me," loudly enough for Evelyn to hear.

Gary glanced up at the rearview mirror again. Evelyn stared at him, dumbfounded.

Or just dumb. Too woozy to puzzle out this strange woman from the woods.

"Gary?" she asked, as if he could hear her from back there. But maybe he could, because he said something to the woman and circled around to the driver's side of the Range Rover. Evelyn watched the woman get into the passenger side of the BMW and slam the door.

"Go home," Gary said.

"Who is that?" Evelyn asked in a low voice, still watching the mirror.

"A patient. I'm driving her home."

"A patient," she repeated.

"I have to take her home. Her car broke down at my office."

She turned her head to look at him, the muscles in her neck screaming as if she'd asked them to perform the impossible. Two spots of color burned high on Gary's cheekbones. "A patient," she said one more time.

"Yes. Go back to bed. We'll talk in the morning when you're not high."

"High?" she yelped. "You gave me that prescription!"

"So I know exactly the effect it's having on you. You can't think straight."

"I can think straight enough to know you're not with a patient at eleven at night!" Her hands burned from gripping the steering wheel. She twisted them harder into the leather. "I'm not *that* damn high."

"Oh, for godssake, Evelyn. If this were anything untoward, would I have called my *wife*?"

She opened her mouth to counter him. To call him out for a ridiculous lie. But her jaw hung there, her brain stunned into stupidity. Because he was right, wasn't he? Even with a car in the ditch, he could've just called a taxi. If the cops found his car in the morning, he would've said a deer had run him off the road. Without a blood alcohol level, there was no proof of impaired driving, no crime. He hadn't needed to involve his wife.

He glanced down the road. "Please, let's get out of here before someone finds us."

"All right," she said, her voice sounding very far away again.

Gary patted the car door as if that resolved everything. His wedding ring ticked hard against the metal. "Go." He softened the word with a smile.

Go.

So she went, head aching from the tightness of her brow. She drove away and watched his headlights get smaller and smaller in the night. Her bed was waiting, and she was so damn tired.

CHAPTER 3
AFTER

This was crazy. The craziest thing she'd done yet. There was no reason for her to return to the Whitman Gallery, not after her ignominious exit the day before.

If she'd walked out like a reasonable person, made an excuse, then she could've walked back in just as calmly: "Hello! I wanted to take another look at that Franklin piece!" or "Silly me, I forgot to ask about local artists yesterday." But now what could she say? Noah Whitman would likely hit the panic button on his alarm system when he saw her coming.

Or maybe he wouldn't. He'd seemed friendly. Genuine. And there was a connection between them, even if he didn't know why. He'd recognized that she'd been searching for something. He'd watched her leave as if he were concerned for her.

Then again, maybe that look of concern had been for himself.

She parked farther down the street this time, in case she changed her mind and stayed in the car. A man with a tiny dog emerged from a nearby door, carrying an insulated cup. A bumper sticker in the store window let her know that friends didn't let friends drink Starbucks.

Evelyn snorted. Yet another little espresso place that hated that cruel caffeine behemoth. Evelyn couldn't understand the hostility. Did they think people in podunk towns would have developed a taste for iced lattes without Starbucks on their grocery shelves? This place owed its very existence to Starbucks.

The frown she felt coming on died before it could fully form, because the coffee shop offered the perfect excuse. She could take Noah a cup of coffee. An apology for spilling the cup he'd brought her. A transparent apology, but if he suspected she was interested in more than the art, what did she care? She was interested in his whole life.

But she shouldn't be. She'd promised herself she was done with all this. That she was ready to let go of her anger. Work on her marriage. But now it didn't seem so simple.

Noah Whitman had stayed with her all day after she'd fled his gallery. He'd stepped along beside her through her grocery shopping and house cleaning. He'd sat at the dinner table with her while her son texted his friends and her husband read his medical journals. He'd floated through her mind after she'd taken her sleeping pill. Only for a few minutes, of course. Then everything had gone comfortingly black.

Was he as clueless as Evelyn had been? Did he love his wife? Did he think everything in his marriage was just fine? He probably had no idea what evil his spouse was capable of. Noah was the mirror image of Evelyn—the innocent, ignorant partner—and just talking to him had brought her comfort. He was handsome, successful, and kind, and he'd been betrayed and lied to, just as she had.

It felt natural to return to his gallery to see him again, but she knew that didn't make it right. If anything, it was a warning that she was truly obsessed with the subject of Juliette and anything that involved her.

Evelyn cleared her throat in an attempt to dislodge the feeling that she was doing something very wrong. After all, wasn't it serendipity that she'd parked right here next to this little espresso place? A good sign. She grabbed her purse and got out of her vehicle before the doubts could settle into place again.

A few minutes later, two cappuccinos in hand, she walked toward the gallery, eyes on the door. She could move faster today in her black boots. Fast enough that her doubts nipped at her heels but didn't catch up.

Yesterday's sleek outfit was the only business attire she owned that still fit well, so today she'd gone casual in skinny jeans, boots, and a long tunic sweater that hid the middle-aged softness of her abdomen. Yesterday she'd been dressed for battle. Today she'd dressed to show she was no danger.

The door of the gallery opened when she was ten feet away, and Evelyn wasn't ready. She nearly panicked, but then Noah stepped out, hand raised in greeting. "You're back," he called, offering a smile that made it clear he wasn't afraid.

Evelyn smiled back in utter relief. "I brought a peace offering," she said, holding out one cup as she met him at the door.

"I didn't know we were at war."

"More of an apology, then. That was . . ." He took the cup and waved her in. She met his eyes as she passed. "I'm really, truly sorry."

"Come on. No apology necessary. It's good to be affected by art. Isn't that what it's for?"

"I suppose. I guess I've been having a bad month. I just wanted to return and offer a little reassurance. You don't have to lie awake at night worrying that you'd hosted a crazy woman in your gallery."

"It's no problem. I think I could take you if you turned on me." He winked, and Evelyn laughed. She actually *laughed*, as if this weren't a terrible, screwed-up situation. Another sign that returning had been the right decision. "But I do appreciate the coffee," he added, touching his cup to hers in a toast. "Cheers."

"Cheers," she answered, still smiling as she tipped the cup to her mouth.

"I'm Noah, by the way."

"Evelyn," she responded.

"Well, Evelyn, your timing is perfect. I was just going to switch out the display pieces in the window. Want to help me choose?"

Of all the scenarios that had been tumbling through her mind all day, this hadn't been one of them. "Seriously?"

"Sure. I'm all on my own here. It'd be great to have another eye."

"But I . . ." *But I'm not qualified. I'm just a housewife. I'm nobody. I'm losing my mind.*

He watched her expectantly. *Expectantly.* Like he really wanted her there and hoped she'd say yes. When was the last time someone had truly wanted something from her? "I'd love to," she heard herself say, and she was rewarded with a wide smile. His eyes crinkled. They were dark brown and so much warmer than her husband's blue.

"Come on. Let's finish our tour so you know what you're working with."

"All right, but I'll warn you, I can be a little opinionated about art."

"That sounds perfect."

Her body flushed with pure pleasure, and for the first time in so long, Evelyn's world settled, and she was calm.

CHAPTER 4

BEFORE

A soft rumble emanated from the kitchen floor, vibrating up through Evelyn's heels, tightening her body as each second passed. She could feel the jolt of Gary's feet hitting the treadmill, a steady beat like a heart. Or perhaps it was more like the march of a faraway army coming closer.

As she stared into her cup of coffee, the whir of the treadmill stopped. When the shower in the exercise room's bathroom wheezed to life, she knew Gary thought she was still sleeping. He planned to shower down here, then sneak out before seven.

Usually he made a big show of turning on lights in the bedroom and opening and shutting doors, letting her know that he found her tendency to sleep late irritating. Some mornings she could feel his irritation tipping more toward contempt. But she hadn't slept late today. The excitement of the night must have worked some of the drugs out of her system. She'd woken with a gasp at 6 a.m., with no fuzziness muffling her thoughts.

Her husband was cheating on her.

What had been merely a wisp of an idea the night before was crystal clear in the morning light. Her husband was cheating, and Evelyn's calm, cozy world was about to fracture in some way. She didn't know how yet, but what she'd built here was done.

The sound of water rushing through pipes stopped with a suddenness that left her ears ringing in the silence. She got up and dumped her cold coffee into the sink. Her stomach was too sour for it anyway.

When she leaned against the counter and closed her eyes, that ghost woman appeared from the woods, blond and beautiful and slim. Gary touched her, his hands on her shoulders as if he'd touched her a hundred times before. As if he'd spent hours touching her.

Tears burned behind Evelyn's eyelids. They scorched her throat, her chest. She was flooded with acid. She couldn't breathe or swallow. A door opened down the hall. She shook her head. She didn't want to have this conversation. She never wanted to have it.

For a moment, the possibility blossomed. She didn't have to say anything. Didn't have to demand answers. She could pretend her medication had erased all but the most basic details from her mind. The car, the road, the deer, the end.

His footsteps came closer, hard-soled shoes on natural stone tile, clack, clack, clacking until they stopped abruptly and that ringing silence returned.

"Evelyn?"

For that one moment, he sounded vulnerable. She'd caught him off guard, exposed, and those three startled syllables made him sound more like the boy she'd fallen in love with than he had in years.

Yes, he'd been cocky even at twenty-six, but he'd been less certain, still unsure of his place in a new residency program. Years later, when she'd realized his confidence was actually arrogance, she'd forgiven him that flaw, hadn't she? Didn't that mean she deserved his respect and love and fidelity?

"What are you doing up?" he asked, that old annoyance with the world seeping back into his voice.

She opened her eyes and faced him. "Who is she?"

His mouth twitched as if he'd caught a whiff of something rancid. She was ruining his plan for the morning. "I told you. She's a patient."

"A beautiful patient."

That twitch again. "I suppose."

"A beautiful patient you were having dinner with."

"No. I was having dinner with Dr. Christiansen. You knew that. A patient called, in crisis. She was panicked. Demanding to see me."

Evelyn frowned, some of her righteous anger slipping away. Could that be the truth? "You don't see patients after hours. You haven't for years."

"What else could I do? She was in the middle of an anxiety attack and already driving to my office."

She felt her stupid, weak-willed head begin to nod in agreement before he'd even finished speaking. But then she realized she had him. She'd caught him. She didn't need to accept this paper-thin lie disguised as an explanation. "If she drove her own car to your office, why would she have been in *your* car at all?"

She expected to see a moment of confusion cross his face. He'd fallen into a trap. He must be surprised. But he only shook his head as if he were disappointed in her.

"I told you. She was having car trouble. Or that's what she said, anyway. I'm not sure I believed it, but she was near panic. I gave her a Klonopin to calm her down. Hell, even after the pill and thirty minutes of reasoning, she was still upset. You saw her. She couldn't drive in that state."

That much was true. The woman had seemed distraught. But had she been distraught because of a panic attack or because Evelyn was there? You wouldn't want to meet your boyfriend's wife that way, after all.

"I saw the way you touched her," Evelyn insisted.

"*Touched* her?" he snapped. "Are you kidding me? I grabbed her to try to stop her hysterics. Jesus, Evelyn."

She saw him gripping that woman's shoulders again and remembered being surprised his hands hadn't sunk right through the flimsy white form of her body.

Evelyn pressed a hand to her forehead. If only she hadn't been so tired, so high, she would *know*. She would trust her instincts. But what kind of instincts made you think a ghost had walked from the forest?

Maybe he was telling the truth.

"Evelyn," he said, her name softer on his lips now. "I'm sorry. Your reaction is totally logical. I was out at night with another woman. Anyone would assume the worst. But I swear, she's just a patient." He moved across the kitchen, his shoes clacking more slowly as he approached. He wiped his face of irritation, and his eyes softened with something like understanding. His favorite Armani blazer was slung over his arm, his graying hair still damp above his ears. It all seemed so *normal*.

Was it?

"I understand why you're suspicious, but it doesn't make any sense that I would've called you if I was with another woman that way. I'm not cheating on you, Evelyn."

It definitely wouldn't make any sense to call her. That much was true. She could grab onto that.

Her hands trembled with relief. Gary wasn't cheating. The cracks that had been expanding through her world stopped their progress. Everything held together. She let out a long, low sigh.

Gary smiled. "I'm really sorry I scared you that way."

"I just thought . . ."

"I know. I should've explained more last night, but I was upset by the whole thing, and you were already asleep when I got home."

She nodded.

"Let's do something nice this weekend. Vigo's?" He named her favorite restaurant, and Evelyn latched onto that kindness in relief.

"Tonight?" She didn't think she'd have the strength. Her muscles felt like rags now that all the adrenaline had leached away.

"Not tonight. I'll be late."

"You're kidding. Even after this?"

Gary held up his hands in surrender. "The AMA dinner, remember? You didn't want to go."

Right. She'd begged off. She never felt as if she had anything in common with the women at these annual dinners. Which was strange, considering so many of them were doctors' wives just like her.

"Tomorrow," Gary suggested.

"All right. Tomorrow. Vigo's."

He kissed her cheek, and despite the way she always poked fun at his ninety-five-dollar shaving lotion, it smelled good. Comforting. Familiar. She tipped her head up for a kiss on the mouth. That was comforting too.

"Can you share the Toyota with Cameron today? I need to get the BMW checked out before we drive it."

"You drove it home last night. Was something wrong?"

"Maybe. The steering felt off. I'll take it in next week."

She didn't want to share her son's car all weekend, but she supposed she couldn't be churlish about it. Gary hadn't been injured in that crash, and her marriage wasn't over. She should be feeling gratitude.

"No problem," she said. "I'll drop him off at school."

He glanced at the clock. "I'd better get going. Shouldn't he be up by now?"

And just like any other day, Gary was annoyed that Cameron had inherited Evelyn's love for sleeping in, which was funny, considering that he'd inherited every other trait from his father. Shouldn't Evelyn be the exasperated one, trapped in a house with two perfectionists?

But she kissed Gary one last time and trudged upstairs to wake her son. She'd drop him off at school and come back to wash the dishes and throw a pot roast in the slow cooker for dinner. Then she'd return to the school for her paid eleven-to-four shift in the office and put in another hour or two of volunteer work organizing the book fair.

Just an average day for her average family. Everything was back to normal.

CHAPTER 5

After

When Noah flipped on the back-room lights, Evelyn found a rather austere storage space instead of the art wonderland she'd been hoping for. Her eyes caught on the nearest object, a square shrouded by a plastic sheet. "What's this?" She lifted the plastic and exposed a white metal stand.

Noah said, "Prints," just as she spotted the edges of rows and rows of matted paper filed like medical records.

"I didn't see any out front." She tipped the first print up and found a watercolor. Not her taste, but she could understand why it would be popular. "Oh," she said then, dropping the print and pulling her hand back. "I'm sorry. I'm poking around as if I belong here." And she didn't belong. Not at all.

"I said I'd show you the whole place. It's no problem. I don't sell many prints, but there are a couple of shop-local events on this street every year, and I have to have something to sell that costs less than nine hundred dollars. Funny enough, those ten-thousand-dollar sculptures don't move at sidewalk sales."

"Surprising."

"I buy prints from regional artists and some of the national folks who are popular at the local art festival. Every once in a while, I roll that stand out on the sidewalk and bring in fifty dollars in sales to buck up my spirits. Now, are you ready to break open some crates?"

The grin that overtook her face startled her. The muscles felt stiff, stretching uncomfortably at the strangeness of such a carefree movement. "Do I get to use a crowbar?"

Noah grimaced. "I'm afraid I oversold that. They're just cardboard boxes. Pretty sturdy ones, though."

"You're ruining my idea of what a gallery is like behind the scenes."

"Yeah, this is as romantic as it gets, I'm afraid." He shoved his hands into the pockets of his jeans and glanced around the room. Evelyn's eyes followed his gaze.

With this second look around, she saw that what looked like gray blobs of plastic were actually covered pieces leaning in stacks against the walls. There were two four-foot-high cardboard boxes near a wall of articulated metal that looked like a smaller version of a garage door. In the farthest corner of the room sat a large table outfitted with all sorts of measuring lines. "You do your own framing?"

"Saves money," he confirmed. "I worked in a frame shop during college. And after. Geology work at its finest."

"You're taking a risk bringing up that geology degree again."

"Are you going to bolt?" His tone stayed as light as hers, and she liked him trying to put her at ease.

"I am really sorry about yesterday."

"Don't worry about it. Let's get to work."

Work.

This wasn't her work. She knew that. Her work was tedious, endless, repeating. Her work was cleaning and washing and planning and ticking boxes for people who only noticed that work when you failed to do it. But as she walked toward the boxes, anticipating what treasures she might find inside, this felt real. More real than any work she'd done in years.

Noah cut the rigid plastic straps that webbed around the thick cardboard. He handed her a screwdriver and together they unsealed the top flap of the first box.

She'd expected to find packing peanuts or clouds of that shredded paper that always fell out of crates in movies. But this was like any other box of goods delivered these days. Bubble wrap and rigid blocks of Styrofoam. A little disappointing.

But then it wasn't disappointing anymore. Then it was the faint scent of oil paint and the promise of three stretched canvases, white edges marked with red and orange and gold. They removed the bars of Styrofoam together and he helped her ease the first canvas free of its prison.

"Oh," Evelyn breathed.

"I thought you'd like her." She could hear the smile in his voice, but she couldn't look away from the painting. Poppies, she thought, though she wasn't a gardener. Orange poppies that were done in such thick, crazed strokes, they'd become almost abstract.

"It's beautiful. Who's the artist?"

"Jennifer Beckenbauer. I went to a tiny art festival in Charleston last year and snatched up two pieces. They sold within a month. You can see why."

She could. The work was beautiful enough to appeal to nearly any consumer, but bold enough to make Evelyn's heart shake.

"She's getting better," Noah said, almost to himself. "And she's only twenty-eight."

Only twenty-eight. *My God.* That felt so far away. This girl was just starting out. Everything was in front of her. And she could do *this*? She was only a baby.

But she wasn't, of course. Evelyn had been a mother at twenty-eight. A wife. A homemaker. At twenty-eight, she'd already been done.

Grief tried to rise inside her. Fury. Horror. But there was the painting, and two more behind it, and a whole other box to unpack, so Evelyn shoved the grief down and made herself feel pleasure instead.

And it wasn't that hard. It felt easy here. Noah talked more about Jennifer Beckenbauer and then about the next booth at that Charleston art festival, where the woman had carved old shriveled-up apples into creepy doll faces. Evelyn was suddenly laughing so hard that tears streamed from her eyes.

They propped the three Beckenbauer pieces on the table to take them in from a distance as they opened the other box. This one wasn't quite as satisfying. More watercolors. That medium had never been Evelyn's favorite. It was too pale and formless. Like her.

After that, Noah uncovered the works he had in storage, determined to give her the fullest range of options for the front window.

She had no awareness of time passing, not until they were interrupted by a soft chime. Noah glanced toward a corner, and for the first time, Evelyn saw the monitor. A small black-and-white screen with a tilted view of the front door, and walking through that front door was all the grief and fury Evelyn had tried to shove down.

Juliette Whitman.

Evelyn drew a breath so sharply that it hurt her throat. She'd forgotten this woman for a moment, for the first time in nearly three weeks, but here she was, walking into her own husband's art gallery. Of course she was. Of course.

But then Noah said, "Lunch is here," and the blonde glanced up toward the camera with a smile, and it wasn't Juliette at all.

"Lunch?" Evelyn whispered.

He winked and slipped past to speak to the girl. Evelyn stayed where she was, knees locked and hands trembling. She'd forgotten. She was with Juliette Whitman's husband, and somehow she'd forgotten why she'd come here in the first place.

How was that possible? It must have been that connection between them, the sticky web that bound them together. He felt it too, obviously. Why else would he have acted so happy to see her?

The girl laughed at something Noah said, and Evelyn looked back to the monitor, but they were somewhere out of range of the camera. It was just the door on the screen, still as a photograph, and she realized he'd been able to see her yesterday when she first entered. The way she'd hesitated and wiped her sweaty palms on her skirt. Had she looked scared? Suspicious? Or had he only seen an utterly nondescript middle-aged woman?

The girl reappeared on the screen just as Noah walked back into the room, a white paper bag clutched in his hand. "Was that your wife?" she asked, deciding that she had to get back to the heart of this. Juliette.

"My wife?" He laughed.

She glanced to his wedding band. "You're married, aren't you?"

"I'm married, yes. But that was a delivery girl."

"Oh, I thought maybe your wife brought you lunch."

"Well, that would be nice, but it's just my favorite sandwich shop. They bring my lunch every day at eleven before they get busy."

If he'd be happy to see Juliette every day, did that mean things were good between them? Evelyn wasn't sure, but he didn't seem inclined to talk more about his wife. "So you get the same lunch every day?"

"No!" He looked vaguely horrified. "Of course not. I have a schedule. Today is Brie with tomato and basil."

"Oh, a *schedule*." She pressed her lips together and nodded.

He ran a hand through his too-long hair and shook his head. "Oh, God. I actually have a sandwich schedule. And it includes Brie." His smile was all charm and wry chagrin, but his cheeks went pink with real embarrassment.

Evelyn laughed too loudly. The sound filled up the space, and then his laughter joined hers and pushed it even bigger.

"It's cute," she assured him as he shook his head.

"No, it's not. I'm going to have to bring you in on this now. Split my Tuesday Brie sandwich and share my shame? It's the only way to keep you quiet."

She had the sudden, strange thought that he could be flirting. That wasn't possible, though. She wasn't the type of woman men flirted with. She hadn't been for years.

But maybe he was a serial cheater. Maybe that was why Juliette was so unhappy. Evelyn cleared her throat. "I don't want to steal your Tuesday Brie sandwich."

"Come on. We still have to make a decision about the window."

"True, but . . ."

"And I've got half a bottle of wine in the fridge."

"It's only eleven!" she protested.

"It's art, though, not business."

It was art. And she was an adult. And she'd obviously decided not to make it in to work again.

But what made the offer truly delicious was the possibility that Noah was coming on to her. If she said yes, she could sit and share a glass of wine with Juliette's husband. Get a few intimate details of his life. Steal back a little of what Juliette had stolen from her. The idea filled Evelyn up with a warm buzz of satisfaction.

"All right." She reached for the bag. "Tell me more about this sandwich schedule."

"You're mean."

"Fine. Tell me a little about yourself then."

He rewarded that with a smile. "Let me get the wine first."

CHAPTER 6

Before

Evelyn fought the urge to unmute the reality show on her bedroom TV. Keeping an eye on the action, she shifted the phone to her other ear as her sister, Sharon, told another story about office politics at the insurance company where she worked. The supposedly real drama flickering on the screen wasn't even one of the shows that Evelyn usually watched, but the editors of these programs were skilled at making the most mundane conflicts compelling. Sharon was not.

Evelyn curled tighter under the covers and made a sympathetic sound as her sister kept talking. It was almost 10:00 p.m. Gary would be home soon. Evelyn had thought maybe she'd stay up so they could have sex. It had been a while—maybe even a month?—and despite the relief she'd felt over his explanation this morning, Evelyn was feeling vulnerable.

"Sharon," she finally interrupted, "can I ask you something?"

"Sure. Anything."

"How did you know Jeff was cheating?" She'd tried to ask it casually, but her sister's silence conveyed far too much understanding. "I'm just curious," Evelyn added quickly.

Sharon cleared her throat. "Well. There were a lot of signs. We stopped having sex, or I guess to be more accurate, he stopped *complaining* that we weren't having sex. He was more interested in his phone. Always checking for emails and texts. He lost twenty pounds. All the typical crap you can find in any article. I'm sure you've heard it before."

"Yes."

"But more than that . . . I just felt it. I suppose it was a shift of energy. *Away* from me and toward someone else. Something was just gone."

"Hm." Evelyn couldn't say that any of those signs struck a chord with her. Gary would never reduce himself to *complaining* about a lack of sex, though he did sometimes make snide comments about how early she went to bed. He wasn't obsessed with his email or phone—he hated texting—and he'd always been in shape. As for the energy . . . Well, she wasn't sure his energy had ever been very focused on her. First it had been school, then starting his career, then the house and Cameron and all the work that went into a successful practice. There'd always been distraction, but she'd understood. She'd had a few jobs over the years, but she'd never had a *career*. His dedication to his job allowed them to have this life.

"Do you think Gary is cheating?" Sharon asked, the words slow and careful as if she were placing them delicately on a table between them.

If she'd expected Evelyn to be upset by the question, she was wrong. Evelyn felt strangely distant from it. "I don't think so. I was jealous over a female patient who called last night. I just wondered if I should be worried."

"Should you?" Sharon asked.

"I'm not sure. Probably not."

"Well, I haven't heard anything. Not that we run in the same circles—"

"It's nothing. Just momentary doubts."

"Okay, but just . . . I don't know."

"What?" Evelyn asked, her body tensing in anticipation of some story that would confirm her worries. Gary at a coffee shop with a blonde. Gary pulling into a hotel. Sharon lived forty minutes away, but wasn't that the kind of distance people went to hide an affair?

"I know how angry I was," Sharon finally said. "How determined I was to kick Jeff out and make him pay. And then I was so triumphant to get more than he wanted to give me in the settlement. But now that it's been a few years, I almost wish I'd never confronted him."

"What?" Evelyn couldn't keep the squeak of shock from her voice. "About the affair?" Sharon had hired the best divorce attorney in town. She'd embraced the fight. She'd been self-righteous and driven and *right*.

Sharon groaned. "I honestly don't know what I was imagining. Did I think at my age I'd meet someone else and fall in love and start over? I'm a forty-five-year-old woman with three kids, and now I have to work fifty hours a week. Who the hell would I date if I even had the time?"

"Well . . . Okay, but Sharon, you couldn't have stayed with him!"

"Couldn't I?"

Evelyn shook her head in confusion. "I . . . I don't get it. Do you wish you'd stayed? Even after you'd found out?"

"I don't know. That's why I said I wished I'd never asked. I wish I'd never *known* about that slut. I'd still be married. I'd still have my family. This is *lonely*, Evie. Lonely and exhausting. The kids are still in therapy, Jeff is already engaged again, and I have no one. All the girl power in the world doesn't change that."

"I'm sorry," Evelyn said. "I didn't realize you felt that way."

Sharon laughed, a quiet, weary sound that brought tears to Evelyn's eyes. "I've had two glasses of wine, or I wouldn't have admitted it even to you. I'm just tired."

"Let's have dinner next week," Evelyn said. "Just you and me."

"That would be nice."

"Somewhere fancy. I'll drive so you can get drunk."

"You're an amazing sister. Thank you."

They said good-bye, and Evelyn found she'd lost her taste for reality drama, so she switched over to the local news, determined to stay up and greet her husband tonight.

Her sister had inspired her. Sure, her own marriage may have lost some spark and fun, but that didn't mean she wanted to be lonely and struggling. They'd almost made it, for godssake. Cameron would be a freshman at MIT next year. That was a benchmark, wasn't it? A claim to success? Their only child was smart, healthy, and ready to head off to a bright future. Evelyn needed to nurture the happiness of this union instead of worrying about what might be missing.

Heck, maybe she'd even offer an olive branch of oral sex when he got home. They could put last night behind them.

Laughing to herself, she unmuted the TV and propped up her pillows. The email alert on her phone dinged, and Evelyn reached to see which parent was sending some excuse for why she couldn't help with this week's homework club or next month's book sale.

It was Heather Smith, who always claimed she couldn't volunteer but could usually be talked into it with just a little wheedling, so Evelyn typed out a polite plea. She was so busy choosing the perfect smiley face that she almost missed the news story. In fact, she wouldn't have looked up at all but for the words *Old Highway 23* spoken in an urgent tone.

Evelyn's eyes went wide at the sight of lights flashing in the dark scene. Red and blue reflected dully off black pavement. A spotlight caught the shadowy outlines of trees. She grabbed the remote and turned up the volume. "Police are asking anyone with information to call the tip hotline."

A phone number appeared on the screen. Evelyn pressed frantically at the remote button that would reverse the story in five-second increments. She hit it too many times, backing up to a story about the funeral of some retired civic leader she'd never heard of.

Afraid she'd push the wrong button and change the channel, Evelyn let the story run, focusing on the coiffed newscasters as if her attention would force them to talk faster, faster.

They finally finished their murmurs of condolence, and the TV filled with those blasts of red-and-blue light again.

"Police have revealed that the death of a juvenile female last night was the result of a hit-and-run. The county sheriff says a passing motorist spotted the body of the seventeen-year-old girl on the shoulder around the ninety-five-hundred block of Old Highway 23 at 11:30 p.m. on Thursday night."

Evelyn's pulse became a living, panicked thing, fighting to burst free of her. Her throat and temples and the base of her skull all felt battered by the assault.

"Authorities are unsure when the accident occurred, but the girl was deceased before paramedics arrived on the scene."

No.

"Her name is being withheld for now, but if you were on Old Highway 23 around this time or know anything about the accident, police are asking anyone with information to call the tip hotline."

"No," Evelyn said aloud, the word thick and guttural as it scraped past the pulse in her throat. "No."

The story was already over, so she backed it up and watched again, then hit "Record." The moment the red light blinked, she regretted the impulse. Would the recording be evidence of wrongdoing? Even if she deleted it, the machine would likely keep a record of what she'd recorded, what she reversed, exactly when she pressed "Record."

Her pulse became violent, threatening to close off her breath completely. She realized she was up on her knees only when she grew dizzy.

"No," she said one more time, trying to draw a slow, steady breath to calm herself down. This was ridiculous. Why was she thinking about *evidence*? There hadn't been any sign of a dead teenager last night. The blonde, as pretty as she'd been, had been thirty or forty, not seventeen.

This was all a terrible coincidence. Nothing more.

She turned off the television and set the remote carefully on her bedside table, then picked up her phone and typed *9500 Old Highway 23* into the map.

Her first reaction to the search result was relief. That wasn't where Gary had gone off the road. There hadn't been a dead body lying a few feet from the reach of Evelyn's headlights, just as there hadn't been a ghost floating out from the woods. It really was a coincidence.

But then Evelyn made the mistake of enlarging the map. Even as she slid her fingertips along the screen, she heard her sister saying, *I wish I'd never asked.* But that wasn't a choice here, was it? This wasn't about jealousy or some personal betrayal. This was a life. A death.

As the roads on her phone stretched out into longer, narrower lines, she saw familiar names attach themselves to the map. Hickory. Then Saddleback. Then tiny James Lane. Finally, she spotted White Oak, the road she'd taken to get to Gary. The road he'd *insisted* she take.

An inch below it, two miles, maybe more, the icon marking the spot of the girl's death glowed like a target. It was just above James. Hickory, then Saddleback, then James and White Oak, all of them crossing Old 23 like rungs on a ladder. Saddleback was the thickest rung, a more developed road with streetlights marching through the night. A main artery meant to feed housing additions that had never been built after the recession. Saddleback was the road she should have used to get to Old 23. It was the safest, the fastest. Why had Gary been so determined to keep her off it?

The target glowed, swelling bigger on the map until Evelyn blinked her eyes and it shrank back down to a dot.

Her heart had slowed, but it thumped hard now. A sick double beat she could feel through her whole chest. Her stomach twisted into a tight, hard mass. Beyond that, she felt strangely calm as she climbed carefully from their king-size bed. It was too tall for her, with the expensive kind of mattress that rose up eighteen inches and stayed still and quiet even when your partner tossed and turned or snuck into bed halfway through the night.

She put her phone on the bedside table and walked out of the room.

Halfway down the hallway, Cameron's door was closed, his room quiet. Sometimes she let herself believe that meant he was getting a good night's sleep, but she knew he likely had his headphones on and his laptop open until two in the morning. But he got good grades and had never been in trouble, so he deserved his privacy.

Aware she was sneaking, she tiptoed past her son. She was also aware of *why* she was trying to be quiet, and that was what scared her as she crept down the stairs and into the kitchen. It scared her, yes. Terrified her, really. But she stared calmly at the door to the garage before she approached, gathering herself to face the quiet horror that could be waiting on the other side.

She briefly considered finding a pair of shoes to put on, but why bother? Gary kept the finished garage floor clean. He sneered at the next-door neighbors, whose garage was just bare two-by-four walls and half-empty paint cans stacked on gritty concrete next to broken sports equipment. Gary took good care of their house. He took good care of their lives.

When she opened the door to the blackness of the garage, she half expected to find Gary standing there, keys in hand, but when she turned on the light, the Range Rover's stall was still a blank space awaiting his return.

The BMW gleamed pale in the sudden light, the depth of the paint lost under the fluorescent bulbs. He hadn't wanted plain white. Too typical. Too pedestrian. They'd waited four weeks for the ice-white model with the exact trim Gary had wanted. Wouldn't that hurt him now? His expensive, atypical paint smeared across some dead girl's skull?

Evelyn had convinced herself at some point between the bedroom and the garage. She knew she'd step in front of the BMW and see Pollock-like splatters of gore across the front. Long hair caught in the grille. A body-shaped dent in the hood. When she walked over and finally looked at the car, she nearly laughed in terrible relief.

No blood. No gore. No hair. Nothing.

"Oh my God," she sobbed, before dragging in a strangled breath. "Oh my *God*." She did giggle then, because it was so ridiculous. Maybe she was losing her mind, suspecting Gary of cheating and scheming and now, good Lord above, even murder. Maybe she was having one of those breakdowns that made nice housewives go away for a few weeks of treatment for exhaustion.

Hadn't that happened to Suzanna Lopez? "A little retreat," she'd said, her eyes shuttered against more questions.

Evelyn laughed harder, leaning over until she had to brace herself on the perfect white hood. "Maybe I just need a little vacation too," she said, the hilarity of it all making the words hiccup out of her.

She spread her fingers over the smooth coolness of the BMW and closed her eyes until the humor had worked its way from her body. Her head dropped. She took a deep breath.

And when she opened her eyes, she saw a shallow wave in the line of the front bumper. A faint concavity. That was all. No blood. No brains. Just a tiny dent on the passenger side of the bumper, almost at the edge. The edge closest to the shoulder of the road.

"Ha." Evelyn managed one last quiet laugh. Funny, how these things hit you.

CHAPTER 7

After

When Noah texted her, Evelyn was surprised, though she wasn't sure why. After all, they'd exchanged numbers so he could let her know when the piece was framed and in the window.

In that back room of his gallery, she'd felt wicked, standing next to him and watching as he typed her number into his phone. "What's your last name?" he'd asked.

Stupid that she hadn't anticipated the question, but she hadn't. Without that glass of wine with lunch, she probably would have stammered and stumbled and exposed herself as a fraud, but the alcohol had kept her from panicking.

She'd said her maiden name immediately—"Farrington"—and watched her long-ago self return to life on his phone as he'd typed. Then he'd murmured it to himself. "Evelyn Farrington."

She'd only meant to keep Gary's name from him. After all, Noah likely knew that his wife's psychiatrist was named Dr. Tester. So she'd lied, and she was so glad she had. The sound of her old name had satisfied something buried inside her. She hadn't always been Evelyn Tester. She hadn't always just been Gary's wife.

It was only 9:00 p.m., but she was already in bed, propped up by pillows, all her comforts at hand: a book, a glass of water, the remote, and her bottle of sleeping pills. She hadn't taken one yet. She'd excused herself early as she did every night lately. Sometimes she was exhausted, but mostly she was just trying to escape Gary.

He'd probably be up until eleven, and she could no longer look at him without wanting to slap him or cry or maybe just fall to her knees and ask why he'd ruined their life.

Tonight she wasn't exhausted. She wasn't even tired. As a matter of fact, tonight she'd listened to music as she'd made dinner. She'd danced a little over the stove. After dinner, she'd even snuggled on the couch with her son, and they'd watched a few funny YouTube videos together. Tonight she felt happy, and before bed she'd emailed her supervisor in the school office to say she'd be returning to work the next day.

After the two hours she'd spent with Noah, she'd assumed that he would get in touch in a week or so, let her know the piece was framed and hung, but he hadn't waited a week. He hadn't even waited a day.

`It's done`, was all his first text said.

When Evelyn saw who the message was from, she scooted higher on the pillows, paused the TV, and cradled the phone in her hands to stare at it. She read the text several times despite its simplicity, then did the same for his name. *Noah.* Just *Noah.* Four letters to make her feel giddy and bright.

She took a deep breath and texted back. `The Beckenbauer piece???`

`Yes.`

`Already???` She hit "Return" and immediately regretted the preposterous number of question marks she'd managed to send him in just two messages, but when he started his next text with a silly winky face, her self-consciousness faded away.

;) I couldn't wait. Stayed late to frame it up, and I'll hang it first thing in the morning. Still need to frame the other two to hang inside, but maybe you could come see the window tomorrow?

She laughed out loud. Before remembering that she didn't care what her husband thought anymore, she glanced at the bedroom door to be sure it was still closed. What a stupid impulse. He'd been screwing someone else and she felt guilty for laughing at another man's texts? She'd do whatever the hell she wanted. I can't, she typed back. I'm working tomorrow.

Where do you work?

At my son's school.

Really? My wife is a teacher.

Yes, I know. She teaches second grade at your children's school, and she stays late to tutor other kids, and she won teacher of the year last year because no one knows she's a whore, not even you.

She didn't type that. In fact, she didn't type anything about his wife at all, which was strange even to her. This was an opening to ask more questions, to dig deeper. But after the lovely day she'd had, Evelyn didn't want to invite Juliette into her bed.

I'm not a teacher, I just help out at the school.

Art department?

Principal's office.

!!!

She laughed and used too many question marks again. What???

Do you have a pair of little black glasses? Because if you paired them with that black skirt and heels, you'd be intimidating as hell.

Her? Intimidating? She pressed a hand to her grinning mouth and shook her head at his flirting. The truth was that she worked in that office in stretchy slacks and comfortable shoes with her hair up in whatever clip was closest at hand in the morning. She wasn't intimidating; she was invisible.

Not at all... she started typing, but then her fingers refused to finish. Didn't she rule over the volunteer programs with an iron fist? Didn't people avert their eyes when they saw her coming? She could be strong and sure when she wanted to be. She could make her presence known. Maybe she should start dressing the part.

Evelyn deleted her original words and went with something entirely different. Be good, she wrote back, or you'll get detention.

She was rewarded with another smiley face. This one wasn't winking; it was a wide, delighted grin that matched the one on her face.

:-D Sorry. I couldn't resist. So you can't come by tomorrow?

No. She had to work. And she needed to buy groceries. And bake cupcakes for her son's water polo team. And try to catch up on the hundred things she'd dropped so abruptly.

Jackie had written to say the book fair had been a fund-raising failure and everything still needed to be packed up and shipped back. No one else knew how to take care of that. Evelyn couldn't drive back out to Noah's gallery just to see a painting she'd seen already this morning. She had responsibilities, and she'd been neglecting them for far too long.

But.

This wasn't just flirting, was it? This was part of solving the mystery. Did Noah flirt with everyone? Was he a womanizer? Was that why Juliette had given herself permission to sleep with Gary? Not that a faithless husband could explain away all of Juliette's heartless behavior.

No, talking to Noah wasn't just flirting. It was also personal justice. A secret for Evelyn to call her own. Gary wasn't the only one dissatisfied with this marriage. Juliette hadn't cornered the market on taking a husband's attention from his wife. Was she right there beside Noah while he texted another woman?

Evelyn hoped she was.

She finally answered Noah's question with a coy response. `I'm off at four.`

`I'm here until seven . . .`

Dot, dot, dot. Those three periods were a tease, a little question that he must know the answer to already. She wanted to go. But would she?

A girl was dead. A marriage was ruined. And the world just kept going on as if that were all okay, when it wasn't okay. *She* wasn't okay.

Despite her promise to her sister, Evelyn wasn't ready to move on. She wasn't ready to forgive Gary. She certainly wasn't ready to let Juliette escape unscathed.

She'd been right about Noah. He was the last piece of the puzzle. But she still hadn't figured out how he fit in. Old Evelyn might have been satisfied to let everything drop and move on, but new Evelyn wanted more than that. She *deserved* more.

A few tiny bits of her awful pain dissolved like salt in warm water as she typed out a new message.

Tomorrow, then. I can't wait.

She spared a glance at the empty space on Gary's side of the bed and smiled.

CHAPTER 8

Before

She didn't drink often, and she never drank hard liquor—but she'd also never accused her husband of a crime, so Evelyn poured herself a shot of his most expensive Scotch. Single malt. Twenty-five years old. She downed it and poured herself another.

Smoky, fruity, nuanced, rich. Bullshit. All she tasted was the burn of alcohol. She wished he was there to watch her waste each fifteen-dollar ounce by tossing it down her throat.

He'd killed a teenage girl. Run over a human being and left her on the side of the road like any other dead animal. That was why he hadn't been able to call the police or a tow truck.

So he wasn't only a cheater and a liar—he was a murderer. Her own husband.

Evelyn had assured herself that she could believe his stupid excuses because *of course* he wouldn't call her with his mistress in the car. Of course he wouldn't! Who would be that dumb?

But it hadn't been dumb. It had been Gary's only option. Off the record. Just a call to his wife. The only witness a sympathetic one. At best, he'd hoped Evelyn would never see the news, never connect the dots, maybe never even remember picking him up, thanks to the sleeping pill. At worst, he thought he could talk her out of turning him in because she was his wife.

Could he?

Hell, no. This wasn't about a personal indiscretion. This wasn't about Evelyn's hurt feelings. Someone was dead.

He was a monster. She was married to a monster.

She closed her eyes and let the room spin around her. The whisky wasn't working fast enough. She could still feel everything.

This was going to be awful. She had a son. A life. A community. A future. That cheating, selfish asshole had ruined everything.

And, she reminded herself, he'd killed a young girl.

She poured another inch or two of Scotch, letting it glug, glug out of the bottle in a way that would have made Gary scream. Her stomach turned at the smell, and she knew if she drank more she'd be sick. She might be sick anyway. At least if she drank more she wouldn't care about vomiting.

Before she could force herself to pick up the glass, the whir of the garage door motor stilled her hand and her heart and all her thoughts. The sound filled the room. She knew it wasn't that loud, but she could feel the shaking of it in her bones, dissolving all her certainty and resolution into sand.

If she got up right now she could ditch the bottle, race upstairs, and be under the covers and feigning sleep before Gary was even in the house. She could pretend this hadn't happened, or at least put it off until tomorrow. Tomorrow was Saturday. She could get a good night's sleep, think it through, make a plan. Maybe she wasn't being rational. Maybe there was another explanation.

There had to be.

Evelyn jumped to her feet and lunged for the bottle, but her sloppy grab pushed it across the table, and when she tried to save it, she knocked it to its side. Bowmore splashed across the table and pooled at the edge. She righted the bottle immediately, but whisky was dripping onto the floor.

A car door closed with a crack. The garage motor began to rumble down. Evelyn stood there paralyzed, whisky falling in a drip, drip, drip that somehow kept her brain from working.

The door opened and Gary was there, putting his keys on the counter just as he had a million times before. "Evelyn!" he said when he finally noticed her. "I thought you'd be asleep."

She should have been. She should have taken her pill at nine and fallen into her normal coma, and she wouldn't have seen the news report and she'd never have known anything.

His gaze fell to the table, eyes ice blue and never missing anything. "What the hell?" he snapped. "Is that my Bowmore?"

"Yes."

That was all she said. *Yes.* More a hiss than a word. But what burned in her lungs was, *Yes, it's your Bowmore, and even though you killed a person last night, you still have it in you to be irritated about a fucking bottle of overpriced alcohol.*

"It isn't cooking sherry, Evelyn! Why the hell would you even get it out?"

Cooking sherry. Because that's all she was good for. Cooking his meals. Piddling around the house. Taking up hobbies and learning how to bake and *definitely* not worthy of single-malt Scotch.

"By all means," he said, "just stand there." He marched over to the counter and tore a bunch of paper towels off the roll, making sure to mutter his disgust as he bunched them up with exaggerated movements.

"She was seventeen," Evelyn finally said, her voice a strange, low croak.

"Who was?" he bit out, lip curling as he approached the table like a holy warrior wielding a paper mace. *It isn't cooking sherry, Evelyn.* He pressed the towels to the table and she watched gold spread into the white between his fingers.

"The girl you killed."

Gary turned to stone. The tendons of his hand strained against the skin, but his face remained scrunched in irritation at the mess she'd made. He stared at the table as if he were having trouble making the transition from stupid wife to criminal accusation.

"They haven't released her name yet." Her voice was working better now, the words smooth and steady, like they were having a conversation about random vandalism in their neighborhood. "They said she was seventeen, but they didn't give her name."

"Who said?" he asked the table.

"What?"

"Who said that?"

"The news."

His tight shoulders slumped almost imperceptibly before he straightened and finally looked at her. "What are you talking about?"

"You know what I'm talking about. You hit someone last night."

"No. I almost hit a deer, but I swerved to avoid it."

"Maybe that happened too."

"That's all that happened, damn it!"

"Then why haven't you taken your car to the dealer?"

He lifted his hand to gesture toward her, and Bowmore splashed her fingers. "I didn't have time. I don't get up at nine and go to work at eleven, in case you've never noticed."

"Ah. I thought it was because there was a dent in the bumper from hitting that girl. Or maybe because—"

His fist hit the table with a sloppy thump. Several dollars' worth of Bowmore sloshed over the edge and onto the floor. Not that it mattered. He wasn't going to wring the towels into his mouth.

"Or maybe because," she tried again, "your custom paint job could be smeared all over her skull. Isn't that what happens in the movies?"

"You're insane," he snarled. "Where was this girl even found?"

"A mile or two south of where I found you."

"Then what the hell are you even talking about, Evelyn?"

She should have felt rage rush through her then. That was how their arguments worked, not that they argued often. She was careful with him and he kept his more hurtful opinions to himself. They worked at it. But when those artfully constructed safety nets failed, he said nasty, snide things and she gathered her hurt up into anger and screamed at him like the irrational animal he knew she was.

But this time she felt weak. Drained. Terrified. She let her legs give out and sat down hard in a chair. Cool liquid soaked into one side of her yoga pants. "Just tell me the truth. I'm your wife. And even if that means nothing to you, this is going to affect me too."

"I didn't hit that girl."

God. She honestly didn't matter to him. She was just another chink he needed to patch up to keep this story solid. Evelyn set her elbows on the table and dropped her head into her hands. Whisky fumes burned her nose and eyes. "Then why were you so careful to direct me to White Oak Road? Why would you care which way I took?"

He stayed silent. Still. The whisky dripped more slowly now, the sound of some old, abandoned building, rain dripping through the deteriorating roof. It would collapse around them soon, and that would be the end of it.

"Gary. Please. Tell me the truth."

He inhaled a long breath. Held it. Then, "I wasn't driving."

"Gary . . ." she sighed, slumping a little more into her hands.

"I wasn't driving. She was."

Evelyn raised her head. "You said she was drugged up."

"That was a lie."

Of course it was. Of course. "So she wasn't at your office because she was having a breakdown."

"No."

"You were in the car together because you're sleeping with her."

"Yes."

She'd hoped the terrible circumstances would soften this blow, but the shock of it still hit her hard. She wondered if the impact was visible around her, a ripple of force as the air gave way before it.

A girl was dead and the police were investigating and Gary might be arrested, but this . . . this was what mattered to Evelyn. That her spouse had chosen another woman. That something belonging to her had been *stolen*. "Who is she?"

"Evelyn . . ." Oh, he wasn't sneering her name now. He wasn't mocking or chastising or correcting. He was pleading. *Please don't make me be honest. Please don't make me tell the ugly truth about who I really am.*

"That would be a strange coincidence," she said.

"What?"

"If her name were Evelyn too."

"Don't be snide." A slipup, but he corrected it with a very gentle, "Please."

"Who is she?" Evelyn repeated.

"She's . . . It doesn't matter. I took her to dinner because I was trying to end it—"

Evelyn snorted her disbelief.

"I was. We argued, and I had one too many drinks. She said she wasn't going anywhere with me like that, so I told her to drive. I just wanted to get out of there. I wanted to get home."

"Home," she muttered. "How long have you been seeing her?" Such a civil sentence. What she meant was, *How long have you been screwing that tiny blond bitch?* Evelyn looked down at herself. At the yoga pants and fleece shirt stretched over the round hump of her belly. She'd never lost the bulge after having Cameron. Even when she'd been thinner, her belly had still been there, soft and striped with pale-silver stretch marks. She would have looked dumpy in a gauzy white sweater. She

wouldn't have looked like a beautiful forest spirit drifting in the night.
"How long?" she repeated.

"That doesn't matter."

"Of course it matters." But then she realized it didn't, because the perfect solution was right there waiting to be plucked like ripe fruit. She sat straight and met his gaze. "I know the truth now, so you can turn her in."

His whole face crumpled, collapsing into a horrified frown. *"What?"*

"You didn't want to be caught with another woman, but it's out now. You can call the police. Tonight. Tell them she was driving. Then we'll be done with this. We'll . . . we'll move on." Whoever the blonde was, she'd be too occupied with her arrest and trial to spend time with Gary. Evelyn wouldn't have to worry about her at all. Problem solved.

"I can't do that!"

"Yes, you can. We'll need counseling, I'm sure, but maybe it would be good for us to—"

"Evelyn, I am *not* calling the police. You're being irrational."

The fury finally woke inside her, stretching out as it roused itself, then clawing higher in her chest. "You're going to risk everything?" she growled. "Your freedom, your marriage, your work . . . everything for this *whore*? And I'm the one being irrational? What if the police track you down? Do you think they're going to believe some story about letting someone else drive your car *after* you've been arrested? You have to tell them *now*."

"I can't do that to her. She has children—"

"*You* have a child!" Evelyn yelled. "You have a wife! Not that we mean a goddamn thing to you, apparently."

"Calm down."

"I won't calm down!" she screamed, but it was an empty threat. A door opened upstairs, and they both looked toward the staircase in horror. Evelyn snapped her mouth shut.

Cameron. She'd forgotten all about him. She tried to frantically rewind the past few seconds to figure out what he might have heard. He couldn't know this about his father.

But he would, wouldn't he? If Gary turned in his lover, he'd have to testify if it went to court. Everything would be public record. She hadn't even thought about that.

The thump of his footsteps descended slowly, and she and Gary both watched the wall that shielded the staircase from view. When Cameron finally came around the corner, his head was ducked and black wires disappeared into both his ears. Maybe he'd heard nothing. Maybe—

"Jesus!" he gasped when he caught sight of them both standing there. "You guys scared me." He tugged one earbud free. "What's wrong?"

"Nothing," they insisted simultaneously. Such an ironically united front.

Cameron aimed a skeptical frown at the table, and Gary leaped into action, grabbing the sopping wad of paper towels. "A spill," he said, as if there were some other explanation for the puddle.

"Whatever," Cameron said. "I'm getting some milk."

Evelyn jumped to her feet. "I'll get it!" she offered, though her son had been getting his own milk for a decade now. He shrugged one bony shoulder and stuck the earbud back in.

She poured him a large glass of milk and handed it over with a bright smile. Cameron muttered thanks and raised an eyebrow to let her know she was being weird.

"You can take it to your room," she offered, but he was already downing it, his big teenage Adam's apple bobbing. What happened to men's Adam's apples as they got older? Did it finally figure out a way to fit into their bodies or did it just get hidden under layers of indulgence?

He was so handsome. Taller than her, taller than Gary, with a fine, wide mouth that had cost five thousand dollars at the orthodontist to perfect, and a flop of brown hair that settled over one eye when Evelyn got too busy and didn't insist on a haircut. He had some of her sturdiness to make him less fine boned than Gary, but he did have Gary's pale-blue eyes. Still, Cameron's were warmer somehow.

When he finally drew in a deep breath and wiped away his milk mustache, Evelyn smoothed his hair off his forehead and rose up on her toes to kiss his cheek.

"Night," he said as she took his glass. He offered a halfhearted, one-armed hug before waving at his dad and disappearing around the corner.

His childhood had been as perfect as any. No serious accidents. No deaths of friends. No bullying. No sudden behavioral problems, traumatic events, or even deep sadness. His life had been nothing like Evelyn's uncertain childhood of depending on relatives to take her in for weeks at a time during school breaks while her mother worked.

He wasn't tough. He'd never had to be. How would he handle what was about to happen?

Her heart seized with sudden dread. What if he'd known the dead girl?

Amazing that this hadn't occurred to her until now. A seventeen-year-old girl who'd died ten miles away? She might be a classmate of Cameron's.

Oh God, what if *Evelyn* knew her? She recognized most of the kids by sight, if not name. She helped them track down lost IDs and pick up school photos and change contact information. She took their forms for ordering graduation gowns and school rings. What if she knew this girl's *parents* and she had to watch them grieve for a child Gary had helped kill?

Worse yet . . . what if she forced Gary to go to the police and then everyone—Cameron's friends, the girl's teachers and parents, Evelyn's coworkers—believed Gary had killed that child?

Suddenly the right thing didn't feel so right.

CHAPTER 9
AFTER

"Evelyn, you made it back," the principal said from the doorway of his office. She'd been out for more than two weeks, but he didn't bother looking up from the sheet of paper he was reading. He always printed out important emails, saying he couldn't absorb information unless he was holding it in his hand. This from a man who wanted to go to all digital textbooks to save money.

"I made it back," she confirmed as she took her normal seat behind the long counter. She was aware of her supervisor, Wanda, watching very quietly from the other side of the office. Evelyn got the distinct feeling she was about to be fired for missing too much work. She also got the distinct feeling that she didn't give a damn. All she wanted to do was drive over to Noah's gallery to see the painting he'd hung. Forcing herself to come in this morning had been an effort worthy of Hercules. She was sure she'd strained a few mental muscles.

"Finally feeling better?" the principal asked dryly.

"Right as rain."

He glanced up then, and his eyes widened over his reading glasses. His hand dropped, the paper fluttering in resistance. "Evelyn?"

She cleared her throat, her eyes darting toward Wanda and the full-time receptionist, who were both watching. "I lost a little weight while I was sick," Evelyn explained.

"I'll say. Are you sure you're all right to return?" The suspicion in his voice had disappeared. Now he sounded genuinely concerned. She tried not to feel disappointed at the return of her job security.

"I feel great today, thank you."

"That's a relief. Welcome back."

She pulled a stack of field trip permission slips into her work space and tried to concentrate on the forms instead of the curiosity of her coworkers. It wasn't just the weight. Instead of throwing on some powder and blush and rushing out the door, she'd applied foundation, shadow, and mascara. Not much, but enough that the other women noticed. And she'd worn her heels, though not with the black skirt and red blouse. Instead, she'd paired them with a sleeveless blue wrap dress that accommodated her change in size. She'd added a black cardigan to tone things down for school, but she'd take it off when she left. After all, she'd shaved under her arms. May as well show off the effort.

It took only two hours to catch up on her work, so apparently she wasn't as needed here as she'd thought she was. Really, what were they even upset about?

Once the lunch-hour rush of students with questions or requests for early-outs had passed, Evelyn excused herself and slipped into the hallway to follow the signs to the book fair.

Her heels clicked too loudly on the polished floors, and she liked it. She also liked the slim black-and-blue reflection she caught of herself in the trophy case as she passed it. Maybe she *would* buy some little black glasses. Surely she'd need reading glasses soon.

A secret smile was still caught on her lips when she turned the corner and found chaos in the library alcove. Boxes were everywhere, surrounded by stacks of books and half-dismantled shelves. In the middle of all of it, like a tornado that had caused this destruction, stood Jackie, a stack of books clutched to her chest. Her wild eyes rose and locked on Evelyn's face.

"Oh, *now* you're back!"

"Yes, I'm feeling much better, thank you for asking."

Jackie's eyes narrowed to slits. "You've made quite a spectacular recovery."

"I have. I'm sorry I missed the fair. How did it go?"

"You saw the emails. You know exactly how it went."

"Ah well. We'll make a big comeback next year."

"And what," Jackie snapped, "is the PTO supposed to do for funds this year?"

Right. Jackie was vice president of the PTO this year. She wasn't concerned about whether or not enough kids were reading books. She was worried about how she'd look at next month's meeting. "I'm sorry my illness inconvenienced the PTO. I'll be sure to apologize at the meeting."

She strode into the middle of the mess and started fixing the mistakes that Jackie had made. They worked in tense silence, slowly packing the books away.

Evelyn should have felt guilty. For her lies, the book fair, and the loss of PTO funds. Any other time in her life she would have been racked with remorse and apologizing profusely. But despite her lies to Jackie and the school, she had honestly been sick, damn it. Sick with rage and hurt and horror. Sick that she was married to a man she didn't know at all.

And as the bell rang and kids began filing past, the sickness returned on a wave.

The girl who'd been killed, she was the age of these children. Evelyn knew she'd be seeing that dead child in these hallways for years to come. And Juliette Whitman wasn't going to pay a price for that.

Evelyn stole a look at the clock and sealed up another box. Two thirty. Four o'clock seemed impossibly far away. She knew her eagerness had little to do with finding justice for that girl, but it didn't matter. Today she'd find out more about Juliette from Noah. Today she wouldn't lose focus. Her goal wasn't to make a new friend, it was . . .

What exactly? What was she planning to do? Expose Juliette? Get revenge? Or just figure out how Juliette had snatched Evelyn's life from her grasp when she hadn't been looking?

What was she doing in these heels and this dress? Trying to impress Juliette's husband?

Evelyn hefted the box off the table and dropped it on the floor. It landed with a satisfying boom that was still echoing through the alcove when she grabbed an empty box and started the whole routine again.

No, this wasn't about looking good for a man. This was about looking good for herself. Her toes ached in the heels, but she felt powerful. Alive. Present. She felt like when she finally decided what to do, people would see her. They'd have to. Because she wasn't disappearing anymore. She wasn't lost in the shadow of Dr. Gary Tester. And whatever she decided to do . . . it was up to her. He couldn't do one damn thing about it.

When she finally walked out of the school at four, her arms ached from the hard work and her toes had gone mercifully numb. She threw the cardigan into the backseat and climbed into the Range Rover. Not an efficient way to traverse busy suburban streets, but she was never getting behind the wheel of the BMW again. As far as she was concerned, it was a murder weapon. That didn't seem to bother Gary. He'd started driving it again a week after the accident. Yet another reason to hate him.

This time, when she got to the gallery, Evelyn parked right in front of it. The painting looked wonderful in the window, the vibrant reds and oranges standing out even on this cloudy day. Evelyn looked at it for a long time, feeling satisfied despite the fact that this wasn't her gallery and she hadn't painted this piece.

Maybe when Cameron left for college next year, she wouldn't return to the school. Maybe she could get work at a gallery or an art museum. Neither would pay much, if anything, but did she really need the money? Whether she stayed with Gary or not, she'd be fine. She could get a little apartment in the city. That was a life she'd never had. The single city girl. The comfortable artist.

The lonely, middle-aged divorcée.

And Juliette would still have all this.

Evelyn got out of the truck and tucked her little black purse under her arm. It matched her heels, and it was only large enough to hold her wallet, phone, and one compact of powder. Her real purse was shoved under the passenger seat, stuffed full of receipts and Kleenex and hand sanitizer and Band-Aids and cough drops and an emergency flashlight and anything else that any person in the world might need from her while she was near. An eternal diaper bag for the eternal mother.

Nobody had better need anything from her right now.

When she walked in, she glanced up at the camera with a sly smile and heard movement from the back room immediately.

"Evelyn!" he said, already grinning when he stepped into the short hallway. "You made it."

"I did."

His eyes swept down her body and she sucked in her belly a little. She should have kept the cardigan on. But his eyes traveled right over her stomach and back to her face. "Driving the teenage boys to distraction?"

That shocked a laugh out of her. "I don't think I quite qualify as a MILF, but thank you."

"I . . ." His mouth stayed open for a long moment. ". . . am going to keep my response to myself."

Laughing at his outrageous teasing, she gestured toward the blank wall to his left. "Are you hanging the other two there?"

"I'm just about to put them up. Stay right there and let me know what you think."

He retreated to the back and reemerged with one of the framed paintings in his arms, then hung it carefully on the white wall. On his second trip, he came back with a stool and adjusted one of the small lights that hung from the unfinished ceiling. The painting glowed. When he finally came back with the second painting, the wall looked perfect.

"I love it," she said.

He held up a finger and took the footstool back. A few seconds later, he reappeared carrying two plastic cups and a wine bottle.

"This is a hell of a workplace," she said.

"There are many benefits to hosting art openings." He poured them both a cup and then touched his container to hers. "You did a good job."

They looked at the paintings together and both took a sip of wine. "You do know I had nothing to do with it, right? You'd ordered these paintings long before I wandered in here."

He shrugged. "You got me excited about them again. This place can get a little . . . discouraging."

Heat rose to her cheeks. She didn't think it was the wine, though alcohol often had that effect on her. "It was nice to help. My place can get a little discouraging too."

"The school?" he asked.

"Yes. That too."

She felt him turn and look at her, but she stared hard at the paintings and took another sip of wine.

"Do you want to get dinner?" he asked.

Her hand tightened, bowing the cheap plastic cup. "Now? It's barely five." She darted a glance at him and caught his shrug. "Isn't the gallery open until seven?"

"I'm in good with the boss if anyone complains."

She needed to get home and prepare dinner. Make sure Cameron finished his homework. Do a load of laundry. Pay the bills. Bake those cupcakes.

"There's a new Indian place not too far away."

Indian was one of her favorites. Gary didn't like anything more adventurous than French or Italian, so she hadn't had Indian in a couple of years.

Screw the cupcakes. "All right. Give me a minute to text my son."

"I'll lock up."

Evelyn assured herself that it would be better this way. She could learn a lot more about this man and his wife over dinner than she could standing awkwardly in his gallery.

She texted Cameron to let him know he could order pizza. `There's $20 in the cubbyhole next to the garage door.`

`Yes! Thx mom.`

`Do your homework.`

`Yeah yeah.`

She rolled her eyes, but her exasperation melted away when he sent a little text heart as a follow-up.

`I love you too`, she wrote back.

"I set the alarm," Noah said from behind her. "We've got thirty seconds to evacuate."

"Oh!" Evelyn gulped the last of her wine and ditched the cup on his small, neat desk before hurrying out the front door with him.

She stared at the desk through the window as he locked up, worried that his wife would come by and see the scene. The gallery closed early and locked up tight. An empty cup on the desk, the plastic marred by a woman's lipstick. Then she remembered that she didn't need to worry about that. It'd be what Juliette deserved.

She stopped to get her sweater from the backseat before following Noah to his car. It wasn't until she got in and buckled up next to him that she realized how unusual this was. She hadn't been alone in a car with any man but her husband for years. She didn't have any good male friends—or any good friends at all, aside from her sister—and a car was an intimate space. His thigh was only inches from hers, his music played on the stereo, and the little details of his life were scattered around him. Sunglasses, a garage door opener, leather gloves lined with sheepskin for the winter that had just passed. And in the backseat, a stuffed bunny and a booster seat.

"How old are your kids?" she asked, though she knew full well that Stephanie was eight and Connor was six.

"Six and eight. Yours?"

"My son is seventeen. Off to college next year."

"Wow. So it'll be just you and your husband?"

"Maybe," she answered honestly.

"Planning on having more?" he asked with a smile.

"No, that is definitely not what I meant."

She'd only meant to give him an opening to talk about problems in his own marriage, but when he stopped at a red light and turned to look at her intently, she wished she could take it back. "You know how it is," she said quickly, staring straight ahead.

"It's not easy," he answered, to her satisfaction. Life with Juliette wasn't smooth either.

"No, it's not. What's your wife like? You said she's a teacher?" Her mind filled in what she couldn't say: *born on August second, age thirty-six, teacher of the year at Oakwood Elementary last year, favorite treat is brownies, favorite movie is—*

"She's a great mom, an amazing teacher. She takes care of everything. She's kind, beautiful. A great mom."

He'd said that twice. A great mom. And an amazing teacher. Nothing about what kind of wife she was. Was it possible he knew she wasn't faithful? "How long have you been married?" she pressed.

"Eleven years. You?"

"Almost twenty."

He nodded, but she wasn't sure what that meant: "That's a long time," or "Congratulations," or "I can't imagine making it that long because my wife is a monster."

One big raindrop plopped onto the windshield just as he pulled into a small parking lot. Before she could get a look at the restaurant sign, the world dissolved into a blur, and the car swelled with the noise of a thousand drops hitting them at once.

"Shit," he murmured. "I don't have an umbrella. I've got a jacket in the trunk. You can—"

"I'm fine. I've got my sweater."

"I don't think that's going to keep you dry."

She looked pointedly at the button-down shirt he was wearing. "I'm sure men are more weather resistant, but I'll survive somehow."

"Am I being sexist?" he asked with a sheepish smile.

"You're being thoughtful, but I'm stronger than I look."

"Then let's just say I wouldn't want you to catch a chill and cut dinner short. How about we wait a moment and see if it stops as quickly as it started."

The small space was even more intimate in the rain. The world outside was gone. They were shrouded in water, utterly alone. She noticed the way his fingers stroked the bottom edge of the steering wheel and forced herself to look away.

"Why did you stop painting?" Noah asked.

"Me? I . . ." She'd already started answering the question before she realized she didn't know. "I-I'm not sure, actually. Life, I guess?"

"Life does have a funny way of happening."

It did, but she was bothered now. She felt like she needed to pin it down. "I painted all through college. And then I worked full time in a bank, just to pay the bills, you know. But I still painted. Not as often, but . . . I suppose it happened when we bought our house."

She frowned at his fingers stroking, stroking the leather seam of the steering wheel. "Funny, because we had more room in the house. I'd imagined I'd have a little studio in the smallest bedroom. It has good light. But then I was decorating the house and I got pregnant, so there was the nursery to outfit and . . . God. I never even unpacked my boxes of art supplies. They're probably still in the basement somewhere. How pitiful is that?"

"It's not pitiful. I thought I was going to move to Oregon and study the Columbia River Gorge. Instead I got married, bought a house. It happens to everyone."

Yes. It happened to everyone. Except it hadn't happened to Gary. He'd fulfilled his dreams. And even if Noah hadn't pursued geology, he owned an art gallery now. He'd created a new dream, and he was living it. But Evelyn? She'd tossed her dreams out with Cameron's dirty diapers, apparently, without even making a decision to do it. She'd just . . . faded.

"I'd like to see them," Noah said.

"See what?"

"Your paintings."

She gasped out a laugh. *"What?"*

"I want to see your style. I'm intrigued."

"That's not happening. I don't even know where they are." That wasn't true. She knew exactly which closet her paintings were in.

"Please?"

She turned an exasperated look on him. "That's ridiculous. Would you want to show me your high school poetry?"

"I'd be happy to, but you can try reading lyrics from The Cure instead. They're pretty much the same, though my poetry came with the rich maturity of a teenage boy's perspective."

"Fine then, look through some of Bob Ross's old work. I'm sure it's close enough."

"I liked Bob Ross," he countered.

She laughed. "I did too." After studying him for a moment, she shook her head. "Are you sure about The Cure? You look more like you were a popular guy. Maybe the varsity quarterback?"

His jaw dropped, and he glared at her. "That's incredibly insulting. I was hip and tortured."

"Come on. You were a geology major."

"Okay, I was nerdy and tortured. Mostly without the torture, though. A lot of the tortured part came from having crushes on artsy girls who wouldn't give me the time of day."

"Oh, this is all coming together now!" she cried. "You're picturing me in little black glasses. You want to see my paintings. This is about your midlife crisis."

His booming laugh filled the car and sank deep into her body. She was grinning stupidly at him. She couldn't help it. It felt so good to have fun. Especially with someone she wasn't even supposed to be near.

"I'm not having a midlife crisis," he insisted.

"That's funny. I think I am." She didn't mean the words to sound pitiful. Heck, she was still smiling. But they sounded sad and small in the gray space of the car.

He went quiet, and she dropped her gaze to her clasped hands. The roar of the rain faded to a drone. The outside began to take shape again, returning them to real life.

"You're not old enough for a midlife crisis," he finally said.

"I'm forty-one."

"You don't look forty-one."

"Liar," she countered, but she forced a laugh. "How old are you?"

"Forty."

"A younger man," she murmured, then got flustered by her words. Letting him flirt was one thing. Saying something that provocative was another. "Should we make a run for it?" she asked. "The rain's slowed."

"Let's go."

She draped the cardigan over her head, vain despite her earlier brave words, and bolted out of the car. She heard the wet splash of his footsteps behind her as she scurried as carefully as she could across the lot.

By the time they made it through the door of the restaurant, she was laughing too hard to breathe and had to bend over to catch her breath. Why was she even laughing? What was so uproariously exhilarating about trying to avoid the rain? "Oh my God," she gasped.

"You move fast in those heels."

"That was pure adrenaline."

"Well, you were right. I needed an umbrella more than you did." He raked a hand through his hair, scattering drops, and God, he looked vulnerable, his hair wet like he'd just stepped from the shower.

"Noah!" someone called.

Evelyn snapped straight, fully aware that she was guilty. Guilty of so many things.

"Ranbir!" Noah called out, stepping forward to shake a man's hand. The guy was young. Maybe twenty-eight, and dressed in very expensive jeans and a fitted gray dress shirt. His short black hair was spiked up in a stylish fake Mohawk, and he had the most incredible angled jawline.

"Welcome back!" Ranbir said. "Is this your wife?"

Her eyes widened, and she met Noah's surprised gaze for a second, then two.

"No," he finally said, his eyes still locked with hers, "this is a colleague of mine. Evelyn. Evelyn, this is Ranbir."

She shook Ranbir's hand, and he led them to a table for two in a secluded corner of the restaurant. Maybe he didn't believe that they were colleagues, but he didn't seem to care either way.

She glanced around as she took the seat Ranbir pulled out for her. The place wasn't like any Indian restaurant she'd ever been to. There were no murals of pastoral India on the walls. The decor was bright and bold, modern-art streaks of color across the walls. And though the music playing was rich with sitar, it also had a bass beat and sounded more like rap.

As soon as Ranbir left them alone with their menus, she leaned closer to Noah. "This place is so *cool.*"

"Isn't it great? It's pescatarian, so I hope you're okay with fish and vegetables."

"Are you a vegetarian?"

"No, I just like good food. Ranbir's girlfriend is an artist, so I knew them before he opened this place, and I'm glad I did or I may not have found it. The outside is a little nondescript." He opened the menu. "I usually just order the chef's selection. Ranbir brings me whatever is best for the night."

"Oh, let's do that. An adventure!"

She regretted the words as soon as they left her lips. What kind of a woman thought ordering food at a nice restaurant was an adventure? The sad truth was that this was the most exciting thing to happen to her since her husband had cheated.

But Noah winked and set the menu aside. "It is an adventure. Ranbir wanted to play with the idea of what Indian food means to Americans. He's becoming a bit of a sensation among the foodies around here."

"Then thank you for bringing me. It's been a while since I was on the cutting edge."

"It's even hipper than you think. Ranbir is also a model. He lived in New York for quite a while."

"Are you kidding me? This is just . . . wow. I'm hanging out with the cool kids."

"True, but we do have to pay for the privilege of getting this close. They wouldn't let us near otherwise. Glass of wine?" he asked over her laughter. "Or maybe a bottle of Indian beer? Kingfisher is good."

"I'll stick with wine."

"Then we're all settled. Let's talk about your paintings again."

She let her head fall back and groaned in exasperation. "Why?"

"I have no creative abilities, so I like to see other people's work. I'm vicariously artistic. And . . ."

"And what?"

"And I think you should get out your painting supplies again. You have an amazing eye."

"I'm sure those supplies are unusable by now."

"You know what I'm saying."

She did. And she didn't like the surge of sweet pain that swept through her at the thought. "What would I even paint now?" she asked. "*Scenes from a Divided PTO*?"

"I don't think PTO drama was what inspired you to come into my gallery. And it definitely wasn't what upset you that day."

A brief shock of alarm flashed through her body. Did he know something? Was he trying to catch her in a lie? "What do you mean?" she breathed.

"I'm sorry. It's none of my business. I don't want to pry." His eyes weren't hard with suspicion. They were as warm as ever. He didn't know anything. Why would he?

Evelyn exhaled and let herself meet his gaze honestly. "I don't understand," she said. "Why do you care?"

One of his shoulders ticked up in a shrug. "I like you."

He liked her. She didn't know what to do with the flare of pleasure his words created, half of it satisfaction that a man like Noah would say that to her and half of it her sick hatred of Juliette.

"And," he added, "if I had an ounce of artistic skill, I wouldn't waste it. I suspect you need painting back in your life. Don't you?"

This wasn't why she'd come here. She'd come for revenge or reconnaissance or just the hope for some answers. She'd come here sure Noah was a puzzle piece that would solve a mystery. That he'd fix *something* for her.

But what if the piece he could fill wasn't the puzzle of Juliette but the puzzle of Evelyn? Her life was more than her husband's affair, surely. She was a whole person, not just a marriage.

Wasn't she?

Her eyes filled with tears. She dropped her head and tried desperately to blink them away. Of course, that was the moment a waitress approached. Evelyn opened her tiny purse as the girl spoke, but there was nothing in there that could help her, because it was too small to be useful. If she'd brought in her giant mom-purse, she'd at least have tissues, but all she had to dry her eyes was a compact of powder. Noah was saying something to the waitress, but Evelyn was busy imagining the way layers of powder would combine with her tears to highlight every fine line around her eyes. She willed the tears to evaporate.

"She's gone," Noah said. "I ordered for us."

Evelyn looked up, and one fat tear dropped from her eye and landed on her hand.

"I'm sorry," he whispered, reaching across the table to grasp her fingers. "I shouldn't have said that."

"No, I'm sorry. It's not your fault. I just . . ."

She used her free hand to snatch up a napkin. The silverware clattered onto the table. Her heart beat too hard as she dabbed at her wet eyes, trying her best not to smudge her makeup.

It took her a moment to calm down, but she finally got the tears under control. That was when she realized that she was clutching Noah's hand in hers. She relaxed her fingers, but he held on.

His thumb stroked over her knuckles, and she remembered the way his fingers had caressed the steering wheel. How long had it been since someone had touched her like she was fragile? Like she needed *care*? Years.

"Maybe I should try painting again," she said, forcing her trembling mouth into a smile. "I guess most people don't cry at the mention of an old hobby. It's not a good sign."

He shrugged, and his thumb brushed over her hand one last time, stroking up between the seam of two fingers in a way that caught her breath. Did he know what he was doing? "You're an artist," he said. "You can be sensitive. It's allowed."

Yes. She was allowed all sorts of things now, wasn't she?

Evelyn pulled her hand away, but she let the pad of her thumb drag over the pale skin of his palm. She wasn't sure he noticed, but her heart beat with panic all the same. She'd felt panic quite a bit in the past couple of weeks, but this time she welcomed the rush of blood that tumbled through her veins.

Maybe panic wasn't such a bad thing after all. Maybe it was a sign that she was determined to keep living.

CHAPTER 10

BEFORE

She and Gary stood quietly in the kitchen, Cameron still between them even after they heard the thud of his bedroom door closing upstairs.

Evelyn had been so sure just a few minutes ago. Gary had to turn this woman in. He had to tell the truth. It was the only way to put this behind them and start over. Now she didn't know anything.

"Explain to me why I should protect this woman," she whispered. "Because it sure doesn't feel like she was looking out for me by sleeping with my husband."

Gary nodded. Seeing Cameron seemed to have had a sobering effect on him too. He looked exhausted now, a few deep lines showing between his eyes as he tossed the paper towels in the trash and gathered up new ones. His motions weren't furious anymore. They were weary.

"She has two little kids," he said quietly as he returned to the table to mop up the rest of the whisky. "I'm not asking you to care about her. I'm asking you to consider that those two children could lose their mother over an accident."

"You've met her children?" The words were as tight as the grief that clutched her heart.

"No! Absolutely not. It wasn't like that."

"What was it like?"

He cleared his throat. "It was just physical."

"Sex."

"Yes. It was sex. Nothing more."

"Yet you want me to help protect her."

Gary knelt at her feet and wiped the edge of the table, then cleaned up the splashes on the floor. Evelyn stared at the top of his head. She hoped her gaze felt hot on the parts of his scalp that weren't protected by quite as much hair as they used to be. He tried so hard to hide that, but he couldn't hide it from Evelyn. Had his lover ever noticed?

Gary tossed the last of the towels in the trash and sat down. His eyes rose to meet Evelyn's. "She's my patient."

"What?" she whispered.

"She didn't come to my office that night. That part wasn't true. But she is my patient."

"Gary . . ." she breathed in horror. He was sleeping with a *patient*? "You could lose your license!"

"If it becomes a criminal case, I definitely will."

"How could you . . . ?" She dropped back into her seat, swallowing hard. Her throat clicked and stuck, too dry to swallow anything. The whisky burned in her stomach and tried to find its way back up her throat. "How could you do this to us?"

"I'm sorry."

"And the girl you hit . . ."

"She came out of nowhere, Evelyn, I swear. She was walking down a pitch-black road. Not on the shoulder. She was in the middle of the lane! She had to have been drunk or high."

"I thought . . . I thought maybe she was on a bike or something."

"No. The headlights only caught her for one second. We had trouble even believing what we'd seen. The road was dark and then suddenly there was a woman there."

"You should have stopped. You should have helped her."

"I couldn't! I'd lose my license, not to mention my reputation. Everything we've worked for, Evelyn. Everything. I got out to look at her. I did. But her skull . . . She'd hit the pavement. Nobody could have helped her. She was already gone."

"Oh God," she croaked. "Oh God, oh God."

"She was wearing black. Dark jeans and a dark shirt. It wasn't our fault, and I just thought . . . why should our lives be ruined for this? Our marriages and our careers . . . I was trying to protect you."

"And you."

"Yes."

"And *her*."

"Yes. Juliette kept driving. She was hysterical. I tried to calm her down, and she accidentally ran off the road. That was when I had to call you. I'm sorry."

Evelyn stared at him.

"The truth is," he added, "that girl would still have been dead no matter what I did."

"But that's not true, is it?" she pressed. "If you'd been at home with your family, *none* of this would have happened. If you hadn't been having an affair, you wouldn't have been on that road."

He exhaled slowly, like he was trying to gather patience. With her. As if she were the one causing problems. "You know what I mean."

"What you mean is I'm being difficult. That I need to be more reasonable about you cheating on me and lying and killing a teenager. You want me to buckle down and help come up with a calm solution to this after *you* dropped a bomb in the middle of our house."

"I'm sorry," he said again, and she had no idea if he was.

"I can't think anymore," she whispered. "I can't." The alcohol was finally hitting her, and she just wanted to collapse onto the table and weep. "I'm going to bed. You're not welcome there tonight."

"And you're not going to call the police?"

She pushed to her feet and stood swaying, staring down at the table, at his hands, at the gold wedding ring that glinted under the light.

Their marriage hadn't been perfect. They'd grown apart over the years, but Evelyn had told herself that was what happened. A normal part of marriage. They didn't fight often. Didn't hate each other. Things were peaceful, calm, steady.

Steady. Like a rock. Or something dead.

"Not tonight," she answered. "I'll decide tomorrow." She hoped he was afraid. She hoped he was *terrified.*

"Evelyn—"

"Shut up." She walked out of the kitchen, up the stairs, and past her son's room. She closed the double doors of her bedroom very softly and turned the lock. Once she was alone, she fell to her knees and pressed her forehead to the soft gray carpet she'd replaced last year, and she cried.

She wished she hadn't asked.

CHAPTER 11
AFTER

For the first time in months, Evelyn didn't take a sleeping pill. She didn't have time for one, because she always took it before ten so she'd have enough hours to sleep the drug off. Now it was ten thirty, and she was sitting on the floor of the guest bedroom, unwrapping paintings she hadn't looked at in eighteen years.

Gary knocked on the door and opened it without waiting for an answer. She shielded the small painting she'd just uncovered and glanced over her shoulder.

"What are you doing?" he asked.

"Nothing." She'd never have answered him that way before all of this, but what she did was none of his business now. They weren't friends. He wasn't her *partner*. He was just her cheating husband, and she was the woman who was choosing to forgive. Or trying to.

He sighed. Not a natural sigh, but a pointed one. "You're not planning to make me move in here again, are you?"

"No." He could sleep in their bed beside her. She didn't care. He politely stayed on his side of the mattress these days. If he tried anything else, she'd shove him back.

"Are you coming to bed?" he asked.

"Not right now."

She felt him standing there for a long while, as if he weren't sure what to say. Another new development in their marriage. Gary had always known exactly what he wanted to say to old Evelyn. Now he treated her like a feral, unpredictable cat.

Good. She wasn't tame anymore.

He left without closing the door, and she was startled at the rage that welled up at that. It was just common courtesy to close a door you'd opened. He wouldn't do that to one of the partners in his practice, but he'd do it to her.

She got up and slammed the door, aware that her anger was disproportional to what he'd done. This obviously wasn't about the door.

She thought she'd been coming to terms with his infidelity, but her rage was back, and now it felt mixed up with disdain and disgust instead of sadness. Was that normal? She knew from what she'd read online that it often took a year to even begin healing from a betrayal like this, so surely some ups and downs were expected.

They'd start therapy soon. Gary had resisted it, of course, dragging his feet, complaining that he couldn't be expected to reveal his personal life to someone he might know professionally. He'd finally agreed, but only if they saw a common therapist who didn't mix in his lofty circles.

Evelyn had agreed to that. She'd also agreed that they wouldn't speak about the accident and they'd say the affair was with a colleague instead of a patient. She'd spent a whole day researching marriage counselors in their area, and she'd given Gary a list to review. He had yet to give an answer. She'd pressed him several times, but it didn't matter quite as much anymore. Her urgency had faded.

She would give herself time to process this new anger, and they'd get to counseling soon enough.

Rolling her shoulders, she took a deep breath and blew it out slowly. She stretched the fingers that were clasping the canvas to her chest, then held the painting out to look at it.

"Oh." She sighed. Nostalgia rolled over her in a bittersweet wave. She didn't know if this was her best painting, but it had been her favorite. Yet she hadn't thought of it in years. How was that even possible?

She still vividly remembered the embarrassment of watching the model drop her robe and stand naked in front of the class. Evelyn had been in classrooms with a nude model before, but she'd never been in the front row. The front had been the only option in the small room that day. There'd been just six other students in the class, and Evelyn had ended up directly in front of the wooden dais.

Even now her cheeks warmed at the thought of how the model had looked directly at Evelyn and nodded in greeting. It had felt so strange to nod back and then blatantly study the woman's breasts for shape and size and coloring.

Not that Evelyn's work was photo-realistic or anything close to realism. She used wild brushstrokes that hinted at a woman's face and form without giving much away, but the emotion was still there. The memory. The belief that she'd been looking at true beauty in the woman's small breasts and shockingly furred armpits and her dark, bushy pubic hair. The model's unselfconsciousness had seduced Evelyn, and she'd poured that onto the canvas, capturing her upraised arms and arched neck and the long line of her nude body all the way down to her thighs.

She'd displayed it in the bedroom of the apartment she and Gary had shared for a year, but when they'd moved to this house, she'd hidden the painting at the back of the closet out of fear that one of their guests would find it or, God forbid, her child.

She'd buried this, the work she'd been proudest of. The work that had inspired her to embrace her love of painting women. Women nude, women with babies, women alone, women laughing. She'd hidden a whole part of herself to fit in better with this neighborhood and life and family.

She had the vaguest memory that she'd thought she should get her paints out again to capture Cameron when he'd been a baby, but she'd been so tired from late nights and breastfeeding. And the oil paints and solvents would be a danger, wouldn't they? If the baby got ahold of them, he could get sick. At the very least, he'd ruin the carpet.

But mostly . . . mostly she'd just been tired. And really, what kind of suburban housewife fancied herself an artist? There were real artists out there, and they didn't use finger paints or work with safety scissors.

It wasn't until her text alert buzzed and she tried to look at the screen that she realized she was crying. The words blurred together into wavy hieroglyphics. She quickly dashed her tears away, hoping it wasn't a message about some school activity.

Are you thinking about it?

Noah. She grinned in shocked delight that he was texting her so late at night. Shouldn't he be in bed with Juliette already?

Evelyn set the painting aside to answer. I'm going to pretend that doesn't sound inappropriate.

HA! Now I'm blushing. I meant your work. Are you going to let me see it?

Still inappropriate.

I had no idea your mind was so deep in the gutter. You seem like such a nice woman.

That was the best part about this. She *was* a nice woman. A harmless, unnoticeable, middle-aged mom. But she'd somehow managed to find the courage to make Noah Whitman blush.

She was flirting with him. There was no denying it now, not even to herself. She was married and he was married and it was a terrible, ugly situation that had broken her heart, and she was *flirting*. Yet it didn't feel wrong. It felt light and happy and right. A sweet reprieve in an ocean of pain. Hadn't she earned this?

She'd been impeccably faithful to her husband for twenty years. She'd never once even fantasized about another man. And who knew how many women Gary had cheated with. She didn't believe his promise that this had been the only time. She'd decided to forgive him, but she didn't believe him.

And she didn't owe one damn thing to Noah's wife. Juliette deserved this. She deserved worse than this.

As for Noah . . . Well. He could stop interacting with Evelyn anytime he wanted. No one was being hurt here. No one who didn't deserve it.

`Is it too late to be texting you?` Noah asked.

`No.`

`Can I call? I'm obviously not great at this texting thing.`

Could he *call*? Exhilaration crashed over her, spinning her into dizziness. Lights danced at the edges of her vision when she looked guiltily at the door. She couldn't let him call, could she? The house was quiet. Someone would notice the sound of her voice, no matter how muffled it was. And then they'd . . . do what exactly?

Her muscles ached with the sudden surge of power. Because this was power. The power to do exactly what she wanted and tell everyone else they could go to hell. She'd spent far too many years worrying about everyone else and not herself.

`You can call`, she typed out quickly, unwilling to give herself time to change her mind.

She scooted up on the bed and propped her back on the dozen decorative pillows that rested against the headboard. Laying the painting across the tops of her thighs, she stared at it and waited for her phone to ring.

Despite that she was anticipating just that thing, the buzz still made her jump when it finally came. She answered with a cautious, "Hello?" as if she didn't already know who it was. Her son laughed at that charade. He'd never lived in a time without caller ID.

"Are you sure it's okay to call?" Noah asked, and she smiled stupidly. "I'm not bothering you?"

"No, it's fine." She pitched her voice low to match his. Was he hiding in a spare room too?

"Are you the night owl in your house?" he asked.

"Not usually." Usually she was comfortingly drugged up. "Are you?"

"Yes. Juliette gets up early to get ready for work, but I only need a few minutes to make the kids their oatmeal and wave good-bye. Then I have an hour to have coffee before I get ready to go to the gallery."

She winced when he said Juliette, but the pain faded quickly. After all, he was choosing to talk to Evelyn instead of Juliette, wasn't he? How deliciously just.

"That's my favorite part of the morning," she said. "Sending everyone off and having the house to myself. It's peaceful. That's why I prefer working in the afternoon."

"Peaceful," he repeated. "Exactly. It's heaven."

"You're not still at the gallery, are you?"

"No. I have an office in the basement."

Evelyn closed her eyes and imagined him there, feet up on a desk, phone to his ear, while Juliette sank into the untroubled sleep of a psychopath upstairs.

"So you haven't answered my question yet . . ."

She smiled at the teasing warmth in his voice. "I'm still thinking about it."

"That's progress. At dinner you told me no. Now you're thinking about it?"

She stroked her hand over the painting in her lap. It wasn't on par with the work he displayed in his gallery. She wasn't that good. "You look at amazing art all day. I'm sure you routinely reject artists who are far better than I am."

"I'm not hoping to discover the next Picasso. I'm just . . ."

She snuggled a little deeper into the pillows and brought her knees up higher, keeping the painting close. "Just what?"

"I guess I'm discovering you."

Evelyn pressed her lips tight together. Shook her head. There was that surge of power again, but this time it was shot through with an awful vulnerability. There wasn't anything good in her to discover. She was just skin and bone and organs. If he discovered anything at all, it would be the lies she'd told him. The barbed and bloodied path she was leading him down. "I'm not—" she rasped, before realizing her throat was too dry and hot to work. She swallowed hard and tried again. "I'm not anything special, Noah."

"Why would you say that?"

"I don't know. I'm just . . . lost."

"Maybe. Or maybe you're not lost at all. Maybe you're wandering. Looking around. Taking stock. Isn't that what a midlife crisis is?"

Was that what she was doing? Taking stock? It did feel like she was making some sort of strange transition. She definitely wasn't the same person anymore. She'd felt that immediately. And Noah was part of her world now, not because she'd asked the Whitman family into her life, but because they'd been forced on her.

She didn't have to feel guilty for trying to get something good out of this horribleness, did she?

"I'm looking at my paintings right now," she murmured.

"Are you?" She heard him shift around. The squeak of a chair. "What do you see?"

"I see my past. Who I was in college. Who I thought I'd be."

"An artist?"

"Yes. I mean, I was realistic about it. I knew I'd have to have a day job. And I wanted to get married, have a family. I just thought I'd manage to . . . I don't know. Stay interesting through it all."

"You did."

That wasn't true, but she let it go. She didn't want him to know how dull she'd been for so long. "And you?" she pressed. "Do you have a secret stash of rocks in your house? Will you bring your favorite geode to show me next time?"

"You don't know much about geology, do you?"

If Gary had said that, she would have prickled and snapped at him in defense. But Noah's laughing words made her chuckle along with him. "Are you saying there's more to it than rock collecting?"

"Yeah, it's pretty much the fiery birth and formation of the entire world over billions of years, all of it recorded in complex patterns of stone like a secret language."

"Ah."

"And yes, I've managed to pick up quite a few supercool rocks over the years, if you must know."

She laughed until tears leaked from her eyes, though she tried to smother any sound by turning her face into a blue satin pillow. "So," she gasped, "can I see your amazing geodes sometime?"

"God, that's sexy," he growled.

She tried her best to ignore the way her body warmed at his words. He was only joking. There was no reason for her to be aroused. But she was.

"Bring some of your work by tomorrow," he insisted.

"I don't know if I can." She'd already thawed the chicken she'd meant to make tonight. She'd have to make it tomorrow or it would go bad.

"Try?" he asked.

Yes. Yes, she'd try.

They spoke about the latest books they'd read and even touched on politics, but at eleven fifteen, when Evelyn yawned for the fourth time, Noah chuckled and said he'd let her get to bed. She liked him saying that, liked him thinking about her undressing and getting under her covers.

Just in case it mattered, she skipped the practical cotton nightgown and put on panties and a silky pajama top before she found her way through the dark bedroom and climbed into bed next to her husband.

Gary turned one way and she turned the other, and she wondered what Noah Whitman was thinking about in bed next to a wife he only thought he knew.

CHAPTER 12
BEFORE

Her head pounded and her mouth was bone dry. She'd forgotten to bring her normal tumbler of water for the bedside table last night, so Evelyn went to the bathroom and cupped her hand under the sink for a sip. She didn't want to leave her room yet. The doors were still closed and locked tight, and she entertained a brief fantasy of staying there forever.

She could hire a housekeeper to cook and clean and run errands. Her family would barely notice. Everything Evelyn did in this house could easily be covered by people working for minimum wage, or for much less if she ignored employment laws.

Cameron might miss the hugs she still gave him every day, or maybe he'd be thankful to be rid of them. He didn't seem to mind her affection, but perhaps he just felt sorry for her.

Possibly the people at school would feel the loss. She did their grunt work, and for nearly minimum wage. And the PTO might miss her. A volunteer like her wasn't easy to come by. Still, there was always someone who could be roped into it. The mother of a freshman, usually. That was how she'd come to the position. Regardless, the school wouldn't crumble without her. If she keeled over today, her death would be a blip. A temporary stumble, even for the people she loved most in the world. Evelyn Tester was utterly replaceable.

After drinking her fill, she brushed her sticky teeth and climbed back into bed. Gary's side was still mostly made. She tugged the covers awry to destroy the reminder that she'd banished him to the guest room.

Turning on the TV, she checked to see if the local news was on, but when she finally found it, they were already covering the weather. The only news they'd discuss after that was sports, so she opened the browser on her phone and went to the website of a local station. There were no updates to be found. No new clues. No name or picture of the girl who'd been killed.

Evelyn wasn't going to receive a sign about what her decision should be. No one would help her with this.

If Gary was telling the truth, then it really had been an accident. The girl had been walking down the middle of a dark road on a stretch of highway with no houses, no lights. Any driver would be caught unawares. Surely even the police wouldn't find Juliette at fault.

But how could she know if Gary was telling the truth? He'd been lying to her for months. Probably years.

Then again, what other story could there be? There were no businesses out there. Unless Gary's mistress had deliberately swerved into a girl standing on the shoulder waving a flashlight, then no one was responsible. It was an accident. So did it need to be reported?

Something inside her screamed, *Yes!* But Evelyn knew that wasn't her moral center. It was hatred. Jealousy. Hurt. Somebody had to pay for this accident, because that somebody had been sleeping with her husband.

Evelyn dropped her head into her hands with a cry of anguish. Why was she the one who had to make this decision? She hadn't done anything wrong. She'd been a good wife, a good mother, a good citizen.

"This isn't fair," she groaned, rocking against her hands, letting her fingers dig into her scalp over and over. What had she done to deserve this? "This isn't fair!"

She gasped out rough, animal sobs and pressed her fingernails hard into her head. The physical pain helped bring her back to reality, and she managed to gradually calm herself until she was panting instead of sobbing.

No, it wasn't fair, but life never was, was it? And this wasn't only about her. If Gary lost his practice, how would they pay for four years at MIT for Cameron? And what would Cameron think of his father? How would he face his schoolmates with his family on the news? Everyone would be talking about Gary's sex life, their marriage, how cheap and sordid it all was.

And the girl would still be dead. Nothing would bring her back.

So . . . maybe Evelyn had made a decision, after all.

She showered first, giving herself time to let the choice settle. She tipped her head back and let the warmth slide over her, but instead of relaxing her, the steam filled up her lungs and made her feel like she was choking.

Was she really going to say okay to this? To all of it? Just go back to her life?

Maybe Gary would bring her flowers. Maybe he'd take her to her favorite restaurant and hold her hand and order expensive wine. Maybe he'd do a good job of being sincere and attentive for weeks, and she'd tell herself he was trying, it wasn't over, he still loved her, they could get past this.

She turned off the water and let her head drop. She stared at her pale legs, cellulite-dimpled thighs, untrimmed pubic hair, and her stretched, striped belly, too fat and white for her to look at long.

She'd used up the best of her body on supporting Gary's burgeoning career, then on carrying and nursing and raising his child. She'd let her youth trickle away like the water dripping from her skin into the dark slime of the drain. Whoever she might have been without Gary was gone now, and he'd moved on to another body. No doubt it was younger and tighter and, above all else, less familiar and contemptible.

Evelyn got out and dried her hair, moisturized the fine lines on her face, put on clothes to cover her never-quite-fit body, and unlocked the doors of the bedroom. Gary wasn't sitting there in the hallway, red-eyed and weeping, waiting for her judgment. She found him downstairs in his study, the same place he'd spend any quiet Saturday. She could tell by the neatness of his hair and clothes that he'd already worked out and showered.

When he looked up, she closed the door behind her and sat in one of the leather armchairs he'd insisted on buying for twelve hundred dollars each. They were as uncomfortable as they looked, the leather ice cold and unyielding beneath her legs. Or maybe it was only that her flesh yielded far too easily.

"Are you okay?" Gary asked.

She ignored his stupid question. "If I agree not to turn her in, I want to know everything."

He sat forward, his hands steepled. "What do you mean?"

"I want to know her name. How it started. What you did with her."

"Evelyn—"

"No. Don't tell me it's not healthy or that it won't help. I want to know what you did with her and any other women. In exchange, I won't send your girlfriend to jail."

"She's not my girlfriend."

"Well, whatever you call the woman you have sex with and take out to dinner and have long talks with in your office . . . I'm not doing this for her. Or you. It's for me and Cameron."

"I understand."

"We'll go to counseling. Assuming you're done with her—"

"I am."

"And assuming you want to save our marriage."

"Evelyn, of course I do."

Oh, *of course*. What the hell did that mean? *Of course*. As if he hadn't nearly ruined everything with his stupid genitals already.

"So you'll be one-hundred-percent honest with me. You'll answer my questions. We'll go to counseling. And you'll never see her again."

"You have my word. It's already over."

"Who is she?"

She saw the way his shoulders relaxed at the question. He looked steady and solemn, but he'd been scared that Evelyn wouldn't agree to keep his secret.

"She's a patient of mine—"

"I know that. I want her name."

His lips parted, his eyebrows snapping down in a frown, but whatever he'd been about to say, he swallowed it. "Her name is Juliette." In response to a jerky, "come on" motion from Evelyn, he sighed and added, "Whitman."

"Juliette Whitman," she repeated, hating the elegant name already. It sounded like the name of a Disney princess. "How did it start?"

His throat strained as he swallowed. "She was my patient. She started coming to me about a year ago."

"For what?"

"You know I can't answer that," he said calmly. So calmly.

Evelyn clenched the arms of her chair and leaned closer to his desk. "Screw your doctor-patient privilege." As soon as she said it, she laughed, a horrible barking sound. "The same way you screwed your patient."

For a moment, he looked genuinely pained, his eyes softening with regret, hand starting across his desk as if he'd reach for her. "Let's sit on the couch," he suggested, but she shook her head. She wanted to do it like this. Like a business discussion. If he touched her she'd cry. She'd let him hug her, and she'd lean into him and be so *weak*.

For all his faults, she'd loved this man for twenty years. And he'd loved her too, once. They'd had picnics and gone to movies and snuck in a late-night round of sex in the hotel swimming pool on their honeymoon. They'd both cried at Cameron's first ultrasound and they'd talked late into the night about who their son would be.

Yes, they'd drifted apart. Life had a way of seeping into the seams of a marriage and slowly prying them open, but things had been so good in the beginning. Gary had been a little older, and he'd been serious and secure and responsible, and after her fatherless childhood, Evelyn had loved that about him so much. She'd needed that. Someone a little better than everyone else. Someone not so casual and unanchored as all the other men she'd dated.

She'd loved him, and she couldn't touch him while they had this conversation or she might remember what they'd had before.

Evelyn crossed her arms. "No. Stay there. And tell me everything about Juliette Whitman." When he hesitated, she lifted her chin and set her jaw. "Everything."

CHAPTER 13
After

Evelyn wiped the sweat from her brow and zipped up the cranberry-red skirt, cursing the stuffiness of the department store dressing room. She was supposed to be at school in fifteen minutes, and she still hadn't found the perfect outfit.

If she was going to stop by the gallery today, she couldn't wear one of the three outfits she'd already worn, but there wasn't much left that fit her. She'd thought she would wear the skinny jeans again with a striped knit shirt, but the shirt had been an ugly, boxy mess when she'd put it on. It had been washed too many times and become almost as short as it was wide. Funny that she'd never noticed until now.

After waiting at the doors for the store to open at ten, she'd spent too much time trying on clothes that seemed as if they'd fit, but were somehow tight in all the worst places.

Grabbing the black cashmere sweater the saleslady had brought her, Evelyn smoothed down the knee-length skirt and tried to ignore the way her flesh bunched above the waistband when she slouched. She wouldn't slouch.

Hoping this last outfit would be a keeper, she tugged the simple, lightweight sweater on and looked in the mirror. "Oh, thank God," she breathed. The sweater skimmed her body closely enough to give her a waist, but it didn't cling. The cranberry skirt was a perfect flash of color between the sweater and her black heels.

The saleswoman knocked.

"I'll take it!" Evelyn called.

"Wonderful! You should get that green blouse too. The color looked amazing on you."

It was probably just an upsell, but Evelyn didn't care. The green had been pretty and . . . what if she saw Noah again soon?

"I'm going to wear it out," she said, tugging off the tags before she opened the door. She paid for the new outfit and the green shirt, shoved her old clothes into a shopping bag, and walked into the school only five minutes late. "Sorry!" she called out as she sat at her desk. "I'll write myself a tardy slip."

She sent emails and text alerts to all the parents whose students had been absent from the first two periods, then helped a sophomore who'd tripped during PE limp his way to the nurse's office. After the lunch rush, she processed fifty-seven permission slips for the annual trip to a local film festival that the theater classes took.

Only two hours into her shift and she was checking the clock every five minutes, hoping to see the little hand swinging closer to four.

She didn't know who she'd been trying to kid last night when she'd told herself she couldn't make it because of a thawed chicken. A thawed chicken. It was such a meaningless excuse that she was embarrassed for herself.

Was that the kind of thing that had been important in her life up to now? Ten dollars' worth of chicken her family would finish in minutes before going back to things they did without her? That was her only hold on them, she supposed. The few nights a week when everyone came home at the right time and she insisted they sit down together.

It meant they were a family. That she'd built something. Or that was what she'd thought. The reality was that she'd had to lure them close to her with scraps of food.

She wished she were home right now so she could throw that goddamn chicken in the trash.

"Evelyn?"

She jumped, and her gaze flew up to find Vonda Jenkins looking down at her with a tight frown of worry.

"Are you all right?" Vonda asked.

"I'm great, thanks!"

Vonda leaned closer and dropped her voice. "You looked upset."

Evelyn forced a laugh for her favorite teacher in the school. She was one of the few people Evelyn believed might actually be concerned and not just nosy. "I was concentrating. Sorry."

"Are you sure? You were out sick for so long. I emailed you, but—"

"I'm so sorry I didn't get back to you. That stomach bug really worked me over."

Vonda patted her arm. "Don't think twice about it. I'm just glad you're back. You look great."

"Thank you."

"Um . . ." Vonda's dark-brown eyes darted to Evelyn's shoulder. "You've got a tag. Want me to clip it?"

Evelyn reached up and her fingers brushed the hard corner of a price tag. "Oh my gosh!" she gasped, immediately hot with embarrassment. "I had to buy new clothes, and—"

"I can see you lost weight while you were out. Here, let me get it."

Vonda plucked the scissors from a cup on the desk and brushed Evelyn's hair aside. "There," she said as she snipped the tag. "No problem." She dropped it onto the desk, and Evelyn saw that it was the brand name's tag, shining gold and black on the desk. She darted a glare toward the two other women in the office. Surely one of them must have seen it and said nothing.

"Thank you so much," she said to Vonda with a little too much enthusiasm. What if she'd waltzed into the gallery like that? What if Noah suspected she'd bought this outfit just for him? She didn't want him to know what a mess she was. She wanted to seem cool and sexy and serene. Or as serene as she could seem after crying every time they'd spent time together.

"How are you?" she asked Vonda. "How's Tyrell?"

They both had only one son, and like Cameron, Vonda's son was a natural at engineering. The boys had been in the robotics club together before Tyrell had left for college.

"He's wonderful. He's really thriving at school. Too busy to call home most weeks."

"It must be lonely."

"Oh, I get by," she said with a shy smile that made Evelyn suddenly curious about Vonda's personal life. She'd been divorced for years. She must date. What was it like at forty-something? Was sex awkward, no-nonsense, or amazing?

But she wasn't close enough to Vonda to ask those kinds of questions. She wasn't that close to anyone except her sister, and as she watched Vonda gather up a stack of papers and walk out of the office, Evelyn wondered why she didn't have real girlfriends. Surely that was odd.

When Cameron had been younger, she'd hung out with other moms, but that had been less like friendship and more of a babysitting club. *If you take Cameron this afternoon, I'll take Cheyenne tomorrow.*

And there was always a strange undercurrent among parents of preschoolers. A competition. Maybe one kid wasn't quite potty trained, but at least he didn't throw violent tantrums. And that other child might know the alphabet, but he also liked to kick the cat anytime it got close. The constant jostling for superiority had made her skittish. She hadn't trusted any of those moms. Certainly not enough to exchange secrets.

Then school had started, and Evelyn had not only been an officer of the elementary school PTO, she'd also been a room mom every year. Busy, busy, busy. No time for girlfriends. No time for painting. No time for keeping up with fashion or music or trendy new restaurants. Life outside the home, besides the school, had been far away and vaguely distasteful.

The same hadn't been true for Gary, of course. Most of his life had been safely outside the reach of Cameron's sticky hands. There was work, of course. And networking. Continuing education. Medical conferences. Prestigious awards. Research. Training for the occasional triathlon. Golfing with colleagues. And sex with other women.

Amazing that it had taken her until now to resent what her life had become. Had she been happy with it?

She would have said yes. Yes, absolutely. But if she'd been happy, why had it been so hard to wake up some mornings? And why had it gotten so impossible to get to sleep at night that she'd resorted to asking Gary for a prescription three years earlier?

Too much responsibility, she'd told herself. Too many obligations, too many threads to weave together. Every month it was something else. Another fundraiser, another field trip, another school event that needed more volunteers. She'd been good at that. Too good. More and more tasks had fallen to her, and she'd never said no to any of them.

She hadn't been able to shut her mind off at night. Instead of drifting to sleep, she'd lie in bed, the hundred tasks awaiting her the next day whipping through her consciousness like weapons. The first time she'd taken a sleeping pill had been the happiest moment she'd felt in years.

Thinking back on it now, she couldn't believe that hadn't terrified her.

Her phone chimed with a reminder she'd set a month before. *Check on tables and chairs for the volunteer awards dinner!!!!!*

The five exclamation points indicated she'd cared a great deal about that message last month. Today, she swiped it away with barely a glance.

The awards dinner. Stupid little plaques handed out to people who'd put in a few hours of work because Evelyn had begged them to. She probably put more time into planning that dinner every spring than they'd put in at the school in a whole year. Screw the awards dinner.

She stared at the clock and willed it to move faster. Two of her canvases were tucked into a tall bag in the backseat of the Range Rover. Her stylish clutch purse was in there as well, just in case. Maybe he'd lock the shop doors and take her to dinner again. Maybe they'd go for a drink.

Unable to concentrate on work, she grabbed her phone and texted Gary. `I've got an awards committee meeting tonight. You and Cameron are on your own for dinner.`

She'd throw the thawed chicken in the garbage as soon as she got home.

Her phone buzzed a few minutes later, and Evelyn smiled, anticipating a cajoling message from Noah. She hadn't yet confirmed that she was coming by. He must be wondering, thinking about it, maybe even hoping.

But a little picture of Gary popped up next to the one-word message. `Again?`

Evelyn put her phone down without answering. It wasn't really a question, was it? It was a complaint. Like poking a miserable animal with a stick.

A dozen students floated in and out of the office with various requests. Evelyn took care of them all without really noticing what she was doing. When the final bell rang at long last, she hopped up from her chair and grabbed her purse. "I need to get to an appointment," she said. "Is it all right if I slip out now?" That wasn't really a question either, because she was already halfway out of the office and waving good-bye. No one could stop her. The principal wasn't even in today. He was at a county meeting with two dozen other high school administrators. Evelyn was free.

Once she got past the doors of the school, she couldn't stop grinning. Even the long line of cars waiting to get out of the parking lot didn't ruin her anticipation. She'd flirted with Noah on the phone last night, and he'd flirted back. Would the same thing happen in person today?

Despite her agonizing doubts about the quality of her art, she wasn't even particularly worried about that. He'd made clear that he wanted to see her paintings because they were part of her, not because he expected to discover a masterpiece. And once he'd said that, she'd wanted to show him. She'd needed to. Because she needed someone to *see* her.

It was nearly thirty minutes before she reached the gallery. She parked on a side street so she could take a moment to check her hair and makeup. She popped a mint into her mouth and dabbed on lipstick that matched her new cranberry skirt almost perfectly. She powdered her forehead and smoothed down her hair, then added a little black liner to her eyes. Between the lipstick and eye makeup, she looked brighter than she had in months. Maybe years.

She'd meant to look at the paintings one more time and decide whether she should bring one or both but, worried that the pause would break her momentum, she just grabbed the tote and locked the SUV behind her before swinging toward Main Street. She deliberately lifted her chin and kept her stride long. Today she wasn't a mom or office worker or school volunteer. She was a confident artist. A sexual being. A woman scorned. She was a force to be reckoned with.

The faint ding of the chime in the back room greeted her when she opened the door, but Noah didn't need the alert. He was behind the desk in the gallery, talking to an elderly gentleman who wore his hair in a wispy silver ponytail.

Noah glanced up, and his eyes widened before creasing with a warm smile. "Evelyn," he said. "Good afternoon. I'll be with you in just a moment."

The older man turned to nod his head in greeting, and Evelyn smiled far too happily at him before she wandered toward one of the walls of paintings to feign interest.

Feigned, because she couldn't pay attention to anything except Noah. He was only a dozen feet from her, and she wondered if he was watching as she moved idly along the wall, her shoulders back and chin up, breasts outlined by the soft black sweater. She wondered if he liked the way her heels tightened the muscles of her calves and made her curves more prominent. Was he paying attention in a way he hadn't before? Was there a new current of interest in the room? There certainly was in her body.

"Thank you, Henri," Noah finally said, coming out from behind the desk to clasp a hand to the man's shoulder. "I'll call you as soon as I've got it shipped. Two days at most. Have a safe trip back to California. I'll see you when you're back in town in July."

Evelyn kept moving along the wall, pretending she wasn't hyper-aware of Noah walking the man to the door. She heard the door chime, a few more words exchanged, and the door whooshing slowly shut. Evelyn stared hard at the mixed-media piece in front of her.

"Did you bring something to show me?" Noah asked, his voice much closer.

She shot him a coy look over her shoulder and found he'd stopped only two feet from her, one eyebrow raised in question and his thumbs hooked into the front pockets of his jeans. Even with the heels she wore, he was taller. Six one, maybe.

"Something like what?" she asked.

His eyebrow twitched a little higher before he grinned. "Let's start with a painting."

She watched him for a moment, as if she were still considering it. "Not here," she finally said. "I don't want you comparing me to the competition." She walked past him, brushing lightly against the sleeve of his shirt as she headed toward the back. He followed, and her neck prickled with the knowledge that his eyes were on her. She could feel him watching.

"Did you make a sale?" she asked.

"In fact I did. The Beckenbauer in the front window."

She gasped and shot a wide-eyed look over her shoulder. "Really? Already?"

"That doesn't sound like excitement."

"No, I'm happy for you, of course. It's just . . ." She pushed open the back door, and the sound of her heels echoed to the metal rafters. "I don't know. I thought it would be here a little longer."

"Yeah. I'll miss it too."

She smiled sheepishly as she stopped and turned toward him. "Not that it belonged to me."

"Not legally, no. But it got under your skin, right?"

She nodded. So had Noah. She had no true claim to him either, but here she was. His voice had gone softer in those last few words, and she had to hold back a shiver at the way he'd mentioned her skin. A turn of phrase, but still a thought that had passed his lips.

They watched each other for a moment before he tipped his head toward her hand. "Do I see two canvases there?"

Now that it was time, the nervousness was back. Evelyn cleared her throat and lifted the oversized tote a couple of inches. "I couldn't decide. One of them is better but . . ."

"But what?"

"But the other is my favorite."

He moved toward the framing table. "Let me guess which is which."

She couldn't back out now. She'd look foolish and weak, but worst of all, she'd miss the opportunity to show him this part of herself. That would be an unbearable regret.

He waited at the table until she finally took the four steps forward to join him. "All right," she breathed, and laid her bag carefully across the grid lines of the surface.

The tote was oversized, but five inches of both canvases still stuck out over the top. She wrapped her fingers around one edge. "You won't laugh?" she whispered, her role as confident artist slipping slowly away.

"Never."

Evelyn took a deep breath and pulled the canvas carefully free. It was her favorite. The nude model. She laid it on the table, excruciatingly aware of the woman's rose-brown nipples and black pubic hair. Aware, but also . . . excited. She'd known when she'd slipped it into the bag that she'd be showing him this. A titillating image—if not for the visual of the woman, then for the fact that Evelyn was the one presenting it to him.

After she laid it down, carefully squaring it with the grid line closest to the edge of the table, she pulled the other painting from the bag. She'd done this two years after the nude, and the brushwork was more confident, more daring, though the subject was modest. An older woman, her white hair wild around her head as she looked out a window toward an unseen view. The colors of both were cool and calm.

Noah didn't say a word as she laid the second painting even with the first. He stared at both canvases, eyes moving back and forth between them. Evelyn nibbled the edge of her thumbnail, trying not to demand an immediate opinion. What did he see? She'd looked at them both far too many times to understand their impact anymore.

He reached one hand slowly toward the first painting, and those long, blunt fingers of his touched the edge of the nude woman's hip before stroking up. His fingertips dragged softly over the woman's waist, then along the curve of one breast. Evelyn watched, her lips wet against the tip of her thumb.

"This is your favorite," he said. He glanced toward her, his gaze falling to her mouth until she pulled her thumb quickly away.

"Did you guess that because the other is better?"

"No." He turned back to the table. "There's more feeling in this. Fear. And excitement."

"Yes," she whispered.

"It's beautiful."

"Is it?" She felt weak. Shaky.

"Yes. They both are. And not what I expected."

Pressing her hand to her chest, she felt the thump of her heart against her knuckles. "What did you expect?"

"Something more careful, I guess. Restrained."

"Oh." She nodded, a nervous bobbing of her head.

"There's wildness here."

Yes. There was. Or there had been. Fear, excitement, lust, and wonder. That had all been part of her, but the most important part must have been her need for security, because she'd abandoned everything else for that.

But the wildness was back now. She could feel it moving. Changing her. Pushing her toward things she shouldn't do.

"How old were you when you did them?"

"Twenty," she whispered. "And twenty-two."

"Wow." His finger stroked the woman's hip again, this time sliding all the way down to her thigh, his finger hovering so intimately near the dark triangle of pubic hair. "That's a lot of potential in a twenty-year-old."

"Now you're just being nice."

"Not true. They're wonderful."

"They're nothing a gallery would sell. Nothing you would sell."

"No, but I'd have wanted to see how your style developed after a few more years."

"Really?"

"Really."

She wasn't sure what she felt at that. Pride, certainly. It swelled beneath her skin. But a sick, hot wash of regret moved through her too. "I thought I was good, but there were so many powerful artists in my classes. People who channeled their anger and passion and disgust into huge works."

"Even professionals sometimes mistake loudness for skill. Your work is quiet, but it's deep."

"Maybe." She stared at his hand, the way he'd spread his fingers over her painting.

"Promise me you'll get back to it?"

"Yes," she answered as his hand slipped off the woman's skin.

"Evelyn . . . I mean it." And now he was touching her instead of the painting, his fingers curling around her elbow as if he needed to get her attention. She raised her eyes slowly, over the glinting hair on his forearm and the dark-blue cotton of his work shirt, up his throat and over his chin and mouth until she was looking into his eyes, drowning in their depths, like a heroine in some romantic movie.

He looked worried, serious, passionate, all of it for her.

"Try it again," he urged. "See how it feels. Find out who you've become."

Painting, he meant, but maybe he meant more than that, because surely no one cared that much about a stranger's oils and brushes. "What if I've forgotten how?"

When she spoke, his gaze fell to her mouth, and suddenly she *remembered.* How this all worked. The nervous dance. The terror and hope. The emotion pushing up and out, needing to emerge through fingers and mouths and skin. Passion was the same, whether for art or sex, and she was feeling it for the first time in so long, and the way it mixed up with this sudden triumph over another woman only made it sweeter.

"Look at you," he murmured. "You haven't forgotten."

He bent his head slowly, unsure of how she'd respond or maybe unsure of what he was doing. She felt too shocked to move, but she shifted closer without realizing, moving into him, lifting her head. She watched his mouth, but somehow still didn't believe he meant to kiss her until his lips brushed hers.

At first it was just that. A brush of skin against skin. Nothing startling about it. But his mouth touched hers again, pressing more firmly, and she realized she was kissing someone. Someone new. A man who wasn't her husband.

Her heart thundered to life, shaking with alarm, punching so hard against her ribs that the vibrations spread through her bones. She sucked in a deep breath, a gasp really, and then his mouth settled against hers, and she could smell him, taste him. A stranger.

His hand slid to her shoulder and she found herself touching him too, wrapping her fingers around his arms to steady her weak body.

But her touch seemed to startle him. His mouth left hers. "I'm sorry," he murmured. "I didn't . . . I shouldn't have done that."

He shouldn't have. She shouldn't have. But their mouths were still only inches apart. Did he want her to stop him? If so, he should have picked an average middle-aged woman who wasn't falling apart, because right now she needed something to hold on to, and his arms were warm and solid under her hands.

She rose up on her toes and kissed him.

He went as still as she had when he'd kissed her, but that moment of silence lasted only an instant. A short, quiet moan rumbled in his chest, and then his lips parted and his hands spread over her shoulders. His tongue touched hers, and she gasped in shock even as she welcomed him deeper.

She'd missed kissing, she realized then. And he was a good kisser. His hands slid up her neck to frame her jaw as he tasted her mouth. He'd turned her body with his, and now her back was against the edge of the table, his legs between hers so he could get closer.

Then he *was* closer. His tongue inside her, his fingers spreading over her neck, chest and hips pressing into her as they kissed.

He broke the kiss and ducked his head. When the wet heat of his mouth touched her neck, she groaned and arched up, baring her whole throat to him. His teeth on her neck was all it took to flash lust through her whole body. The sucking pleasure of his mouth stirred up blood that had long ago sunk into useless pools inside her. Now it coursed through her, waking dead nerves.

She panted like an animal, needing more oxygen for that new blood. Her arms wrapped around his waist and spread over his back to pull him closer.

It was as exciting and uncertain and dangerous as a high school make-out session, yet it was so much better. Because when she felt him grow hard against her, she wasn't embarrassed or worried; she was thrilled. Thrilled to her very bones that she could make this handsome, hot, forbidden man hard for her. She wanted him hard. Wanted him so wild and hot that he had to apologize for it. Because he wasn't only a stranger. He was a spoil of war, and Evelyn was claiming him.

When he picked her up, Evelyn felt sure she was observing a scene from someone else's life. This woman wore tight skirts and black pumps, and she kissed strange men and arched her neck for more and let herself be lifted onto tables so he could spread her knees and force her skirt higher.

Oh God, Noah's hips were between her thighs now, the high table lining up their bodies perfectly. They were kissing again, hands roaming. His palms framed her hips, then her waist while she explored the wide strength of his back, and then her skirt was higher and his hardness was pressed against her. Her panties were soaked, and she knew she should be embarrassed, but she wasn't. She was proud. She wasn't some used-up, soul-dead mother and wife. She was alive, and she needed this.

Would she let him fuck her if he tried? Let him unzip his pants and take her right here on his worktable? She didn't even know. It felt as if the choice were beyond her, something larger than herself. Fate or kismet or whatever people called it these days.

Old Evelyn would never have been capable of such a thing. She would have been too worried about morality and responsibility and the wrongness of it all. But for new Evelyn, this felt right. She'd *earned* this. Damn the consequences. This was hers.

Noah's hand gripped her bare thigh, and she had to turn from his kiss to draw a shuddering gasp of air. Unfortunately, that seemed to break the spell. Noah's hand pressed hot into her skin, but it didn't rise higher.

"I'm sorry," he rasped against her temple. "I'm sorry, Evelyn. I've never done anything like this."

"Never?" She realized then that she'd begun to assume that this was something he did. That maybe he was to blame for Juliette's trespass.

But he shook his head, rubbing his chin against her hair, and she dared to press a kiss to his neck and breathe in the strange new smell of him. "Never," he repeated.

"Me neither."

He drew back a little to look at her, though his hand stayed on her leg, a torturous connection. "Really?"

"Yes. You're the only man besides my husband I've touched in . . . God. Over twenty years now."

"Jesus," he sighed. "What is this?"

She could have given him an answer. She could have said it was her own obsession driving this. But that couldn't be true, could it? Yes, her obsession with his wife had brought her here, but Noah didn't know anything about that. If he felt it too, then it was real, wasn't it? It was something deeper than this awful thing that had happened. It was *good.*

"I'm sorry," he said again.

"Are you? Truly?"

He looked into her eyes, and his thumb stroked slowly along her inner thigh. When she shivered, his eyes closed and he inhaled sharply. "I don't know. Are you?"

"If I say I'm not, will you think I'm a horrible person?"

"No." He must have meant it, because he kissed her again, more slowly, though. More gently. He took his hand from her leg, leaving a spot that felt cooler than the rest of her body. With a sigh, he rested his forehead against hers. "We shouldn't do this."

"I know."

"I love my wife."

She nodded, but bitterness filled her mouth and chased away the taste of him. He didn't know the truth about his wife. That wasn't his fault. He couldn't know that every time he brought her up, Juliette stuck a knife in again.

Evelyn didn't bother proclaiming any love for her husband. She wasn't sure of it anymore, and Gary didn't belong here between her and Noah.

Noah sighed one more time, then pressed a quick peck to her lips before he stepped back. "God, you're sexy," he groaned, running a hand through his hair.

Evelyn laughed in delight. "I am?"

"Yes." His gaze swept down her body, and she realized she was still sitting there with her legs open and skirt hiked up to her black panties. She didn't close her legs immediately. She let him look for another few seconds before she scooted off the table.

He thought she was *sexy*. What utterly perfect revenge.

"What are we going to do?" he asked.

"I don't know." She hadn't known before, at least. She'd wanted to flirt with him, and boy, she'd pulled that off. But now . . . now she wanted to do so much more. She had a free pass. So did Noah, but he didn't know it, so she'd have to give him a little space. "Do you want me to leave?" she asked.

"No, I don't. That's the problem. I'd like to set you back up on that table and . . ."

Evelyn smiled, charmed by his desire for her. It was more power she'd never expected to have. "And what?"

"God, Evelyn," he said on a laugh. "Don't make me think about it."

"I want you to think about it."

He ran a rough hand over his face and shook his head. "Yeah, I think that's pretty inevitable at this point."

"Good."

"If this is—" Whatever he'd been about to say was cut off by the door chime. They both swung toward the monitor and watched two women walk through the door. "Stay here. I'll see who it is."

She let out the breath she'd been holding. She knew his wife was off work by now. What if Juliette had walked in with his two young children? Evelyn had no idea what she would have done. Her mind rocked unsteadily between guilt and hatred.

Noah's voice drifted back to her, the courteous tone indicating the women were customers. Evelyn slumped against the table and drew a shaky breath. Her exhalation broke into a laugh, and she had to cover her mouth to hide the sound.

This was insane. She'd made out with Noah Whitman. Noah Whitman. If this had been her idea, she'd say it had been a terrible one, but it hadn't been an idea. It had just happened.

And God, she'd loved it. Was that what Gary had felt with Juliette? That beating, driving, joyful feeling of just being alive? If that was what he'd felt, she could almost forgive him.

But only almost, because Evelyn had had an excuse. What excuse had Gary invented for letting himself get close enough to another woman to feel that? Evelyn would never have flirted, never have wanted, never have touched . . . if only Gary hadn't cheated on her.

But now . . . now she had. And it filled her up with power. A different kind. A sweet, soulful power, nothing like the vengeance she'd been wreaking on Gary.

"I'm sorry," Noah said as he stepped into the back room. "They're just browsing, but I should—"

"It's fine." She reached behind her for the bag. "I didn't mean to interfere with your work. I should go."

"I . . ." The word died in his throat, and he just watched her, his hands raised a few inches, as if he didn't know what to do with them.

"It's okay. I'll go." She slid the paintings into the bag and ran a hand down her skirt to be sure everything was in place.

"Can I text you tonight?" he asked as she swung around.

"Yes."

"Evelyn . . ." He looked so helpless, his face creased with worry.

"Please don't say you're sorry again. Not unless you are."

He closed his mouth. Shook his head. The worry didn't clear from his face. "I'm not a guy who cheats on his wife."

Good. She wouldn't want him as much if he were. "All right," she drawled. "Then you don't have anything to worry about, do you?"

His laugh was mostly a groan of exasperation.

"I'll go," she repeated, but as she moved to walk by him, she realized his mouth was pinker than it should be and reached up to swipe her thumb over the faint ghost of her lipstick. "But you'd better clean up, because you look like a man who cheats on his wife."

As she walked through the gallery, she didn't have to tell herself to put her shoulders back and keep her chin up. She might have come in the gallery faking the stride of a sexual, confident, dangerous woman, but on the way out, it was all real.

CHAPTER 14
BEFORE

"She came to me for the normal kind of thing," he started, still trying to keep it vague.

"You're a clinical psychiatrist," Evelyn snapped. "You don't deal in normal."

Gary cleared his throat. "All right. The normal kind of abnormal that plagues most people in our society. Depression, but mostly anxiety. Everyday anxiety made worse by severe anxiety attacks. After the first few sessions, she seemed to think I was helping her. She . . . flirted with me."

Evelyn sat back. "So this has been going on for a year?"

"No. I didn't just *succumb* to her overtures. Do you know how many patients develop crushes on their doctors?"

"A lot. So how many have you slept with?"

His jaw clenched like he was already irritated with her questions. Poor baby. He was in for a long day. "She's the only one."

"How many women have you slept with who weren't patients?"

"Evelyn, I swear I've never done this before. It was only her."

"So she was special?"

He took a deep breath and seemed to give up some of the fight, sinking back into his chair as he exhaled. "I don't know what happened. I just . . . I guess I was flattered by her attention. And maybe I developed a bit of a savior complex. I don't know. She was so fragile, and I felt pulled in. It was a . . . connection."

"And she's pretty," Evelyn pointed out.

He wisely kept his mouth shut.

"When did it turn sexual?"

"Six months ago."

Evelyn closed her eyes. He'd been making love to another woman for six months. Had there been a change in him? She knew she would spend days and weeks turning over the question, but she couldn't think of anything now.

Six months ago had been the start of winter. There'd been holiday preparation and awards dinners and plenty of his events Evelyn had said no to. She'd been too busy buying gifts and decorating and baking things for neighbors. There'd been homecoming, then winter fundraisers, then Thanksgiving and Christmas and . . .

"In your office?" she asked.

He shifted, his gaze drifting down to the desk. "The first time, yes."

"And the others?"

"Evelyn—"

"Tell me." She stared straight at him until he answered.

"Sometimes hotel rooms."

"How? I pay your credit card bills."

A flush climbed up his neck. She tried to imagine him frequenting some no-tell motel where he could pay with cash, but she couldn't picture it. Not with Gary. He liked his high-thread-count sheets too much. He was picky about shower heads and cheap carpet. He'd never have sex on a stained polyester coverlet. Unless, of course, there were a thousand more ways she didn't know him.

"I . . . I paid cash for debit cards that you fill up at the store."

Her own face burned at that. The heat climbed up her throat to her cheeks and all the way to the top of her head. He hadn't just had sex with this woman. He'd thought about her. Planned for her. Schemed and strategized. How many nights of his "work" distractions had actually been about this Juliette?

God, he must have loved it when Evelyn and her sister had driven to Iowa for their aunt's funeral. Three nights of freedom in February. Had he spent all of them with her?

"Do you love her?"

"No. I told you, it was only physical."

"But it wasn't only physical. You said you felt a connection."

"I thought so at first. It was exciting. Exhilarating. But I knew it was wrong. After a while, it became more of a complication than anything else. She was needy, of course. Her anxiety problems . . ." Whatever he'd been thinking, his words faded away.

"So *why*? Why did you do it? Why did you keep doing it if you weren't even in love with her?"

He shrugged, shaking his head as if to loosen his thoughts. "I don't know. Ego. And . . ."

"And?"

"Sex."

Here was the part of the conversation she didn't want to have. Her face grew so hot she wanted to press her palms against her cheeks to cool them. "Because you weren't getting enough at home?"

He didn't answer.

"Well?" she demanded.

"You're not interested," he said.

She wanted to scream at him that it wasn't true, but the reality was she just didn't care about sex anymore. She didn't even want to be naked with him, because she knew he'd be quietly judging her for not working out more. She'd rather protect herself than be vulnerable to the weary judgment in his eyes. Not that they never had sex, but surely he could tell that she was doing it out of guilt.

She couldn't even tell him about her self-consciousness, because he'd deny it. He'd say, "I've never once called you fat," and that would be true. But he'd sneered at her snacks, raised eyebrows at her complaints that her knees hurt and she couldn't work out. He'd been too smart to ever say a word, but he'd made it clear that he was superior.

She'd stopped feeling attractive, and eventually she'd also stopped *being* attracted. And hadn't every woman heard those warnings her whole life? *If he's not getting it at home, he'll get it somewhere else.*

"And her?" Evelyn croaked. "*Juliette.* Was she just tired of her husband and kids? Looking for a little excitement?"

"I don't know."

"You don't *know*? You're her fucking psychiatrist." A moment passed, then she burst into harsh laughter. "Get it?" she gasped. "Her fucking psychiatrist. Literally!"

He didn't seem to find it amusing. His face wrinkled in distaste, and she had the strangest urge to stand up and give him the finger. Both middle fingers, actually. She usually found cursing as vulgar as Gary did, but today it felt really, really good.

"Sorry," she managed to choke out. "Should I call it making love?" But she'd taken it too far now, because an image suddenly sprang to mind of Gary naked with that woman. Both of them fit and beautiful, stretched out on fine white cotton in a high-end hotel room as they kissed and caressed each other.

He would've loved showing off his body. His stamina. His athleticism. He was a man. He didn't need just sex; he needed ego stroking, and Evelyn had long been too self-conscious to give him that.

He was a doctor to her stay-at-home parenting. He earned a healthy six figures to her hourly wage. He had a six-pack, and her stomach looked like a bag of marshmallows. The silver peppered through his hair made him look distinguished, while she tried desperately to make her signs of aging disappear. Evelyn didn't have enough ego for herself. She couldn't share with him, so she'd left him to his own devices. Why was she so surprised that one of those devices had been a pretty blond girl who needed his help?

"How many times did you have sex with her?" she asked.

"Jesus Christ, Evelyn. I'm not going to tell you that."

"Yes, you are."

"I'm not. Even if I were willing to, do you really think I counted?"

"So it was that many times? Too many times to count? Hundreds?"

"No," he answered.

"Dozens?"

Gary sighed, blowing a long, weary breath through his flared nostrils.

"How many times did you rent a room?" she pressed.

"I don't know. Five times, I think."

"And how much sex each time? You're nothing if not logical. You wouldn't have wanted to waste a room once you'd rented it. Time with her must have been hard to come by, and you could have had sex at least a couple of times even if you didn't stay the night. Did you spend whole nights with her?"

"No."

"So a few hours in each hotel room. And you still had sex in your office, right? A whole hour together uninterrupted every week? Multiply that by six months. What does that add up to?"

"This isn't going to help you—" he started, but she leaned forward and slapped both hands onto the surface of his desk. The sound cracked through the room and he jumped, eyes flying wide.

"You don't get to decide what helps me," she snarled. "You agreed to tell me everything not *five* minutes ago. In exchange I keep your sordid, awful, disgusting secret. *Remember?*"

Anger flooded her veins, and she became aware of her own strength again. Her visceral, undeniable force. If he wanted his career, then he had to give her what she asked for.

He stared at her. His cheeks weren't flushed with anger or embarrassment now. They were pale as old ash.

Evelyn took a deep breath and sat back. "So . . . you met her in a hotel room five times. And then there was your office. Probably your car too? Isn't that what cheaters do?" She interlocked her fingers and stared down at the weaving of her own flesh, wondering when she'd last held Gary's hand. Last year when they'd taken that vacation to Mexico? She'd held his hand as they'd watched the sun set. He'd pulled away soon after. "So," she said lightly, "how many times did you have sex with Juliette Whitman? Just an estimate."

He held out for a few more seconds before answering. "I don't know. Maybe twenty times. Twenty-five."

She looked up and aimed a hard look at him.

"I didn't see her every week," he said. "Her appointments were twice a month."

"Was she in love with you?"

"I don't know."

"Did she *tell* you she loved you?"

"Once."

"And what did you say to that?" she asked, just the question causing enough of a wound that it felt as if her heart were swelling inside her chest like a ruined, useless limb. She needed to know everything, but why? What difference could it make? Whatever he'd said, it wouldn't change what had happened. He'd still had sex with another woman dozens of times. He'd still wanted and needed her more than he had Evelyn.

"I . . . I told her I wasn't sure what I was feeling."

"So maybe you loved her?"

"Whatever it was, it was temporary."

Oh boy, wasn't everything?

Love was temporary. So was lust. And happiness, confidence, trust. And marriage. Especially that. Gary was probably ready to move on. Trade his old wife in for a newer model. Wasn't that what successful men did?

But he couldn't leave now. Hell, not only did he have to stay, but he couldn't even be in charge anymore.

Evelyn suspected there was never true equality in marriage. Someone always had stronger feelings, or held the purse strings, or was more persuasive, powerful, and pushy. For all of these years, Gary had wielded all those advantages. He'd been the king of his castle. But not anymore.

She told herself that it could be better this way. She'd be stronger. Maybe, in the end, her marriage would be better off with a little more honesty and balance between them.

Or maybe not. Because every time that new power burned through her, it left scorched emptiness behind, and Evelyn suspected she might eventually disappear altogether.

CHAPTER 15
AFTER

`I've been thinking about it`, he wrote at ten thirty.

Evelyn had been in the guest room for hours, organizing the new supplies she'd picked up on the drive home from Noah's gallery. Paints, brushes, easels, cleaners, canvases. A hopeful, satisfying haul . . . and the only thing in the world that could have distracted her from the afternoon with Noah. Still, she'd checked her phone obsessively, one minute sure that he'd send a titillating message, and the next convinced that he wouldn't contact her at all.

He was a good man. He didn't want to cheat on a woman he must assume had been faithful. But . . . he couldn't resist thinking about it, at least.

She grinned at her phone as she read his message several times, looking for secret hints. `What have you been thinking about?` she finally texted back.

`You. Today. Everything.`

Evelyn almost melted onto the bed, her body pooling down to curl into the throw pillows. She'd been planning to move the bed out of here tomorrow to make space for all three easels, but now she wasn't sure. Where would she curl up to talk to Noah?

`And what did you think about me?`

`I can't tell you that.`

Her pulse sped up as if he'd touched her. `Why?`

`Bcuz then this would turn into sexting, and I'd like to maintain some dignity.`

She didn't even try to muffle her laughter at that. There were so many kinds of happiness swirling through her right now. Amusement, lust, anticipation, delight, flattery, triumph. She didn't care about dignity. She'd try sexting with him. Not tonight, though. She was already far too eager for this, and she couldn't let him know.

`And what did you think about what happened today?` she typed instead of demanding to know every detail of his sexual fantasies.

`I still don't know. Could we talk? Is it safe for me to call you?`

That was different from *is it all right. Is it safe* made clear that they had something to hide. Something dangerous. Evelyn wasn't a safe woman anymore. Good.

She glanced at the locking doorknob she'd installed on the guest room door. That had been another stop on the way home. After all, she'd needed to waste time. Those committee meetings could go on for hours. She'd bought a new doorknob at a little hardware store, then walked four doors down to grab sushi, another food that Gary didn't like and she loved.

She'd brought all of it to the small corner bedroom upstairs, aware that Gary was in his study but not bothering to check in with him. First, she'd eaten the sushi and washed it down with a glass of wine, then she'd installed the new lock, and finally she'd unpacked the boxes and bags of supplies. Gary had closed the door of the master bedroom twenty minutes earlier without even asking when she was coming to bed. Now it was time for real fun. Noah.

`Is it safe for you to call?`

`She's asleep.`

"Ha." Evelyn should have been disturbed by the hard, sharp sound that sprang from her mouth, but she wasn't. Juliette was asleep and her husband wanted Evelyn.

`I can talk`, she typed.

It took a few minutes for her phone to buzz. She tried to picture what he might be doing. Checking to see if Juliette was still sleeping, getting a beer, locking the door of his basement office. Maybe she was wrong about all of it, but she liked imagining him.

When it finally buzzed, she took a few deep breaths to calm herself before she answered the phone. "Hi," she said softly, dropping any polite deception. She knew exactly who it was and what she wanted.

"Hi. Are you okay?"

"I'm fine. I'm good, actually. What about you?"

"Aren't you worried?"

"About what?"

"You know what." There was warmth in his words, as if he were remembering.

"I doubt anyone would care," she said honestly. If Gary caught her cheating he'd probably be thrilled. It'd be something for him to use against her. Leverage against the great weight of his crime.

"That bad?" Noah asked softly.

"It's complicated. You must know that. You love your wife, but you kissed me today."

He blew out a long sigh. "I did."

"And did you decide if you're sorry or not?"

"Jesus, Evelyn. How am I supposed to answer that? I loved every second of it, but I don't want to cheat on my wife."

"You never have?"

"No," he said immediately, but the silence that followed that decisive answer eroded the edges of it.

"Are you sure?"

"I . . . God, I've never told anyone this."

"What?" she pressed, half afraid that this was no longer special and half excited to hear his secrets.

"Before we got married . . . a month before the wedding . . . I think I got jitters. I don't know."

"You slept with another woman?"

"It was a one-night stand." She felt inexplicably aroused. Maybe because it was something that could hurt Juliette. Or maybe just that it was scandalous and titillating, and the woman was already no competition for Evelyn. A nameless, faceless woman he'd chosen never to see again. Noah had taken Evelyn out for dinner. Shared his coffee. Begged to see her paintings. She was already more than a one-night stand.

"Tell me about it," she whispered, stunned at this new Evelyn's boldness.

"There isn't much to tell. I was at a bar with a friend. He left with some girl and I started flirting with a woman who was a few years older. She was in town on business. We went to her hotel room."

"You had sex?"

"Yes."

"Was it good?"

"It was . . . different. New. Wrong."

"Did you regret it afterward?"

"Yes. Immediately."

"But you don't regret today?" she asked. Her heart beat so quickly that it thumped a dozen times before he finally answered.

"I don't think I do."

She closed her eyes and tipped her head back joyously. The way her skin stretched made her remember how she'd arched for him. "No one's kissed my neck like that in years."

He whispered her name, and she knew right then and there that they were going to sleep together. Everything in the world was pushing her toward him, and he could feel it too.

"We could do what we want, Noah. This doesn't have to change anything. No one has to know." The words tripped from her without will. She could hardly believe they were hers.

But they were true. No one had to know. It could just be a balm for her soul. A secret way to heal. If she had Noah, then surely she'd lose a little of her anger at Gary. Surely she could forgive Juliette. She'd have her revenge, and no one would know, and their lives would go on.

"What do you want?" he asked very carefully.

She meant to say something sexy. A bold invitation from a femme fatale. But she lost her nerve. That wasn't who she was. And it wasn't who she wanted to be with Noah. He'd looked at her art and glimpsed the real her, and the exposure had been intoxicating.

She squeezed her eyes shut and tried to speak honestly. "I've never done this before either. All I know is I want to feel what you made me feel today. I want that again. I want your mouth on me. I want . . ." She had to pause to catch her breath. "Maybe I'll chicken out."

"That's okay," he said quickly. "It's all right. That's what I want too. I want to see you again. Touch you. Kiss you. We don't have to do anything else."

"When?" she asked.

"Tomorrow. Can you come back?"

Tomorrow. She could hear the urgency in his voice. The need. She was exquisitely aroused at just the thought of him. If she said yes, she'd see him in only a few hours. Feel his hands and mouth and teeth on her skin. And maybe this time he'd touch between her legs.

She thought of the endless hours of waiting at the school today. She couldn't get through that again, knowing what was coming. "In the morning?" she asked.

"Yes. I'd love that. I'll get there early. You can knock if I'm not in the front."

"Okay."

"Okay," he repeated. "I'd better go. I just . . . Evelyn?"

"Yes?"

"I don't regret it. I loved every second."

Her hands were shaking as she set the phone down on the bed. This wasn't about Gary or Juliette anymore. It had nothing to do with anyone except Evelyn and Noah. He wanted her. She wanted him. And there was no one around to stop them.

Was he as aroused as she was? As hard as she was wet? Suddenly, all the vulgar things she'd never understood made perfect sense. People caught in affairs had always seemed so dumb to her, like rutting dogs in the street. What kind of stupid women pretended to want penis pictures? What kind of adolescent men took them? And what exactly was arousing about humping in a back room or dirty texting or phone sex? It had all seemed so desperate.

And it was. Desperate. Needy. Consuming. Dignity had nothing to do with it, despite Noah's words. Today she'd allowed a man to set her on a table and spread her legs and rub his erection against her, and she'd loved it. She would love it again tomorrow. She'd want even more.

She was alive. Living. Clawing for more life.

Aware that she was a different person than she'd been this morning, she rose slowly from the bed and walked into the attached bathroom. She clicked on the light and stared at herself in the mirror.

Was she still desirable? If she'd ever had to consider the question before, she would have chosen *Gary's only option* over *desirable*. But that hadn't been true. She hadn't been his only option at all. Which still left the initial question.

Tonight she looked tired, the makeup she'd put on for Noah smudged beneath her eyes and settling into her laugh lines.

After wetting some toilet paper, she scrubbed away all the black, then finger-combed her hair and took a good look at herself.

She was back in her comfortable clothes, yoga pants and a sweatshirt. This wasn't how Noah would see her, ever. Crossing her arms over her torso, she grasped the waistband of her shirt and yanked it up to reveal the black bra beneath.

She cupped her covered breasts, then ran her hands over her new waist. Not smooth. Not young. But maybe still appealing in soft lighting? She stripped off her pants and stood up straight in her bra and panties.

If she'd had any hint that a new man was going to see her naked this year, she would have put a little more effort into her New Year's resolution to get in shape.

She knew from Facebook posts that Noah's wife was a runner. Evelyn had never had a runner's body, even as a teenager. Her breasts were too big, her stride too unsure. She got dizzy after only a mile of jogging, and her body would overheat and strain for air. But Juliette didn't have that problem. She was lean and strong and probably graceful.

Evelyn slipped off her simple black briefs, unhooked her bra, and looked hard at the mirrored image of her nude body.

The bathroom light cast shadows on every dimple and bulge. She straightened her spine and tightened her core, and that helped. A little. But there was no mistaking the softness of her body. She was a forty-one-year-old woman who'd never gotten back into shape after having a child. What could Noah possibly find attractive about this?

His wife was petite and tan and blond. That must be his type. He'd married her. And if Juliette was his type, then tall, curvy, dark-haired Evelyn couldn't possibly be.

She couldn't have sex with him. Not like this. Maybe she could leave her skirt on and just slide her panties off. That would hide the stretch marks on her belly. She could unbutton her shirt and just push her bra down to her waist. He could see her breasts, touch them, kiss them. That would be a nice compromise.

Evelyn took a deep breath and cupped her naked breasts. They were still pretty, at least. Still full despite the breastfeeding. Her dark-pink nipples peaked in the cool air, and she stroked her thumbs over them, imagining how they'd feel to Noah. Suddenly bolder, she eased her hands down her stomach and waist and hips, and the sensation made her stretch proudly under her own touch. Maybe he was bored with Juliette's tight body. Maybe he'd be charmed by Evelyn's softness.

Her gaze dropped to her pubic hair, and she winced. She'd never shaved more than the edges of her bikini line, but Juliette looked like the kind of woman who had monthly appointments with a waxer. Was that what all men expected these days? Evelyn was well aware of how bare the girls were in porn, but to her it always looked like their sex organs were heiling Hitler. Why did they leave a little mustache of hair above their vaginas? Did men really like that? Was it like a blinking arrow pointing them to sex?

Evelyn gingerly patted her dark curls. She could trim them, maybe. Or spend half the night trying to shave all her hair off and make herself into a sex toy. Her frown turned to a grimace of disgust. She would cut herself or cause razor burn, then show up at his gallery like a newly shorn sheep—pink, wrinkled, and traumatized.

Sighing, she let her hands drop and looked back to the mirror. Appealing or not, this was all she had. She flicked off the bathroom light. Now she was only vaguely illuminated, and with the stark white light gone, she relaxed a little.

The curves of her silhouette pleased her, at least. And Noah knew what she looked like. Her pale, plump thighs had been spread across his framing table when he'd called her sexy. This would be okay. If he wanted a tight-bodied twenty-year-old, he wouldn't have chosen Evelyn. There was chemistry between them. White-hot chemistry. Surely that mattered more than cellulite.

She jerked her sweatshirt over her head and closed the bathroom door before she finished dressing. A tiny voice in the back of her mind told her there were bigger things than her body image at stake here, but she ignored it. She'd spent her whole life doing the right thing. That could be someone else's job now. She was moving on.

CHAPTER 16

BEFORE

That night her most important ally failed her. After Evelyn had gotten through the long, tense quiet of Saturday, she'd rewarded herself with an early dose of her medication. The sleeping pill had done its job quickly, thanks to Evelyn's emotional exhaustion. She'd fallen into her solitary bed at nine and had sunk thankfully into sleep, expecting to wake to a new day, maybe find a little hope waiting.

Instead, she'd awoken to darkness and anxiety, sweat dripping from her skin. She couldn't remember whatever demons she'd been fighting in her sleep, but there were plenty more crouched and waiting for her when she woke.

She squinted at the clock as she wiped a hand over her wet forehead. Only 3:00 a.m. She should still be drugged and groggy. Why was she wide eyed and panicking?

Aware of the clammy dampness of the sheets under her, she shifted to the middle of the bed and wrapped the covers around her. It wasn't as if there were a husband nearby to disturb. He was at the end of the hall, probably sleeping the sleep of angels, because what the hell did he care about how Evelyn was feeling?

She closed her eyes and steadied her breathing, trying to relax back into sleep. It didn't happen. Her heartbeat didn't even slow; it kept kicking, kicking, kicking.

The darkness was no help. Instead of quieting her, it served as a perfect backdrop for the movies her mind had been crafting all day. They were all pornographic. A strange twisting of ugly, rutting, grunting scenes mixed with tender, romantic moments. Gary whispering sweet words into another woman's ear, Gary screwing someone on the floor of his office, Gary pushing a blond stranger up against a hotel door, unable to wait for the bed.

Evelyn squeezed her eyes shut and hid her face in the pillows. She hated him. *Hated* him. She'd spent all of today imagining the steps she'd take to rebuild her marriage, but how could she even touch him again, much less forgive him?

They'd made love during the past six months. Not very often, but a couple of times each month. Had he been fantasizing about Juliette Whitman while he'd had sex with Evelyn? Had he closed his eyes to the sight of her body and pretended he was sliding himself into *her*? He must have, with all the planning and rearranging and lying he'd done to see Juliette. He must have been a little obsessed, a little in love, a little mad for her.

Evelyn moaned into her pillow, her throat burning with her pain, but somehow the tears didn't come. She needed to cry or scream or *something*, but she just lay there, rocking herself into the mattress, trying to force her panicking body to calm down.

The next time she looked at the clock, it was three fifteen, and her pulse was still racing. Maybe she should just take another pill. She could sleep through Sunday. She always made a big breakfast for her and Cameron on Sundays, and Gary too if he hadn't already left to golf, but she didn't feel like pouring chocolate chip pancakes into a pan and whisking up homemade whipped cream while she danced around the kitchen to her favorite songs. She didn't even feel like opening the drapes. She didn't want food. Didn't want to face her son. She'd stay in bed. Feign illness. Sleep until two.

Jesus, how had she become this? Her life had been deep and rich and complex once. She'd lived with her single mother and her older sister, and they'd been strong, resilient, quick. She'd taken city buses and negotiated dangerous neighborhoods even as a child, and she'd imagined herself growing into an artist with wild, creative friends who had little money but so much heart.

Now everything about her was dull. Whitewashed. Placid. She lived in a safe neighborhood with little diversity and no creativity at all. She was married to a man who golfed and wore expensive loafers and drove a fancy European sedan. And *she* wasn't interesting to *him*. Even in a ranking of American stereotypes, she was lifeless and vanilla. She was one of those moms she'd watched on TV as a child. The pleasant owner of a home on a cul-de-sac, a sight she'd only witnessed in movies until she'd bought that home for herself.

In her teens, she'd scorned the safety of suburbia, but now she knew that scorn hadn't emerged from disdain. It had been yearning. It had been desire. Because at the very first opportunity, she'd thrown herself into that life wholeheartedly. Her first new car. Her first home. Her first *yard*. First fireplace, lawn mower, garage, mortgage. The first nuclear family she'd ever experienced.

She'd thought this was a guarantee. She'd thought it was safety. She'd clipped her own wings and settled down as deep as she could get with the assurance that it was *security*. She'd willingly traded herself for this life.

Now it was all teetering on an abyss.

Evelyn growled in fury. This was her life now. *Hers*. For better or worse. She wasn't going to let some dirty blond bitch take that away from her. As stupid, boring, and steady as this life might be, it was *hers*.

She untangled herself from the sheets and comforter and crawled from the bed. She pulled on a sweater over her nightgown and slipped into warm socks. She had to do something. She couldn't just lie there and rage.

As quietly as she could, she unlocked the doors of the master bedroom and tiptoed to Cameron's room to ease his door open and make sure he was fine. Of course he was. He wasn't an infant. He was a teenager who'd be furious that she'd entered his room without knocking, but she'd needed to feel sure of him tonight.

She stood for a moment, taking in his mussed hair and the slightly curled fingers of his open palms. He was such a good boy. He still had time for movie nights with Mom when he didn't have too much homework. He came down from his bedroom when she remembered to propose a board game, even if his, "Sure, Mom," was always faintly laced with indulgence. He was a good boy, and Juliette Whitman hadn't given a damn that she might hurt him.

With only a glance at the closed door of the guest room, she headed downstairs and went straight to Gary's study. The overhead light speared through her swollen, scratchy eyes, so she switched it off and turned on his desk lamp.

She'd never once violated his privacy in all their years together, but now she could do it with impunity. What could he even say if he came downstairs and caught her? She'd laugh in his face.

Evelyn opened every drawer in his desk, carelessly moving things around, searching for evidence of something, anything. Looking to see if what he'd told her was true. She only found pens, pencils, paper clips, highlighters. There were files full of psychiatric journals, though any that mentioned Gary were already framed and hung on the walls to remind him of how smart and successful he was.

His patient files were all at his office, so there weren't even any locked drawers. She found one thumb drive, but when she fired up his laptop, she discovered that it was password protected. Of course it was. He stored other people's privacy in there.

She sat back in his chair, realizing now that she needed those files. She needed to see this woman. That was what she'd come here for.

Hoping that real life was as simple as the movies, she leaned quickly forward and tried typing *PASSWORD* into his computer. It beeped angrily. She tried his birthday, Cameron's birthday, then *PASSWORD123*. More angry beeps. She tried the name of his favorite golf club. She typed in *Juliette*. She even tried *Evelyn*. Nothing.

This wasn't a movie, and Evelyn wasn't a kick-ass spy. She wasn't even smart enough to figure out her own husband's password. Frustrated, she picked up his laptop and set it down with a crack, half hoping she'd accidentally destroy it. But no. This time it didn't even beep. It just stared at her as if she didn't matter. She wanted to throw it across the room. It would crash into his bookshelves, maybe knock down some of those framed accomplishments, cracking the glass into hundreds of pieces, ruining something he was proud of.

But there was a more likely way to get what she wanted. She closed all his drawers, turned off the desk lamp, and shut the door of his study behind her. Her laptop was at the desk built into the kitchen cabinets. It was the household laptop, but she was the only one who used it, because Evelyn was just a household, not a person. And her office was a few square feet of kitchen countertop, because she belonged in the kitchen, didn't she? All her stupid little hobbies, bills, and letters crammed into a junk drawer and one overhead cabinet.

Scowling, she waited for her eight-year-old laptop to slowly rouse its tired brain. When it finally stopped its whirring, she typed *Juliette Whitman* into the search engine and held her breath. It didn't take long to find her. There were a few false starts with a Realtor in Georgia and some links to genealogy sites, but then Evelyn spotted a Facebook page for a local woman. The page opened, and Evelyn choked on her own spit. There was the blond ghost, only she wasn't pale and ethereal and angry. She was vibrant. Pretty. *Happy.*

Her wide smile lit up her profile picture, bright-white teeth shining. She was adorable, and so were the pictures of the children who hovered near her.

"Oh." Evelyn sighed, the anger leaking past her parted lips. Juliette's children. The ones Evelyn was supposed to help protect. A boy and a girl, both sweet and shy with curly blond hair, smiling for whoever had taken the picture. They were perfect. Juliette was perfect.

The whole page wasn't open to the public, but Evelyn could see enough. More than enough. Juliette wasn't only a beautiful wife and mother; she was also a beloved second-grade teacher. There were pictures of her with adorable children gathered around, all of them beaming and earnest. She was crouched next to them or pointing out a word on a whiteboard or helping them dress as tiny animals.

This whore. This home-wrecker. This *killer*. Every molecule of her was a lie, and no one could see it.

Evelyn recognized the name of the elementary school where Juliette taught. It was in the next suburb, separated from Evelyn's town by undeveloped farmland. Old Highway 23 led right to it.

She wanted to call the school. Leave a message. An anonymous tip that adorable Mrs. Whitman was an adulteress and a murderer, and someone should look into it. Her hand itched to grab the phone.

But she couldn't. Partly because she'd promised Gary she wouldn't. Mostly because she had no idea what was traceable these days. They'd call her back. Or maybe the police would come by. Evelyn couldn't risk it.

She tried to click on a picture of Juliette, but Facebook wouldn't allow her to do that without signing in. Another traceable action Evelyn wanted to avoid. If she signed in to her account, Facebook would see what she was doing at least, and for all she knew there were apps to let Juliette know who'd visited her page.

So Evelyn went back to the public view of Juliette's life and zoomed in. The picture went too blurry, so she shrank it again, trying to get a sense of just how pretty Juliette was. Just how thin and young.

Her teeth were an impossibly white row of perfection. Her green eyes twinkled and didn't crease into lines when she smiled. Her small breasts seemed to levitate somewhere near her collarbone. Were they real or subtle implants? Was she waxed and tanned and tweaked to perfection?

Evelyn stared at her, wondering if her voice was high and breathy and sweet when she begged someone else's husband to take her. When she tore off those schoolteacher blouses, was she wearing sheer lace beneath? Did her flat, tan stomach lead down to a smooth, polished sex? Had Gary begged her for it? Had he loved her? Did he love her still?

She slammed the laptop shut with a cry.

Knowing more hadn't helped. Nothing would ever help. Evelyn would be in pain forever.

CHAPTER 17

AFTER

Gary always woke earlier than she did, so Evelyn's body had grown used to ignoring his alarm and the noise he made as he got ready, but today was different. Today her eyes popped open as soon as his alarm trilled. Facing away from him, she smiled into the dark, then deliberately shut her eyes again until he'd left the room.

She didn't get up. It was still early, and the promise of the day was too delicious. Evelyn bundled the warm covers around her and opened her phone. She had reread his texts over and over last night, but she was ready to read them again this morning. She wished there were more. She wished she could replay their entire phone conversation on a loop.

She'd have to ask when it was okay to text him. Or maybe they could email each other sometimes. An email at 6:00 a.m. wouldn't be nearly as curious to others as a text.

But for now, she couldn't reach out to him. She'd have to show up and hope he hadn't changed his mind. Take a leap of faith. A funny way to think of an affair.

She stroked her hands down the silky material of her nightgown, amazed to think that he might touch her just this way in a couple of hours. She'd had a few lovers before Gary, but she could barely remember their names now, much less what it had felt like to make love with them. She only knew Gary now. The techniques, the turn-ons, the routines. She knew his likes in bed and he knew hers. Whatever years of exciting exploration they'd had together had been over long ago.

She'd never wanted more than that. Not really. Not until now.

When Gary finally left, she leaped from bed and headed straight to the shower to shampoo and soap and shave and exfoliate until she glowed like a welcome sign.

She dried her hair and put on makeup, complete with eyeliner and mascara again, but she went with a neutral lipstick this time. Best to leave no incriminating evidence behind.

She'd already made a mental inventory of her underwear, and she had a black lace pair that would be perfect. She'd bought them on impulse last year, wondering if she'd exaggerated the comfort of cotton panties in her own mind, but no. Definitely not. There was nothing comfortable about lace, and the size "XL" on the tag had been an outright lie.

Evelyn dug them out of her drawer and put them on. They fit perfectly now, and comfort was the least of her concerns today. She topped it off with her least practical bra, a low-cut number she'd bought to wear with a specific cocktail dress. It didn't do much to stop her breasts from bouncing when she walked, but she imagined Noah wouldn't give a damn about that.

Actual clothes were another matter. She wanted to wear a skirt. Wanted him to shove it high on her legs again so he could get closer. Jeans would be far too much of a hindrance.

It would have to be the black skirt again, but at least she had the new green top to wear it with. As she fastened the small buttons of the blouse, she pictured Noah's hands opening them back up, exposing her.

"Oh, God," she whispered, suddenly light-headed. This was mad. Wonderful. Terrifying. Maybe it was all a fantasy. Maybe she'd finally broken from reality and was sedated in a hospital, creating this imaginary life for herself. It was a comforting thought, actually. Freeing.

Luckily, a glance at her phone put a stop to her worrying. She hadn't wanted to be too early, but now she was anxious about losing time. The gallery opened at ten. If she got there at nine, they'd have an hour of privacy. He'd said early, but had he meant that early?

Unwilling to slide into an ocean of worry about it, she slipped on her black heels, checked her makeup one more time, then headed downstairs.

"Hey, Mom," Cameron said from the kitchen. Evelyn tripped over her own feet and nearly fell.

"Cameron!" she gasped. "You're still here!" Her hands shook. Her heart trembled.

"There's a late start today. I'm leaving now. Are you okay?"

"Just startled. Sorry. I forgot about the assembly."

"You seem different," he said, frowning as he looked her up and down.

"Do I?" Her voice squeaked in fear, but his teenage maleness worked in her favor. He just shrugged and stuffed half an English muffin into his mouth before waving good-bye. He grabbed his backpack and headed out the door.

The rumble of the garage door opening drowned out her hyperventilating gasps as she collapsed into a kitchen chair. How had she forgotten her own son? What the hell was wrong with her? She'd almost been caught.

But that was silly. So she'd dressed up and put on a little extra makeup. The most her family would suspect her of was trying too hard to look younger. No one would think she was off to have an affair, for godssake. That wasn't something that Evelyn Tester did. It wasn't something she was capable of.

Gary obviously hadn't been thinking about Cameron when he'd set about screwing Juliette for six months. And that woman clearly hadn't been prioritizing her children. Her kids were still small. They still needed all her time. She'd cheated them out of more than a couple of home-cooked meals.

Cameron was practically self-sufficient. Evelyn wasn't *supposed* to be thinking about him all the time. That was unhealthy. He'd be out of the house in six months. He'd take girls back to his dorm room, and he wouldn't once think about Evelyn and her life. No one would. She was the only one looking out for herself.

This wasn't about her family. The past twenty years had been about her husband and son, but today was about her. One day. One week. One month to take what she wanted. That couldn't possibly be too much to ask of the world.

Once the strength returned to her knees, Evelyn grabbed her purse—the smaller, sexy clutch now tucked inside—and headed out.

The drive there was over in a flash. Too fast. The only thing left to do was walk down the street and knock on his door. But now she wished it weren't morning. She wished she'd come in the afternoon. They could have a glass of wine. Two glasses. It would be less like an appointment and more like a date.

Then she saw Noah. He was only a few feet inside the door of the gallery, leaning against the wall, his arms crossed. When he spotted her, he waved and moved quickly to open the lock. She would never have waited that way, but he seemed unconcerned that she'd know he was eager to see her again. He wasn't nurturing some fragile ego, too worried about pride to show his hand.

His face bloomed into a smile as he opened the door. "Good morning."

"Hi." She was happy to see him too, but her smile was all nervousness as she eased beneath his arm and heard him lock the door behind her. "I wasn't sure what time to come," she said.

"I wasn't sure what time you'd be here."

"Have you been waiting long?"

He winked. "Long enough. Want some coffee?"

"Sure," she answered automatically, but as she followed him toward the back, she reconsidered. Were they going to sit around and sip coffee and wait awkwardly for a moment to kiss? Would she have coffee breath? She wanted to taste him again, not what he was drinking.

But she was too quick to worry, apparently. As soon as they crossed the threshold into the back room, Noah turned and stopped her. He put one finger beneath her chin and lifted her face so he could press a lingering kiss to her mouth. "Is that okay?" he whispered, his breath flowing into her when she inhaled.

"Yes."

"Good. Because I feel like I'm losing my mind. You're all I could think about last night." He kissed her again. "And this morning."

"Me too."

He walked her slowly backward to the table. "Wanna make out?" he asked, and she laughed as he lifted her up and set her on the table exactly where she'd been before. It was just what she wanted. Just what she'd imagined. Her laughter died when his mouth touched her neck. She couldn't stop a quiet moan.

"You like being kissed there," he whispered against her skin.

"Yes."

"Good. I like kissing you there."

She twisted her fingers into the wild waves of his hair and held him to her neck as he sucked her skin. She had a vague idea that she should be concerned about any marks he might leave, but it felt so good she didn't care. She'd wear turtlenecks all summer if he'd just keep sucking at that spot.

It felt as if time had ended with their embrace yesterday and had only now resumed. He was between her legs again, his erection pressed against her as she arched her neck for more. In fact, she breathed that very word, "More," and Noah moaned and pushed closer, her legs spreading around his hips as he ducked his head to lick the hollow of her neck.

She might die from this, she realized then. It was so sweet and wild and terrifying that her thundering heart might just give out. How had she lived for so many years without feeling this way? She tugged him up, bringing his mouth to hers, and she kissed him too hard, too deep, trying to devour him, but he didn't seem to mind. He kissed her just as roughly, his tongue sweeping along hers over and over as she curled her fingers too tightly into his hair.

He cupped one of her breasts. His other hand gripped her hip and pulled her to the edge of the table. She could feel him through his jeans, thick and hard and pushing into her.

She let go of his hair and reached for the top button of his shirt. Her knuckles grazed soft chest hair as she worked his shirt open, then tugged it free of his jeans.

She ducked her head and kissed his neck, his collarbone. "Evelyn," he groaned, her name a sweet, secret intimacy on his tongue.

His body smelled so different, so new. A spice unlike Gary's skin, with no discreet touch of expensive aftershave to distract her. She curved her arms around his chest, spread her fingers over the heat of his back. She wanted all of her skin pressed to his, so she sighed in relief when he eased away to unbutton her shirt.

He opened it quickly. She had a brief moment to remember she was supposed to be self-conscious when he pushed the blouse off her arms and reached to unfasten her bra. But then her bra was off, and his breath was ragged with lust as he caught her nipple between his fingers.

She hissed at the shock of pleasure. Any self-consciousness fell away as he laid her back on the table and bent over to take her nipple into his mouth. Sensation swelled inside her, pushing her soul out. She didn't have the space to imagine what she looked like; all she could do was feel.

His mouth sucked at her, drawing pleasure through her body as he reached beneath her hiked skirt and slid her panties down. They both grunted in shock when he touched her. Her hips tilted up to invite his fingers deeper.

"I bought condoms," he whispered. "I didn't know. I haven't . . ."

Evelyn shook her head. "I have an IUD."

Nodding, he stood straight and unbuckled his belt.

This was somebody else, not her. Somebody else watching as he unbuttoned his jeans and pushed down his briefs and lined up his body with hers. Somebody feeling the touch of him against the most vulnerable part of her. And then he was pushing in, the tightness of it widening her eyes. He was thicker than Gary, and she was glad for that, because she could close her eyes and know it was Noah, not her husband.

"Jesus," he rasped. "You're so hot."

And she was. She was hot and wild and guiltless. An animal, spreading for him, taking him in, taking her due. She wrapped her legs around him and pulled him deep, her breath catching with the pressure. But she was so aroused that the pressure quickly eased, and then it was all liquid indulgence. All slipping and sliding while their sounds of pleasure wound around each other.

His hands slid up her belly and cupped her breasts as he sank himself into her again and again. She arched up and stretched her arms high above her head. She didn't need to hold on to anything. He could do what he wanted, use her any way he pleased.

He took her harder, faster, and she urged him on, whimpering, "Yes, yes, yes," until he finally climaxed with a desperate cry. Then her body was filled with him. A man she barely knew. A man she should never have met.

His loud panting grew softer. His hands slid from her breasts to her waist. She thought he'd withdraw then, but he surprised her by curling over her and resting his forehead on her breastbone. He pressed a gentle kiss to one breast and sighed. "Wow."

Her laughter surprised her, bouncing from her throat in relief. "Yes." She giggled, wrapping her arms around him, cradling him. "Wow."

"That was insane."

"Yes!"

Over her own laughter, she felt his chuckle rumble through her ribs. "Hold on one second," he said, and slipped free of her.

Closing her eyes, she heard the clink of his belt as he pulled up his pants. She slid her knees together, but other than that, she didn't move. She couldn't. When she heard him return, she peeked through her lashes to see that he held some sort of padded shipping blanket.

"Here." He eased it beneath her head, then lay down beside her on the table, legs bent, feet hanging down just like hers. He nudged her foot with his, and she realized she was still wearing her heels. She'd just had extramarital sex on a storage room table while wearing black heels.

"I'm sorry about the accommodations."

"I guess it worked just fine," she said, and they both laughed again, wheezing with stupid amusement until tears leaked from her eyes.

When they quieted, he cleared his throat. "I don't want you to think I thought . . . I bought the condoms just in case. Because I didn't want to be an idiot. Not because I thought we'd . . ."

"I know. Was it strange?"

He turned toward her, his eyebrows raised in question.

"Buying condoms," she said. "Not . . ." She waved a hand down their bodies. "This."

"Oh! Yes. Like being seventeen again. I was sure everyone was watching. I took off my wedding ring." He raised his hand to show a pale indentation on his ring finger. "Which was stupid in a number of ways, I guess. As if married people never use condoms."

She wondered then if Gary had used protection with Juliette. But it was an idle thought. Evelyn didn't care anymore. She didn't care about anything but this.

She rubbed her thumb over her own ring. It hadn't even occurred to her to take off her wedding band for this. Why bother? "I'm glad you thought of the condoms. That was nice. *This* was nice."

His forehead creased. "I didn't even take care of you," he murmured. "I'm sorry."

"Next time," she said, and he smiled with the joy of a little boy offered a treat.

"Next time?"

She smiled back. "Definitely." Funny, but she didn't care that she hadn't had an orgasm. Even without, it was the hottest sex she'd ever had. If he thought she wasn't coming back for more, he was a fool. An adorable fool. "But maybe you could put a couch back here or something."

"That might be a good idea. We have one in the basement we never use. I could bring it in." He swept a stray lock of hair off her cheek. "Are you okay?"

"You didn't hurt me, if that's what you're asking."

He blushed, his cheeks turning the sweetest shade of pink. "No, not that. I meant . . . emotionally."

"Honestly?" When he nodded, she shrugged. "I'm fine. In fact, I kind of feel like that was one of the best things I've ever done."

He chuckled. "Yeah, I'm having a similar thought. But I feel guilty as hell too."

"About your wife?"

"Yes."

She wanted to reassure him. Tell him why Juliette didn't matter. But she could never tell him that. He thought Evelyn had just wandered into his gallery, and if he learned the truth, he'd think she was some sort of crazed stalker. But it wasn't like that with him, not anymore.

Instead of explaining, she took his hand and brushed a kiss over his knuckles. "If you love your wife so much, then why do this?"

He turned to stare at the ceiling, but he wrapped his fingers between hers and held her hand. "Because I'm a terrible person?"

"I don't think that's true. And if it is, then I am too."

"I just . . . I love her. I love my kids. My family. My life. But something's missing."

"Geology?" she asked, only half teasing.

"Something like that, I guess. Dreams. Youth. Adventure. Sex." He slid a quick look at her. "I hate to be so typical. My wife is . . . she's working through some things."

Yeah, she was working her way through Evelyn's life like a disease.

"I've tried to be patient," he said. "I *was* patient. I didn't think I was going to be that guy."

"So why now?" she asked, but that wasn't what she really wanted to know, so she rephrased it. "Why *me*?"

He tipped his head toward her and squeezed her hand, watching her as if studying her face. She thought he'd tell her she was beautiful then, a pretty little lie woven of flattery and gratitude. "I don't know," he finally admitted, and she tried not to let the disappointment squash her satisfaction.

But he made up for it. "You're sexy as hell, of course."

She laughed. "Oh, of course!"

"And you're an amazing artist." He slid a fingertip down her jaw, down her neck, then feathered it softly along the curve of her breast, his eyes locked on the trail of his finger. "Did I mention my affinity for cute artsy girls?"

"You did. And I'm beginning to wonder if you're a breast man, as well."

His grin was a bright neon sign of chagrin. "Who, me?"

Her sigh sounded decidedly like a purr as he cupped her in his hand again. Good. That was something she had over perfect, petite

Juliette. Size Ds. Purely an accident of nature, but Evelyn would take any advantage.

"But I think," he continued, "it was mostly the way you looked at me."

"What do you mean?"

"That first day you came in, you were a stranger, but . . . I don't know. You *saw* me. Stared right into me. God, that sounds ridiculous. My youthful bad poetry cropping up."

"No," she said. "I did see you." She wouldn't tell him why, of course, and she felt a cold trickle of fear along her spine as he watched her. Did he suspect anything?

"When you ran out, I wondered if you'd come back," he finally said.

"I did."

"Yes, you definitely did."

The strange tension vanished back into humor. When the hardness of the table began to press into her joints, Evelyn didn't care. She didn't even care that she was sprawled half-naked in front of this man, her skirt bunched up and digging into her soft abdomen. His abdomen wasn't rock hard and tight either. She loved that. Loved the slight curve of his belly, his love handles and wide chest, and the sprinkling of freckles across his shoulders. He was nothing like Gary. He was someone *new*.

"Do you want to do this again?" she asked.

"Yes," he answered before her last syllable was out.

"Good. Maybe we could—"

"I have an idea," he interrupted, the words rushing together. "Just an idea. Maybe it's crazy."

"This is all crazy."

"True. But you said your husband is . . . I guess he's not inclined to suspicion?"

"He's not."

"Well, I'm going to an art show in Monterey next weekend. I don't suppose you could join me?"

"Monterey? *California?*"

"See? Insane. I just thought I'd throw it out there."

"I don't think I could," she started, but the idea floated up inside her like a balloon. "How would I—" She snapped her mouth shut and shook her head. "You'd honestly want me to go?"

"It's just two nights. And I'm sure it's impossible, but lying here next to you . . . hell, I thought how nice it would be if this were a bed, in the dark, and we had more time."

Something inside her melted. Something hard and cold and tight. To lie in bed with this man in the dark, touching and laughing and whispering. She wanted that. For hours. For days. "Let me think about it."

"Of course. Think about it. And think about this." He turned and drew her to him for a kiss, but then he pulled back with a wince. "I might be too old for table sex," he admitted.

"Nonsense. We did that part just fine. It's the table pillow talk we can't handle."

"So it's not just me?" He rose up and offered a hand to pull her up as well.

Once she slid off the table, her self-consciousness made a brief return. She snatched up her shirt and tugged it on as quickly as she could, then realized she'd forgotten her bra. "Turn around!" she ordered, and he did, laughing.

"Are you working today?" he asked over his shoulder as she struggled into the scratchy black bra.

"Yes, but I don't want to. I want to go home and paint."

"Paint!"

He'd turned toward her again, and she would have scolded him, but she was already rebuttoning her shirt. "I bought supplies on my way home last night. I haven't started anything yet."

"Will you show me when you do?"

"You're just using me for my paintings, aren't you?" But she was flattered. Even when they'd first been dating, Gary had only shown polite interest in her work. She must have been more confident back then. It hadn't bothered her. After all, she hadn't been that interested in his psychiatry papers either. Maybe they'd been mismatched from the start.

Gary had been attracted to her free spirit, her resilience, her good humor and loud laugh. She'd loved his steadiness, intelligence, and decisiveness. But attributes became annoyances over time. Yes, she could laugh at anything, but that meant she never took anything seriously. And he had rock-solid beliefs, but that meant he couldn't be budged. Free-spirited became unambitious. Steadiness was stubbornness. Opposites might attract, but there were so many jagged seams where they tried to fit together.

Noah finished dressing, and she straightened his collar and his mussed hair without even thinking. He didn't belong to her. She shouldn't be touching him like this. But he smiled like he liked it.

"I don't want you to regret this," she said.

"I'm going to feel guilty. I already do."

"I know. But . . ." If she'd only started this off with honesty, she could've told him the truth now. *Your wife doesn't deserve your faithfulness. You don't need to feel bad. She's been sleeping with my husband for months, and their affair killed a teenage girl.*

If she could tell him all that, then he could be as happy with this as Evelyn was. She wanted to erase the worry from his eyes and replace it with all the joy she was feeling. But she'd lied, and there was no taking that back. So instead of saying anything, she kissed him, a long, soft kiss to take away his pain.

"I'm sorry," she whispered against his mouth.

He shook his head. "It's not your fault I want you so much."

But it was, of course.

Just before ten, she said good-bye and headed for the school. She'd get there early to make up for yesterday's lateness. But as she pulled into the parking lot, she got a text from Noah.

`You're all I can think about.`

So she texted back and talked to him until eleven fifteen, then walked in late without a trace of guilt.

CHAPTER 18

Before

The girl's name was Kaylee Brigham. The picture used on every news site showed a smiling, round-faced teen with blue eyes that stood out in bright contrast with her brown hair. She was hugging a dog in that picture, captured in a moment of pure happiness.

But the truth was more complicated. She'd run away from home several times. She'd dropped out of school. Her parents were heartbroken and just wanted answers.

Barely breathing, Evelyn opened her school's published student directory and looked through the list of names, addresses, and parents' phone numbers. No Kaylee Brigham. She checked the one from the year before. Still no Kaylee. The girl hadn't been a student at Cameron's school. Evelyn hadn't greeted her or helped her with a school excuse or walked her to the nurse's office. Thank God.

She was a stranger, and now the story Gary had told made sense. Only a lost girl high on drugs would be wandering that highway at that hour. He'd been telling the truth.

Evelyn's relief was short-lived. She needed to know more. To find out exactly what Kaylee had been doing on that road, to make sure no one was at fault. If no one was at fault, then this would all be okay and Evelyn would have made the right decision in protecting Gary.

The news sites had little information. There had obviously been only a brief statement released by the police, and they all had the same paltry details. Evelyn searched Kaylee's name online, hoping to find out more.

The first dozen hits were more of the same, but then she found a blog entry posted by a friend years before, an innocuous little shout-out to her volleyball teammates, and it contained a link to Kaylee's Facebook page.

"Oh, God," Evelyn whispered, pressing trembling fingers to her mouth.

Kaylee hadn't posted anything in the past few months, but before that, her timeline had been dusted with the usual teenage angst and excitement. Squees of joy about seeing friends, snippets of poems about sadness, funny memes shared by a million other kids. She'd been just like Cameron, really, if Cameron had been the type of kid to be on Facebook. He wasn't. His friends teased him. Evelyn was secretly proud that he didn't feel the need to join up.

But all his friends were on social media, just like Kaylee. Some of them even followed Evelyn, calling her Mrs. T. She suspected a few of them wanted to get in good with the woman who decided whether school excuses were real or forged, but maybe some were honestly friendly.

Some of Kaylee's pictures were hidden from Evelyn because she wasn't a designated friend, but most of the posts on her wall were public for all to see. The latest was from her mother, Dawn. A poignant good-bye to a daughter she'd "lost too soon."

Evelyn covered her face and cried. Was there any difference at all between Evelyn and Kaylee's mom, Dawn? She must be living through hell. Not only was her baby dead, but she'd never know what had really happened. In fact, in the last line of the post, she asked for help. *If you have any information at all, please come forward.* Evelyn's stomach churned. She had information. She could come forward.

She clicked over to Juliette's page, looking for some confirmation that she was doing the right thing. There was a new post. A sweet story repeating what one of the kids in her class had said about love.

Love. As if Juliette knew anything about it.

Evelyn tried to click through to find out who was connected to Juliette's page, but she didn't have access. The page was fairly public. There seemed to be quite a few responses from parents of her students. But like Kaylee's page, Evelyn could only see some of it.

This time, when Evelyn backed up to Kaylee's page, there was a brand-new post. A fundraising drive to contribute to funeral costs. Dawn Brigham was online right now, just like Evelyn. She was right there, pleading for help.

Tears dripped down Evelyn's cheeks. She couldn't bring this woman's daughter back. She couldn't fix what Juliette and Gary had done. Even if she came forward, nothing would change for Dawn Brigham.

Pressing her hands hard to the keyboard, she watched random letters trickle across the white bar of the search field. She pressed harder, but they didn't move faster.

What the hell was she going to do? Could she find some way to live with this? She couldn't even offer condolences. Her account was under her real name and connected to friends, family, and volunteers, not to mention the school page she often posted to. It would be too dangerous.

But . . . *But.*

If she had a different account, she could at least follow Dawn Brigham's page. Absorb the pain. And she could find out what was going on. Get news about any developments. It would be *something*.

Evelyn searched for tricks to creating a fake Facebook account, but it was nothing difficult. All she needed was a new email address. Within minutes, she had it all set up under a name she pulled from thin air.

Heart beating far too hard, she pressed the button requesting a friendship with Dawn Brigham. She was instantly approved.

Then panic slapped her in the face. What if Dawn grew suspicious of this stranger following her? What if she pointed police in Evelyn's direction?

"No, no, no," she whispered, wishing she could take it back. But when she calmed down enough to look at Dawn's personal page, she saw that the message pinned to the top was a thank-you.

> *To all of the parents, friends, reporters, and strangers who've come here to offer support, thank you for caring about Kaylee. I've no idea what the coming days will bring, but it's comforting to know I can talk about her here.*

"I'm so sorry," Evelyn said aloud.

She was sorry. Sorry for so many things. She cried silent tears as she clicked through the Brigham family pictures. Several had been posted today of Kaylee when she was young, all happy smiles and parental hope. The wrong path she'd taken in more recent years would probably have been just a stage. She would have grown past it, surely. Gone on to have a full, rich life.

Now her parents had to live forever with whatever conflict they'd had with her. The unfortunate words they must have flung at each other. The last, sad thing Kaylee had said before she'd disappeared.

When her cell phone rang, Evelyn nearly knocked the mouse off her desk, sure in that moment that the police had already tracked her down. But it wasn't the police; it was the school. A glance at the clock had her cursing. It was nearly noon. She'd had all weekend to wallow in her grief, but she was supposed to be at work today.

"Hello?"

"Evelyn? Are you coming in?"

She winced at the irritated tone of the office manager. She and Wanda weren't close, but they were usually polite to each other. "I'm so sorry. I'm sick and I accidentally fell asleep."

"You don't sound good."

No, she was hoarse, stuffed up, and miserable. That was true, at least. "School germs, I'm sure. I'm really sorry I forgot to call."

"It's fine. Let me know how you're feeling in the morning."

Another thing to feel guilty about. Evelyn had never played hooky before. In fact, in the three years she'd been working at the school, she'd called in sick only one day, and she'd been relieved it was a Friday. By Monday her strep throat had been cured by antibiotics, and she'd been back to making herself feel useful.

But there was no way she could work at the school today. She couldn't deal with all those children who were the same age as Kaylee. Bad enough she had to face her own son when he got home.

Evelyn retrieved the mouse from the edge of the desk and rubbed a hand over her tight forehead. She couldn't only follow Dawn Brigham with this new account. She was already paranoid and sick about the charade. She could either delete the fake account or improve upon it.

After a brief prayer that she was doing the right thing, she began to build her false identity. She added more details to her profile and followed quite a few local businesses from a nearby town, just to be safe. By the end of her online tour, four individuals had friended her, and she gratefully returned the favor. She was beginning to look like a real person.

CHAPTER 19
AFTER

"The Monterey Life Center and Spa." Evelyn let the name run over her tongue. Just the name of a resort. There was nothing inherently naughty about it, but she smiled at the words. She was smiling about everything after what she and Noah had done this morning.

Though she'd gotten through her five hours of work, she'd spent most of it looking up information on the art festival and then trying to imagine herself there.

Aside from family funerals, she'd never taken a trip without Gary before. If she went to California, it would be a first. Well . . . *another* first, after the first that had happened today.

Smiling, she picked up a brush, dipped it into the blob of dark yellow on her palette, and inhaled enough air to pump up her chest and make her feel brave.

When she got tired of her own cowardice, she swiped the brush across the stretched canvas in front of her, then stared at the golden stripe she'd left behind. This painting wouldn't be anything. It wouldn't be impressive. She knew that and didn't care. The purpose of this canvas was to open her up. That was all. To *start* her again. And she could already feel it working.

She shifted the brush up to the right corner and began shading in the white, dragging the color close to the original line but not touching it.

God, it felt good.

Picking up a new brush, she pulled a sage-green line over the canvas. She'd hardly ever done landscapes, but she knew what this was. A cliff pictured on the website of the Monterey Life Center.

It wouldn't take much to pull off this trip. If she wanted a spa trip to California, there was nothing Gary could say to stop her. Nothing at all. His infidelity had freed Evelyn. Of course, her freedom meant his. At this point, Gary would be relieved to be left alone for seventy-two hours. He'd wish her bon voyage and put her out of his mind.

And she'd be with Noah. Two whole nights with him. Three days.

But did she have the guts to do it?

Evelyn laughed and almost painted her cheek green when she raised her hand to smother the sound.

Hell, yes, she had the guts to do it. After this morning, nothing would be a big step for her. She'd given her body to another man. She'd reveled in it.

God, this was just insane. She'd actually held another man inside her body. Such an intimate vulnerability with a virtual stranger. And she didn't even feel bad. She wanted more.

The rooms at the spa were expensive, but she wouldn't shy away from that either. Gary loved expensive places, so he couldn't deny her that. The spa was ten miles from the art festival, and she assumed Noah would be staying somewhere more modest, but she could rent a car.

Rent a car. Book a room. Buy a flight. Have an affair.

Would she do it?

The doorknob rattled behind her. Evelyn didn't even startle; she only glanced over her shoulder in annoyance.

"Evelyn?" Gary asked.

When she didn't answer, he knocked softly. If he didn't know how to use manners with her anymore, she'd teach him. "Yes?"

"Can I come in?"

Could he? She turned back to the painting with a scowl. She didn't want him seeing her work. Didn't want his careless disregard anywhere near her paintings. Not anymore.

She set down her brush and palette, then slid the easel around to face the far wall. When she unlocked the door, she stood in the way so he wouldn't come in, but he gestured past her as if asking permission. Churlishness not being her natural state, Evelyn rolled her eyes and stepped aside.

"What are you up to in here?"

"Setting up easels."

He glanced at the freshly marked palette but didn't press her. The smell of the oil paints must be obvious in the small room. She was clearly doing more than setting up.

"You put a lock on the door?"

"I wanted privacy."

"Well . . . it's good to see you getting back to painting."

She didn't know how that could be true when he'd literally never brought it up in eighteen years, but she let the lie go and waited to see why he'd interrupted her.

"I think I'll turn in early," he said.

"Okay."

"I guess you're not taking the sleeping pills anymore?"

"No. I don't need them."

"That's good. Really great."

"Yes. It's great."

He tucked his hands into his pockets and rocked back on his heels. For some reason, the sight of him wearing loafers in the house suddenly infuriated her. Who wore shoes *all* the time? Why couldn't he just relax, for godssake?

"I took a look at that list of therapists," he said casually, as if they were talking about a trip to the movies. "You're right. We need to go. It will be good for us. I think your first choice is fine. That woman. Smith?"

Boy, he'd really put a lot of thought and research into it. He could almost pretend to care. "It's Schmidt," she muttered.

"Right. She looks good."

She stared at him. After giving him the list of therapists weeks ago, she'd waited anxiously, asked him to hurry and choose someone so she could call about an appointment. It had felt urgent then. Lifesaving. And he'd ignored it. He'd scowled when she pressed him. Told her he'd get to it as soon as he could, but he was *busy*, obviously. So busy.

Now he was standing here like some stupid lost puppy bringing her an offering. She hated him.

He cleared his throat. "Maybe you could call her? I'll have to check my schedule, of course."

"I'll get to it when I can."

"All right. Probably Wednesday mornings are best."

"Wonderful."

He stood there for a few more awkward moments, waiting for what, she couldn't imagine. When she crossed her arms, he finally moved toward the door. "Good night, Evelyn."

Evelyn suddenly made her decision. She didn't need to think anymore. "I'm going away next weekend. To a spa."

"A spa?"

"Yes. In California."

"Do you even go to spas?" He looked completely dumbfounded.

"No, which makes me think it's time."

Gary shook his head. "Okay. Is Sharon going too?"

"No. Just me." Technically true. She would be traveling alone.

They stared at each other past the threshold of the door until he nodded. "I'm sure it will be wonderful."

"Oh, I'd imagine so." She closed the door and locked it with a sharp snick.

Once his footsteps moved away, Evelyn picked up her phone and typed a simple message to Noah. `I'll book my ticket tonight.`

Then she turned the easel back around and rolled her shoulders. The Monterey cliffs took shape quickly. Her first painting of her new life. She was finished with it by midnight. She'd let it dry for a couple of days and then take it to Noah.

CHAPTER 20

BEFORE

Evelyn chose her outfit very carefully. Lycra leggings made for running that she'd only ever used for walking. A plain black T-shirt topped by a black-and-pink hoodie made with a sweat-wicking fabric. A dark-gray baseball cap with no markings. Running shoes. A water bottle. Sunglasses.

When she was fully dressed, she raced to the bathroom and threw up.

This was a dangerous, stupid idea.

After she retched into the bowl until there was nothing left in her stomach, she rinsed her mouth, washed her hands, and set off with only her keys and license. The license she locked in the glove compartment of the Toyota before she pulled out of the garage.

It had been five days since the accident, and she was going back to Old Highway 23.

Trying her best to ignore the panic banging at the inside of her skull, Evelyn followed the route she'd taken to rescue Gary. Thank God it was simply done, or she might not have remembered even that. She'd been in a haze that night. Or she'd been in a haze her whole life. Who could tell at this point?

Once she made the turn onto Old Highway 23, she had to clutch the steering wheel to keep her hands from trembling. The quaking of her muscles vibrated up into her elbows and then her shoulders, but she drove on. She didn't stop.

Everything looked different in the afternoon sun, and she had no sense of where she'd pulled over to tow Gary from the ditch. For miles, the highway was nothing but an asphalt line through woods, paralleled by that earthen drainage ditch. Even at this time of day she passed only three cars as she drove.

She crested a small hill, and at the bottom of a long, shallow dip in the road, she saw it. The memorial.

A picture had been posted of it online, but there'd been no need. It looked the same as any other roadside memorial erected hastily by loved ones. She'd seen them her whole life on the sides of freeways. A white wooden cross. Fake pink flowers. A mound of teddy bears. Being so new, Kaylee's memorial had balloons attached too. Three white balloons that bobbed and dipped in the cool breeze.

Evelyn drove slowly past it. She couldn't pull over here. Her parked car would be a glaring memory for anyone who passed. She drove on, watching the cross get smaller in her rearview mirror.

When she heard a strange buzzing noise, she was consumed with fear for a second or two. Terror flashed through her that her car would break down here and she'd babble out a confession to anyone who stopped to help. She couldn't be seen here. Couldn't be remembered.

But no, it wasn't her car. When she sucked in a gasping breath, she realized the strange noise was her. An odd, low hum her throat was making in an attempt to soothe her.

Switching on the radio, she let the commercials mask the sound.

She'd thought she might pull over when she got to a housing development, but two miles up the road she'd passed only one intersection,

James Lane, and there'd been no houses there either. Evelyn doubled back. When she got to James, a road she'd never been on, she turned right. Within a quarter mile, the wooded wetlands continued on the left side of the road, but there were fenced horse pastures on the right, dotted by scattered homes.

At half a mile, she found the perfect spot. A sign indicated that the wetlands were a protected open space. A small brown square pointed the way to a trailhead. Evelyn turned left onto a dirt road that cut through the forest.

The parking area was really just a circle of rutted dirt, so Evelyn pulled as close to the trees as she could and turned off the car. The engine ticked itself cool. Her breath rasped. Her heart thumped, the pulse beating hard in every part of her body.

"Okay. No big deal. You're out for a run. Or a walk. You're out for a walk." If she tried to run, her heart would explode and they'd find her body in the woods near Kaylee Brigham's death site. Surely that would lead back to her husband.

Then again, what would Evelyn care at that point? She'd be comfortably deceased.

When she finally emerged from the car, she saw there were two narrow trails heading into the woods. One looked as if it set off in the direction of the highway, so she headed for that one, only checking over her shoulder twice to see if anyone was watching as she ducked into the woods.

A few seconds in, she felt as if she were entirely cut off from the world. There was no traffic noise here. No sign of houses or streetlights or power lines. There was the packed-dirt trail, the tumbling green of the woods, and the occasional pockets of cattails and opaque water.

She'd always thought of forests as quiet, but it wasn't quiet here. Tree branches clicked above her in the breeze, and everywhere frogs and crickets sang and screeched. A fly occasionally buzzed too close to her ear. Evelyn brushed it away as a trickle of sweat itched its way down her scalp. It was only fifty-five degrees. She wasn't warm; she was terrified.

She'd planned to jog along the road and pass idly by the site of the accident, but this was better. She doubted anyone would pass her on these trails, but if they did, she'd be a woman who didn't even *know* Highway 23 was on the other side of this open space. Just a suburban mom out here getting in shape, like hundreds of others before her.

The trail felt like it went on forever. The slant of the afternoon sun didn't penetrate the woods, and the light got dimmer and dimmer. She eased off her sunglasses and slipped them into her pocket. When it felt like she should be nearing the highway, she opened the GPS map on her phone and zoomed in.

If it was accurate, she wasn't too far away, but the trail was going straight north now, no longer cutting toward the road.

She moved more slowly, looking for a likely spot. It took another five minutes, but she finally found a ridge of a low hill that she hoped could help her avoid water. Easing aside the branches of a sprawling bush, she headed into the woods.

She had to pick her way slowly through the underbrush, and her leggings were covered with burrs before she'd even gone ten feet. But it was dry. A few minutes later, the dimness of the woods gave way to brighter light, and she could see blue sky ahead. When she spotted blacktop through the trees, she stopped.

She couldn't possibly have estimated the location of the memorial with any precision, so she'd have to make herself visible now. She could stay hidden in the woods and walk parallel to the road, but there'd be no point when she didn't even know if she was too far north or south.

After shaking out her numb hands and catching her breath, Evelyn slipped her sunglasses back on and walked toward the highway. At the edge of the trees she hung back, waiting for the sound of cars, but it seemed she was alone for now. She walked to the ditch, then looked left and right.

It was there. Not too far away. About a hundred feet north of her. She stepped into a jog, adrenaline giving an assist for the quick trip. After leaping over the ditch, she ran the last dozen feet on the gravel shoulder.

She'd thought she would just get a look at the spot and jog on past, but she couldn't make herself do it. Four feet from the cross, she stopped in her tracks and stared. Even if someone saw her, stopping at a memorial was a normal reaction. Anyone would be sympathetic or at least curious. It wasn't suspicious. It didn't mark her.

This was where it had happened. Right here. Her husband and his lover had driven on this asphalt and run over Kaylee Brigham. Gary had gotten out of the car and looked at the girl lying on the ground. He may have even walked in this exact spot where Evelyn stood.

The road itself was too dark to show any bloodstains. There must have been some. Gary had said she'd suffered an obvious skull fracture. Evelyn stepped forward, the gravel crunching beneath her feet as she studied the dirt. Kaylee had been found on the shoulder, according to the news. But wherever the poor child had lain, Evelyn could find no evidence of it.

Looking around, she took in the looming branches of the trees above and the green, slimy water in the ditch, and she hoped Kaylee had been knocked immediately unconscious. She would have been scared lying here in the dark, alone and cold in the forest, the hard pebbles of the highway digging into her skin. Hopefully she hadn't known. Hopefully she hadn't hurt.

When the faint sound of a car reached her ears, Evelyn leaped into motion, resuming her jog north. She kept her head down, her ears straining for a sign that anything was wrong, but the car seemed to keep a steady speed. It didn't slow to check her out or, God forbid, pull over because it was a police officer with a few questions about whether she jogged here often and what she—

The car zoomed past, a harmless green sedan. Evelyn immediately leaped over the ditch and sprinted into the woods. It wasn't until she'd crashed through the bushes that she realized how stupid she'd been. If the driver had glanced in the mirror, he'd have seen her fleeing toward the trees. Why hadn't she just kept jogging?

"Dumb, dumb," she muttered to herself, pushing the heel of her hand into her temple. She'd panicked. Run without thinking.

Was that what Gary and Juliette had done? She couldn't believe they'd left that girl there, but it must have all been confusing and terrifying and so unexpected. Could Evelyn know without a doubt that she wouldn't have done the same?

She didn't want to forgive them. They didn't deserve her sympathy. Juliette was a monster. She had to be. How could Evelyn even guess at how a monster thought?

Then again, wasn't that why she'd come out here? To try to *understand*? She couldn't be sure anymore. She was losing her hold on reality. What could she possibly have thought she'd understand from jogging down the side of an empty highway? A road was just a road. There weren't answers here.

The light was growing truly dim when she turned and headed back through the woods. Clouds had blown in to cover the sun. She stuffed her sunglasses away and picked her way over fallen trees and little water-filled pits. This wasn't high ground anymore, and she felt the moist dirt give beneath her shoes with each step. It felt like walking over graves. Like hands would reach up and grab her, the sharp bones poking out through rotting flesh, pleading with her feet to just give in and stop.

Was Kaylee's spirit still here? Was it stuck here because of the injustice of it all? Evelyn wasn't sure if she believed in ghosts, but if they existed, these were the circumstances that must create them. A life cut short. No justice in sight.

Was Kaylee's ghost rising up from this soft ground? Was she watching Evelyn? Would she want to protect her or hurt her? Evelyn wanted to do the right thing, but she couldn't. Would a ghost sense that?

Something caught at the lace of Evelyn's right shoe and tried to tug her backward.

She grunted in shock and reached out to a tree to steady herself. Off balance now, she leaned into the trunk, then wrapped her arms around it. When her foot didn't come free, she pressed her forehead to the bark and whined, pulling harder at her foot. The frogs and crickets whirred more loudly around her.

She didn't deserve this. It wasn't her fault. She'd done everything right and nothing wrong, and she couldn't be the one haunted by these ghosts. It hadn't been her. She couldn't bring Kaylee back.

"Help," she whispered as something tickled the knuckles of her right hand. An ant probably. Or a spider. Or Kaylee Brigham's hair. *"Help me!"*

Her shout echoed against the trees. The forest seemed to take a breath. The bugs stopped their incessant trilling, and the frogs went silent. Evelyn could hear her lungs working now. She could hear the blood rushing through her. Her mind calmed enough to let her think.

There were no ghosts here. It was just the woods. Mud and bugs and shadows and twigs.

"You're okay," she whispered. A lie, of course. She was losing her mind. But she lifted her head from the bark and opened her eyes. After shielding her vision for so long, it wasn't so dim in here. Evelyn blew out a hard breath and lifted her foot up and back. Wiggled it a little. Whatever had caught her let go.

Evelyn unwrapped her arms. She looked back and couldn't decide which branch had grabbed her, but there definitely was no hand. The crickets had started up again before she stepped away.

To tie herself to the real world, Evelyn pulled out her phone and called up the GPS again. It was a comforting, no-nonsense sight after picturing spirits trying to catch her.

According to the map, Evelyn was exactly where she thought she was, so she pressed forward, staring at the ground beneath her feet, half to avoid tripping and half to remind herself there were no skeletal fingers emerging from the soil.

As she was trying to find her way past a seemingly impenetrable line of dogwood bushes, a blackbird suddenly startled from the leaves. Then there was a whole flock of them, rising up, their little bodies joining into a comma-shaped cloud high above the trees before they all veered toward the east and disappeared. They reminded her of the birds in her dream the night of the accident. Was it a sign?

Maybe it was, because when Evelyn dropped her gaze from the patch of sky, she was startled to see something beyond the tall bushes. A wooden shack stood about fifteen feet away, blocking her path.

Actually, *shack* was too generous a word. It looked more like an ancient lean-to, plopped in the middle of the woods, held up only by the generosity of the large tree it was angled against.

She edged around the bushes and approached the dark-gray structure cautiously. Broken windows stared menacingly at her. She circled around the shack, and when she finally found the door, she gasped.

Striped across the crooked door was a bright banner of yellow plastic. Black letters marched across it: "Police Line. Do Not Cross."

Evelyn stumbled back. When her foot caught on the edge of something, she sat down hard, sharp edges of wood and rock poking into her soft flesh. But the pain barely reached her. She sprang back up, spinning in a frantic circle, trying to spot the officers who were likely descending on her, guns drawn.

Already, her mind was forming lies, excuses. *I was just out for a run, I got lost, I took a shortcut, I didn't know,* I didn't know*!*

She held up her hands, turned more slowly. No one appeared.

Evelyn closed her eyes, straining to hear something new. But the forest sounded the same. Frogs, crickets, flies. Now the screaming of a crow somewhere distant. There were no crashing boots or shouted orders. She'd seen too many movies. There weren't any cops here, just like there weren't any ghosts.

She was an idiot. A stupid, helpless, foolish idiot.

Dropping her hands, she turned back to face the shack.

Now that she looked more carefully, she could see that two more strips of the police tape hung limp along the inside of the door, as if the tape had been put up days ago and never touched since. It didn't look like an active scene. In a week, the police tape would likely all blow away and be forgotten forever.

But it was here for a reason. This building must be related to Kaylee's death. It couldn't be a coincidence. Not this close.

She scanned the small clearing one more time before taking a step toward the shack. When nothing bad happened, she took two more.

The door had seemed to be hanging by only one hinge, but now she saw it wasn't hanging at all. It was propped against the doorway, covering most of the opening, but not all. Daring to draw nearer, she leaned her face close to one of the cracks, but not enough light stole through the broken windows, and she was too afraid to scoot the door aside.

After listening one more time for any alarming sounds, Evelyn moved carefully along the line of the wall until she reached one of those blank black windows. She turned on the flashlight on her phone and held it high.

As the beam of light swept over the interior of the shack, Evelyn frowned in confusion. Despite outward appearances, this place wasn't exactly abandoned. A stained ancient mattress lay on the dirt floor, and fast-food trash was scattered everywhere. She could see several bent spoons as well. Sheltered as she was, even Evelyn knew what that meant.

Someone had been living here, using drugs here, and Kaylee had been missing for weeks. This was it. The reason the teenager had been on Old Highway 23 in the middle of the night. She'd been high or just cold and confused. Maybe she'd thought she would hitch a ride somewhere. Or maybe she'd just wandered onto the road and started walking.

Whatever had happened, this was where it had started.

When Evelyn decided to leave, it didn't take long to find the trail. The shack sat only about forty feet from it, which made sense. Local kids wouldn't know this place was here if it weren't accessible.

As she trekked back to her car, Evelyn found she felt a little better, which was strange. Nothing had changed, after all, but she had discovered *something*.

Maybe she wasn't such an idiot. Whether she'd crossed a line—or several lines—or not, she was piecing together what she needed to know of the story. Digging at the nastiness infecting her. If she could get the wound clean, it might have a chance to heal. She could get back to her life. Move on.

If she could gather all the information, maybe there'd be hope for her marriage. Maybe there'd be hope for her.

CHAPTER 21

AFTER

Evelyn stretched hard, loving the way her belly went flat for a moment under Noah's sprawled hand. She pointed her toes past the arm of the ugly brown couch, then relaxed back into the cushions. "I can't believe you moved the couch in here so quickly."

"I was motivated."

"By little ol' me?"

"Mm." He nuzzled her neck, then chuckled at the way she immediately arched for more. "I live to satisfy."

"You certainly did earlier."

There was that adorably proud little-boy smile again. She shook her head, but he'd earned it. He'd pushed her onto the couch, pulled off her panties, and proceeded to give her the best orgasm of her life. She'd read that sex got better with age, but she hadn't believed it until now.

Of course, she'd returned the favor. And she'd enjoyed that more than any oral sex she'd ever *given* too. She was floating now. Buzzing with hormones that felt as intense as drugs. And Noah was her path to more.

She sighed. "I can't wait for California."

"Five more days."

She loved that he was counting down. "You should come stay in my spa room. It's got a huge tub. A shower for two."

Noah groaned and ducked his head to kiss her breast. "Okay, you talked me into it. I'll be there as often as I can."

"Three days of this," she whispered.

"Three days of better than this."

"I don't think I can take any better," she said honestly. "That was so good. Am I supposed to say that? Or am I supposed to play coy?"

"No, you're absolutely supposed to say that. You're supposed to tell me I'm an unbelievably good lover and you've never had better."

"I've never had better," she repeated, and it was true. He was certainly attentive, but it wasn't just that. Whatever electricity was arcing between them intensified even the barest touch into a torturous, shivery stroke. She still felt too conscious of her body when she was looking at herself in the mirror, but once she was with him, all her modesty drowned in a tsunami of lust and she no longer cared.

"What time is it?" she asked.

He glanced at his watch. "Only nine thirty."

"Good." She snuggled even closer than she needed to on the narrow couch cushions, his naked body pressed all along her side. "I like talking to you this way."

"Me too."

"I finished another painting."

"Another woman?" he asked.

"Yes."

"Do you always paint women?"

"Almost always. There's something . . . I don't know. There's something powerful about women, isn't there? But it's a quiet power. It lends itself to being revealed on canvas." She smiled. "Or maybe it's just a yearning for my mother."

"How old were you when she died?"

"Nineteen."

"I'm sorry," he whispered, and kissed the top of her head.

She'd met Gary not long after. Maybe that was why she'd been so thoroughly seduced by the security of a life with him. No father, and her mother just lost. She didn't want to think about it now. Gary was her past.

"I thought maybe I'd bring it next time. See what you think."

"Yes," he said immediately. "Tomorrow."

"Okay. If it's dry, I'll bring it in the morning." They'd do this again tomorrow. "Do you think . . . ?" She abruptly reconsidered her idle question and swallowed it.

"What?"

Evelyn shook her head. "It's stupid."

"Nothing is stupid. I want to know what you're thinking. I wish I could know everything about you. Read your mind."

"Now, *that* would be a bit much. But . . . do you think we could do this forever? Meet like this? I was in an incredibly good mood at work the other day."

"You mean we could do this like coffee? Just a regular part of our days?"

"Why not?"

Laughing, he kissed her, a quick peck that turned into something softer. "I'd like that. A lot."

That was something. She knew Noah loved his wife. He didn't want to hurt her, but despite that, he didn't want to give up Evelyn either. He wanted both, and Evelyn was willing to give him that. For now.

But only for now. Because at long last, there had been a new development in Kaylee's case.

Just that morning, Dawn had announced that the police believed Kaylee was with a friend when she died, and they were calling for anyone who had information to come forward.

Please, if you've heard something, PLEASE call the hotline, even if you don't want to leave your name. Kaylee may be gone, but she loved you and you are still her friends! If you're the one who knows what happened that night, please come forward. We just want to know.

A couple of weeks ago, this message would have sent Evelyn into a tailspin. The terror, anxiety, and uncertainty would have broken her into tiny, quaking pieces. But today? Today she'd felt only a deep sense of rightness.

She could see everything now. She'd chosen to follow all the unraveled threads of that terrible night, and they'd led her here. To this couch. With this man.

She'd never been a big believer in destiny or fate, but she'd always believed in silver linings. Out of something awful, something wonderful could grow. And this was her wonderful. Noah.

She wasn't foolish enough to believe she loved him yet. They hardly knew each other, really. But they had *something*. Something meaningful. She saw him. He saw her. They brought out art and laughter and daring in each other.

And they both deserved better than their spouses had given. They both deserved *this*.

"What's your favorite spot in the world?" she asked him, settling her head against his chest so his heartbeat filled her head.

His hand slipped gently between her legs.

"Stop!" she shrieked, laughing as she wiggled away.

"Okay, besides that? I don't know. Somewhere on the coast, I think."

"Monterey will be beautiful," she said, picturing the cliff she'd painted.

"It will be. But there's a little island on the East Coast I like even more. I went to an art festival there a couple of times, but the show was canceled three years ago. I can't imagine when I'll ever get back."

"Oh, no! Where is it?"

"Off the coast of Rhode Island."

Evelyn gasped. "Are you talking about Block Island?"

"You've heard of it?"

"I've been there!"

He lifted his head to look at her. "No. Nobody I know has even heard about it."

"We rented a home there for a week when Cameron was four! I don't even remember why. One of my husband's colleagues was going on about it or something. I loved it! I've fantasized for years about living there."

"Can you imagine how beautiful it must be once the tourists are gone?"

"Totally isolated. Totally quiet. I used to think about it all the time."

"Man, I love that place."

"You could open a gallery there!"

He laughed. "You could move there and paint."

God, wouldn't that be lovely? It was a ridiculous fantasy—not even a fantasy, really, just a wild story to tell herself—but she could imagine strolling on the beach with Noah, no one else around for miles. It'd be so isolated they could make love on the beach before going back to a room of windows that looked over the ocean, easels set up so she could capture the waves.

Warmth started at the top of her head and slid slowly down her body. "That's a crazy coincidence, Noah." The warmth swept back through her when she felt his name in her mouth. She loved saying it. Loved sighing it out.

"Maybe that's our connection," he offered.

No. That wasn't their connection. Not even close. But it was another sign. Jesus, maybe she did believe in destiny. She'd loved Block Island so much. Even Gary had relaxed there. He'd never even curled his lip at the mediocre restaurant meals.

On their last full day of the vacation, Evelyn had walked almost the entire perimeter of the island, stopping to look at every "For Sale" sign she'd seen.

It was a true island, surrounded by the sea, thirteen miles from the nearest coast. The place had been crowded with summer visitors like them, ferried over from the mainland for a day or a week. But how idyllic it must be for the other nine months of the year. A fairy-tale setting. Old clapboard houses and churches and two lighthouses. She'd wanted it. But there wasn't enough of a population to support a psychiatrist. It had been a fleeting dream.

But now the dream was back. "Maybe they'll start the art festival back up again," she said.

"If they do, you could meet me there."

Her heart tightened to an ache. Yes. She could meet him there. Steal a few days. Maybe a week. They could browse the little bookstore and buy homemade candy and watch a fireworks show over the water. They could sleep with the windows open to the sea and order breakfast in bed and charter a sailboat for one perfect afternoon.

A distant knock made them both jerk in guilty shock. Their heads swung to the monitor. A UPS man stood at the door.

"Shit," Noah cursed as he climbed naked over her body and grabbed his pants. She relaxed back into the couch and watched him dress, smiling at the way he jumped from one foot to the other. His buttocks were lightly furred with nearly invisible hair, and she already liked the feel of it under her hands. He skipped the shoes and buttoned his shirt on the way to the hallway.

Evelyn watched on the monitor as Noah's back filled the camera, then as he exchanged words she couldn't hear with the delivery person. It felt strangely exhilarating to lie naked only a few dozen feet away.

In less than a minute, Noah was back with two boxes. "Thank God it wasn't my regular guy. He comes to the back door. That would have been a scramble."

Evelyn stretched an arm idly over her head. "Nonsense. I'm obviously an artist's model. Nothing strange about that."

"No, you look distinctly like a woman who's just had the best sex of her life."

When he didn't rejoin her on the couch, she groaned. "Is it time to get dressed? Or have you already tired of me?"

"Time to get dressed. Though if it were up to me, you could stay there all day just like that."

"While you work?" She laughed.

"Yes. A nice little treat whenever I need coffee."

"I know I'm not supposed to be flattered at being made into a sexual object for your enjoyment, but I'm a little flattered."

"I'd volunteer to do the same at your job."

Snorting with laughter over the image of him sprawled naked on the couch in the teachers' lounge, Evelyn sat up and grabbed her wrap dress. "Where did you throw my panties this time?" she asked, feeling like the most thrillingly decadent woman in the world.

He found her underwear and brought her a kiss as well. After school, she'd need to do more shopping. She was quickly running out of sexy options, and she was someone's filthy lover now. That took care.

She made it into work on time, though she did take a few extra minutes in her car to check out the rumor mill on Facebook. So far there was nothing but more conjecture. It felt strange to think that, out of all the people in the world, Evelyn was the one who knew the most about this crime.

Gary and Juliette had been there, of course, but Evelyn had heard Gary's story, and she also knew what was going on with Kaylee's family. She even knew about the shack where Kaylee had likely been living.

Dawn Brigham and the police knew those last details, but they had no idea who had been driving the car or why they hadn't stopped. Evelyn was the only link between all of them, and she was just waiting for someone else to connect the dots.

Whichever junkie friend had been with Kaylee that night would eventually be tracked down. At the very least, there'd be a description of the car and the man who'd gotten out to check on Kaylee. There might even be part of a license plate.

It had only taken ten days for Gary to feel safe enough to get the small dent in the BMW repaired and drive it again. That was on the record now for the police to find.

There would be fallout, of course. Gary would lose his practice. Cameron would find out the truth, but he'd go off to college and move on. And Evelyn . . . well, Evelyn just wasn't afraid anymore. She didn't need Gary or this community or her reputation. She'd happily leave it all behind. And Noah would be free of Juliette.

Granted, there'd be some discomfort in explaining Evelyn's connection to his wife, but surely Noah would understand the horror of what she'd been going through. She hadn't been in her right mind. Maybe she'd even gone a little mad. But she was fine now. She'd never, ever felt so right.

Evelyn hadn't quite made it down the hallway to the school office when she was accosted.

Jackie Arthur stood in her way, arms and legs akimbo as if she'd been working herself up for this confrontation. "Everybody wants to know what's going on with the volunteer dinner. There're only five weeks of school left."

Instead of answering immediately, Evelyn looked idly at her phone, swiped through a couple of messages, and then raised one eyebrow. "There's not going to be a volunteer dinner."

"Excuse me?"

"I said there won't be a dinner."

"What are you *talking* about?"

Irritated by having to stand in the hall only a few steps from her office, Evelyn moved forward and refused to alter her path. Jackie squeaked and twitched to the side just in time to avoid being pushed.

"What I'm talking about," Evelyn said as she rounded the counter and dropped her purse on the desk, "is the fact that I put in more hours organizing that dinner than any of the award winners put into doing actual school stuff."

"It's their reward for the work!"

"And where's my reward?"

Jackie scoffed. "Is that what this is about? You want someone to give you an award too? Fine! Have a plaque engraved for yourself! But we're having this dinner."

"No. It's stupid to waste so much money and energy in order to pat people on the back for things they should've been happy to do in the first place. We can have an assembly in the theater and hand out awards there. No renting tables, no paying caterers, no asking the Honor Society kids to act as waiters. Frankly, they're never very good at it."

"What is going on with you?" Jackie demanded. "You used to be good at this; now you're worse than useless. You're a detriment to the volunteer program."

"Fine," Evelyn growled. "I quit. You can be the volunteer coordinator. Have at it."

"You can't . . . You can't *quit*! You have work to do! The graduation celebrations! Seniors' Day! The volunteer dinner! If you—"

"They're all your problems now. Better get to it."

Jackie sputtered out something incomprehensible.

"I'll forward you the relevant emails," Evelyn offered.

When Jackie spun and stomped out of the office, the silence in the room felt like physical pressure. Evelyn glanced around at the other two women in the office. They both looked away. "Sorry about that. A small disagreement."

Old Evelyn would have been consumed with worry over what she'd done. Actually, old Evelyn would never have done that in a million years. New Evelyn was too busy thinking about her weekend in California to care. Screw Jackie Arthur. That woman needed to find a few more hobbies to fill her days. Being volunteer coordinator would be perfect for her. She couldn't keep her fingers out of the damn pie anyway.

Evelyn processed her biggest pile of work, then logged into her email account. Wanda was in the principal's office with him, going over a report he needed to present to the school board. She'd never know that Evelyn wasn't exactly doing her paid duties.

During the chaos of the past month, Evelyn's inbox had exploded from 15 crucial items to 534.

"Good Lord," she muttered. Life really crept up during a nervous breakdown. Or maybe it hadn't been a breakdown. Maybe it had just been a metamorphosis. She felt so sure of herself now. As if she'd been just a blur of a person before and now she was solid, made of dark lines and bright colors. She was stronger now. Better.

A lot of the emails were easy to delete. The dozens of book-fair-related messages were gone in a second. Any mail related to the volunteer dinner Evelyn forwarded to Jackie before dropping her copy in the trash. She rolled her shoulders and bit back a smile.

Seniors' Day was a stickier issue, because her son was involved and Evelyn didn't particularly want to screw it up for him. Coming up with the event's permission slip was easy enough. Evelyn pulled up the one she'd written the previous year and changed the dates. The trip to a local amusement park had already been arranged, but the buses still needed to be reserved and parent chaperones collected.

Evelyn was no longer interested in coordinating the chaperoning, so she filled out all the necessary forms to reserve the buses and typed up another email to Jackie titled SENIORS' DAY VOLUNTEERS NEEDED. She generously included the date and time information, along with how many parents would be required. Surely Jackie could handle the rest.

The rest of the Seniors' Day emails went in the trash too. It took a full hour to wrap up her remaining duties and shove everything else at Jackie. Afterward, Evelyn breathed a huge sigh of relief and got back to her paid work for the school. Life felt even sweeter than it had when she'd driven here, and it had been pretty damn sweet then.

Wanda stopped on her way out of the principal's office. "I got your request for Friday off. There's standardized testing that day, so I'll need you here."

Evelyn didn't feel even a twinge at that. "Well, I'll be in California. I've already bought the ticket."

"I'm sorry, but I can't accommodate that request."

No one said no to Wanda. Everyone in the school was terrified of her, even the principal. After all, she'd outlasted every single person in the administration and most of the teachers too. Evelyn stared into the woman's faded-gray eyes. She lifted her chin. There was nothing here she was afraid of losing. Not anymore.

"I won't be here on Friday. I'm sure the testing will go just fine. If you can't manage without me, then I do believe I'm due a raise and a promotion. Don't you?"

Wanda's eyes widened. Her lips disappeared entirely. "You've already missed eleven days of work this month. If you think—"

"According to the school district, sick days are entirely separate from vacation days. You know that. I can't be denied a vacation day—an *unpaid* vacation day—because of a documented illness. I brought in a note."

"It was from your husband."

"He's a doctor."

The woman bristled. "I won't be—"

"Wanda." Evelyn leaned forward until she was only six inches from Wanda's quivering chin so she could whisper her next words. "You don't scare me." Then she smiled with all the joy bubbling up inside her chest. "There. That's settled. I'm going to run this requisition form over to the nurse's office for her signature so we can get these supplies ordered. Thanks for the chat."

New Evelyn was really kind of kick-ass. No wonder Noah thought she was sexy.

CHAPTER 22
Before

One week after her death, there were still no developments in Kaylee Brigham's case. No real news—only deeper heartache. Her friends began posting stories of Kaylee on Dawn's page, memories and pictures. Evelyn, hunched over the laptop for hours on end, devoured every one.

There were rumors to keep up with too. Stories from her classmates that started with "I heard," or "Someone told me," or "A boy who used to date her friend said," all of them weaving fantasies about what had happened that night on Old Highway 23. The prevailing theory seemed to be a drug deal gone bad or a cover-up of an overdose. Others posited that she'd been kidnapped and had heroically jumped from a moving vehicle.

Evelyn found herself strangely disappointed that no one was on the right track. Acknowledging that filled her stomach with acid and bile. She couldn't hope that the truth came out. It would devastate her family, her life, her world. She'd die to protect Cameron, so how could she wish for that kind of destruction?

But even if she wanted the best for her son, she wanted the worst for Juliette Whitman. Jealousy and pain and a yearning for justice braided themselves into a thick rope of hatred that wound through Evelyn. It squeezed her, twisting her nerves, changing her body. It *hurt*.

The only way to ease the burning pain was to do more, to know more, so she haunted Juliette's public posts, reading every word, every reply. It all infuriated her. Everyone thought this woman was a saint. Her cousins and friends loved her. Her students adored her. The parents admired her and heaped praise on every post.

Everything she wrote was gentle and sweet. Glowing with good intention. Orphans in Bangladesh. Elephants in Africa. Local children who went hungry during the summer. She cared about everyone. Everything! Except Evelyn's family, of course. Except Kaylee Brigham. Except her marriage vows.

During the fourth day of Evelyn's unofficial sick break from work, she couldn't take it anymore. She had to be missing something. There had to be a glimmer of the real Juliette somewhere, and Evelyn *needed* to understand.

Clenching her teeth, Evelyn signed in to her fake account and hit the "Like" button for Juliette's elementary school. Then she sent a friend request to Juliette.

She was accepted within an hour. After all, what would Juliette Whitman have to hide? She was everyone's friend. All comers welcome!

Evelyn's head buzzed as she flipped through photos she'd had no access to before. This was wrong. She knew this was wrong. Grieving for her marriage, raging over her husband's infidelity, even investigating what had happened that night . . . those things were all logical. Assuming a false identity to spy and interact with other people online? Even she understood this was probably not rational.

But she couldn't fathom what else to do. Something terrible had happened. Something awful. And Evelyn had to swallow it down like poison. Every day she woke and took another dose. It was killing her.

The personal photos provided no relief. Juliette's children were so happy. The Halloween costumes homemade every year. The holiday turkeys golden brown. At the start of April, she and the children had gone to a local senior citizens' center to play games and teach little Stephanie and Connor about giving back to the community.

Evelyn swallowed hard. Less than a week after that, Juliette had killed a girl.

But she did find something that stayed the progress of her rage. Juliette's Facebook posts had slowed down after that terrible night. Evelyn had thought maybe the newest posts were restricted to only friends and hadn't been visible before. Maybe Juliette had been lying low. But no. The posts simply weren't there. It was possible Juliette wasn't a complete sociopath, after all. Maybe she had real feelings behind that fake perfection.

After the accident there were school-related posts, but nothing else. No pictures of her children. No recipes of what she'd fixed for dinner. No adorable stories of the darnedest things her kids had said.

The tightness of that awful coil inside Evelyn's gut eased a little. She wanted Juliette to suffer. She *needed* it. Maybe Evelyn could relax a little if she just *knew* it was happening.

Was it?

She moved down in the time line, searching for more answers. About a year back, she found something she hadn't seen before: a picture of the whole family, including Juliette's husband.

Evelyn leaned in close to study him, wondering about this man who'd been cuckolded by his adorable little wife. He stood about a foot taller than Juliette, and his tan skin was darker than hers, his brown hair a little too long and shaggy. Other than that, he was unremarkable. Decent looking but not gorgeous. Smiling at the camera, but a little distracted.

Evelyn read the comments below the picture and found an important detail to add to her collection. Noah. His name was Noah, assuming that the woman who'd commented on the picture was correct.

Noah Whitman.

She searched for his page and found nothing. A man of mystery. Maybe he—

The garage door banged open only a few feet from Evelyn's desk, and she yelped in surprise.

"Hey, Mom!" Cameron said. "Are you still sick?"

"I am," she said, meeting Gary's eyes as he followed Cameron in through the front door.

He still wasn't driving the BMW, so he'd dropped Cameron at school in the morning and had picked him up from an extra-long water polo practice. The big state tournament was coming up. Cameron and his team put in hours whenever they could.

"I guess you didn't get to the store today?" Gary asked, his eyes dipping to take in Evelyn's robe and slippers.

"No," she snapped, "I was feeling pretty sick all day." She closed the lid of the laptop before he passed. "There's a roast in the oven. It's ready. You can serve yourselves."

Evelyn grabbed a glass of wine and escaped to her bedroom. Gary was still sleeping in the guest room, but she'd heard him tell Cameron it was to avoid catching whatever bug Mom had, so Evelyn didn't even have to hide it.

She shut the bedroom door and clicked the lock just as her cell phone rang. Turning it over, she saw her sister's name and ignored it. She couldn't tell anyone what was going on. Not even her sister. The phone stopped ringing, but it immediately chirped with a text alert.

```
Call me! I need to figure out my schedule.
When are we going to dinner?
```

Dinner? She felt her face crease in confusion and wondered how many deep wrinkles she had now. It felt as if she must have acquired a dozen in the past few days.

Dinner. Right. She'd told her sister they would go out this week. That obviously wasn't happening.

`I can't`, she texted back.

`Can't what?`

`Do dinner this week.`

`You promised to take me out! I need cheering up, remember?`

Evelyn almost wept at that. Yes, her sister had been a little down, and Evelyn had been excited about the prospect of a girls' night out. Her unhappiness had been only a vague fear then. An easily appeased worry.

`I'm really sorry`, she wrote. `I'm sick. I've already missed four days of work. I'll be scrambling to catch up.`

`Oh no! Want me to bring some soup?`

`No, I don't have an appetite.`

`Good, cuz it was going to be a can of Campbell's anyway.`

Evelyn smiled briefly at her sister's joke, then said good night, glad they weren't on the phone, because her throat was thick with tears again.

Gary's and Cameron's deep voices rumbled briefly up through the floor, a distant reminder that she still had a family. But she'd fed them. They were done with her.

It was only six thirty, but Evelyn climbed into bed. Sunlight still leaked through the window, so she leaned over and tipped the blinds tightly shut, then turned on the TV. Once she'd found something comforting and quiet to watch, she washed down two sleeping pills with the wine and pulled the covers to her nose.

Sick people slept a lot. It was the only way to recover. And God knew Evelyn had never felt this sick in her life.

CHAPTER 23

After

Noah rolled off her, and they both lay there, panting, sweating, laughing. They'd left the windows open to the sound of the sea, and the morning air was ice on Evelyn's damp skin, so she pulled up the covers and curled close to Noah's heat. Even after sex she didn't want to stop touching him. "I love sleeping with you."

"I love waking up with you," he countered. "But sleeping with you is almost as nice."

"I just can't believe we're leaving," she whispered.

"Yeah. It went way too fast."

"Two nights wasn't enough."

"No," he murmured as she tucked her head under his chin. "Never."

Despite the heavy satisfaction in her limbs, her heart ached. A physical pain lodged between her lungs. Every sore breath reminded her that she had to go back to her real life today.

"I'd better hit the shower," he said, and she found her hand wrapping tight around his wrist.

"No. It's so early. Stay a few more minutes."

"I still have to get back to my hotel to pack and check out."

"I know. But Noah . . ." Tears filled her eyes and spilled quickly onto her cheeks. She was horrified. She didn't want to waste their last hour together grieving. But she was going to miss this so much. How could she go back to her husband? How could she wake up every morning with him instead of Noah?

"Hey," he breathed. "Don't. I'm not leaving yet. We've got breakfast coming, remember?"

She nodded, but the tears kept coming.

"Oh, sweetheart. I know." He pulled her into his arms and let her cry against his skin. "I know."

"This is so good," she whispered.

"It is. On top of everything else, it's so easy to talk to you. I wish we could . . ." He stopped speaking and shook his head, the stubble of his morning beard dragging against her hair.

"What?"

"It doesn't matter. I'll jump in the shower, and then we'll have breakfast. We've still got time. All right?"

"All right. But wait one second." Turning to face him, she wrapped her arms around his body and slipped a leg between his thighs. "I just want to feel you for one more second," she whispered, burying her nose against him to breathe him in. He'd smelled different to her at first. His skin and hair and sex had all been a glaring reminder that he was not Gary. Not her husband. Not her man. But now he was familiar. As comforting as if she'd loved him for years.

"I love the way you smell," she murmured. "It's beautiful."

He held her tightly for a long time before easing away.

Once he was in the bathroom, she lay in his warmth, unwilling to drag herself from bed until it had faded. The shower rumbled as she pulled on a robe and retrieved his scattered pieces of clothing from the floor, smiling at the memory of stripping them off him the night before.

The weekend had been perfect, and she wanted to do it all over again. He'd been busy with the festival, but not too busy for dinner on Friday and Saturday. They'd eaten in the spa restaurant both nights, surrounded by twinkling candles and graced with a view of the sun falling slowly into the ocean.

Even the time without him had been magical. She'd walked along the ocean, treated herself to a full-body sugar scrub, wandered through the booths at the art festival.

Perfect, perfect, perfect.

She'd hoped they could have breakfast on the little balcony of her room this morning, but it was far too cold and the sea was blanketed with the usual Pacific fog. Evelyn shut the open window and turned up the heat, then cleared off the indoor dining table.

By the time she heard a soft knock on the door, she'd left her momentary unhappiness behind. She wouldn't ruin these last few moments together. She wanted to treasure them.

Aware she wasn't exactly being discreet, Evelyn signed for the two meals. It didn't matter. Evelyn paid the credit card bills in her house. Plus, she didn't particularly care if she was caught. Maybe she'd even welcome it.

When the shower went quiet, she called out to let him know the food was here, then made sure to arrange herself carefully in her chair. Her robe was closed, but not too closed. Her hair was tamed but still tousled enough to remind him who had messed it up.

He came out in only his towel but quickly dressed, much to her disappointment.

"I turned up the heat," she complained. "You don't have to put on clothes."

"I do have to put on clothes or I'll let you talk me into staying."

She crossed her leg and let the robe fall open all the way to the top of her thigh, but he only murmured, "I'm starving," as he sat down, so Evelyn gave up and ate too.

A few minutes later, he poured them both coffee. She took a careful sip and found him watching her. "What?" she asked.

"Thank you for coming here."

"You're very welcome," she responded with a grin. "I was wrong when I said I couldn't take anything better than that first morning on the couch. Apparently I can take a lot."

He blushed at that, popping a piece of bacon into his mouth to hide his embarrassment. He'd been sexually insatiable all weekend, and she'd teased him about it every chance.

"Listen," he finally said. "I've been thinking, and . . . I guess we should probably leave this here."

She added a little cream to the strong coffee. "Leave what here?"

Noah cleared his throat. "This."

"This?" she teased, but her amusement fell away when she looked up from stirring her coffee and found his forehead creased into deep wrinkles. "Noah? What are you talking about?"

"I thought I could do this, but it isn't natural for me. I feel . . . Jesus, I feel sick."

He felt *sick*? She shook her head.

"My wife is texting me pictures the kids drew for me. Telling me I don't have to travel because they'll supply plenty of work for the gallery. They miss me. And I'm . . ."

Evelyn felt herself blinking rapidly, as if her brain were trying to hit "Reset." "We just had sex," she said, the coffee doing a slow turn inside her stomach.

"I know."

"You didn't feel sick then."

"I know. Evelyn, I'm *sorry*. This is a shitty thing to say to you now. I get that."

She pressed a hand to her spinning stomach. "I don't understand. Noah, this has been . . ."

"A fantasy," he said quietly. "A dream. It felt . . . separate. But now I'm going back to my real life, and I just keep thinking, what if Juliette finds out? What if we weren't careful enough? She called while we were having dinner last night. And I just . . . I can't do that to her."

"I see."

"She's an amazing person. She doesn't deserve to be hurt."

An amazing person. His slutty, psychotic, *sick* wife. Noah couldn't do this to *her*?

Right then, Evelyn wanted to tell him. Blurt it all out. The whole truth. It hovered on her tongue, the words a metal weight in her mouth, the taste like copper. At the very least, he should know Juliette had cheated. That he was free to enjoy Evelyn as much and as often as he wanted.

"I can't do this to my kids," Noah whispered. "I can't bear for them to look at me and see a man who did this."

Who did *this*. Her. Evelyn.

Coffee sloshed over the rim of her mug and burned her fingers. She tightened her grip on the handle. "So this whole weekend? These nights together? You knew they were a one-shot deal?"

"No, I—"

"Because I wish you would have told me. Before."

"Evelyn, I—"

"*Before* you pushed through your sickness enough to have sex with me. In the evening. In the middle of the night. Before dinner. This morning. Ha! When, exactly, did this all make you so *sick*? Because you seemed to be in raging good health for quite a few hours of every single day."

He grabbed her free hand, wrapped his fingers around her clenching fist. "That wasn't how it was. It didn't hit me until last night. I was thinking about going home. Panicking a little, honestly. I couldn't get back to sleep. Being here with you felt like a different world, but now we're going back to real life, Evelyn."

"No," she whispered.

"I'm sorry. I swear to God, I'm sorry. If things were different, then maybe we could have this. But I'm married. *You're* married."

"People get divorced all the time, Noah."

"I don't want that for me or my kids. I honestly don't."

Right. Of course. Was she actually pleading with him to leave his wife for her? How disgustingly pitiful was that? He was trying to break it off, and she was trying to talk him out of it? She looked down, away from him, and saw that her robe was gaping open, showing half her breasts. She jerked her hand from his and pulled the collar tightly closed. She didn't want him seeing her body anymore. Looking and laughing.

"Okay," she bit out. "Sure. We had this weekend. It was lovely. Thanks for that. You can go."

Noah sighed and stayed where he was, his pained look the perfect expression of sad regret. She wished she hated him enough to slap him.

"It was just sex. I get it. Now go."

"It wasn't just sex."

"But you're going to walk away like it was?"

"I've said this all wrong. I'm sorry. I just . . . Shit, I didn't want to tell you later on the phone. I didn't want to be a coward about it."

"Yes, of course. Thank you."

"Don't say *thank you*," he growled. "I know I'm not doing the right thing. There is no right thing. I'm just trying to be honest about it. I swear, Evelyn. This has meant . . . God, it wasn't just sex to me."

"Okay," she said, but she wasn't okay. Because if it wasn't just sex, how could he go back to his life and never have this again? How could he even imagine living without it?

"If we weren't married, this would all be different."

Yes, it would have been 100 percent different, because he would have been single and dating twenty-nine-year-old artsy girls, and he wouldn't have looked twice at Evelyn if she'd walked into his gallery.

She'd thought about that yesterday. How lucky she was to have someone like him. How everything had pushed them together at just the right time.

So lucky.

"We both knew this was an affair," he said softly.

"Yes."

When she'd asked if they could do this forever, he'd said yes, but he hadn't meant it, and now she felt so, so stupid. He hadn't meant any of it. She'd been too far removed from college and dating to remember that men would say anything in the pursuit of sex. Hell, they probably even meant it at the time. But once they were satisfied and showered, they suddenly had no idea what you were talking about: "I'm not looking for a girlfriend right now." "I don't want things to get too serious." "I forgot to mention I'm in a relationship." All of it designed to make the woman feel he'd been saying it all along and she hadn't paid attention.

This was just the newest version of the same old thing: "Now that we've had sex two dozen times, I don't want to hurt my children."

Well, she didn't want to hurt his children either, but they were going to be hurt. He'd probably come crawling back then. He'd need some comfort when the police found that friend of Kaylee's and announced his wife was a cheating killer.

"So you've told me in person," she said, staring at the coffeepot as if it were the one breaking up with her. "I want you to go now."

"I'm sorry," Noah said again, his voice pleading. What the hell did he want from her? Gratitude? Forgiveness? Was it her responsibility to make him feel better about this?

"I'm sorry too," she answered. She got up, tightened the belt of her robe, and walked to the bathroom. "Please be gone when I get out."

The sound of the shower covered her weeping and took her tears down the drain. She soaped up, then cried more when she realized she was washing the last of Noah away. They'd never have sex again. Never even touch. This was the start of her life without him.

She missed him already. Because the truth was, no matter how much she was hurting, he wasn't a bad guy. He was torn. She understood that. Even if he wanted more with Evelyn, he was trying to do the right thing. Granted, this pious sacrifice came a little late, but Evelyn had known he loved his wife. He'd been honest about that from the start.

By the time she got out, the bathroom was a solid square of steam. She wrapped one of the thick, oversized towels around her and opened the door, pretending she meant to dissipate the moisture, but in all honesty she was looking for Noah. Her lips parted to tell him she'd been harsh, that she understood his fears and regrets. Of course she did.

It wasn't until she saw the empty room that she realized she hadn't believed he'd go. He should have been waiting there, sorry and sheepish, too worried about her to leave that way. He wasn't.

Evelyn closed the door again and curled against the steam-slick wall to cry.

CHAPTER 24

Before

The buzzing of her cell phone woke Evelyn at noon. She dug it from under her pillow and squinted at the screen. *Gary.* She tossed the phone to the other side of the bed and closed her eyes. She didn't want him to know she was still in bed, and if she answered he'd hear it in her voice.

He was probably calling to remind her that she'd promised to go to the grocery store today. She hadn't forgotten. It was just that she had other things to do.

Like sleep. Didn't he know she was sick?

It had only been eight days since her life had blown up into little pieces, but it felt like she'd been crawling through the rubble for months. She was empty. Exhausted. Ill. But after his call, she couldn't doze off again. She tried valiantly for ten more minutes before reluctantly pulling herself from bed to shuffle downstairs to make coffee and check Facebook.

The phone buzzed again, and she saw that Gary had left a message. She put it on speakerphone and got coffee beans from the cupboard. "I got your list of therapists," Gary said. "I'll give you an answer when I have time to look at them. When you go to the store today, don't forget to grab that vitamin C I like. And maybe I should call Vigo's. We never did go. It would be good for you to get out."

Good for her. Was he playing superior doctor, or did he really care? Did he want to take her to dinner, or was he desperate for her to wash her hair and put on clean clothes? The joke was on him. She'd showered yesterday; Gary just hadn't gotten close enough to smell the soap.

She didn't bother to smile at her bitter joke. Her own cynicism was exhausting her. She wanted to get back to being who she used to be. Someone who saw the sunny side of life, who laughed off her husband's quirks, who thought she was good enough for *someone*. She wanted to love him again. Wanted to be happy. Or at least content. Maybe she hadn't been jumping-up-in-the-air happy, but her life had been good before this.

After listening to his message once more, she brewed her coffee—organic, medium roast, single origin from Ethiopia, just as Gary liked—and sat down at the desk to browse Facebook. Wincing, she shifted her weight on the wooden kitchen chair.

Her butt was marked with tiny purple bruises where twigs had stabbed into her from her fall. It was worse today than yesterday. She wouldn't forget that adventure for a while.

Not that she would have forgotten. Pulling up Dawn's page, Evelyn checked for new evidence that the woman knew about the sad place her daughter had likely spent her last days. Surely the police must have told her, but it seemed Dawn didn't want to dwell on that knowledge. There was still no mention of it anywhere.

Evelyn read the latest shared memory of Kaylee, then headed over to Juliette's page to check in on her. Yesterday had been field-trip day, apparently. Juliette had taken the kids to a local petting zoo. There were five pictures of the kids, but the last one showed Juliette Whitman herself, holding a baby goat.

She was smiling brightly, as usual, but she did look different. Curious, Evelyn enlarged the picture. Juliette's normally bouncy blond hair was pulled back in a tight ponytail, and if she was wearing makeup, it didn't cover the dark circles under her eyes. She looked tired. Maybe a little gaunt.

"Hm." Evelyn regarded the picture skeptically. Maybe the hit-and-run had brought her pain. But even if she was suffering, that didn't mean she was sorry. She could be scared. Even a sick, evil sociopath didn't want to go to jail.

Evelyn moved back through posts she'd already memorized, hoping to glean something she hadn't before. But she'd mined this page for what it was worth. She'd learn nothing new here. She needed to see Juliette in person.

Not a confrontation. Not yet, anyway. But if she saw Juliette, maybe Evelyn could detect what kind of regret she was experiencing. Heck, she might even decide the woman wasn't as pretty and perfect as she seemed.

Evelyn sipped her coffee and noted that it was twelve thirty. Plenty of time for her to drive the thirty minutes to Juliette's school. She wouldn't try to sneak in the building or anything. That would be crazy. She just wanted to check it out. After all, the trip to Old Highway 23 had been well worth it.

Invigorated by the plan or the coffee, she pulled a pad from the desk and made a grocery list. She'd stop at the store on the way home. She could make Cameron's favorite spaghetti, spicy meat sauce with fresh mushrooms. Mushrooms weren't her favorite, but they were easy to pick out.

When her phone buzzed, she grabbed it with a quick hello, happy she could tell Gary that she was getting out of the house.

"Evelyn," a woman's voice drawled coolly.

She pulled the phone from her face to look at the caller ID. Crap. It was Wanda. "Hi, Wanda," she said in a duller voice.

"Do you have any idea when you'll make it back to work?"

"I'm still very sick to my stomach. I couldn't come in if I wanted to. I'm hoping by Monday I'll be on the road to recovery."

"All right. Just be sure you bring in a doctor's note. It's been a bit more than three days."

"Of course," she answered. It hardly mattered. Her husband was a doctor. Surely Wanda knew that.

"Jackie Arthur has been in to ask about you several times. She says you're not returning her emails."

"Yes, I've been in bed all week."

"Well, you might want to get in touch."

"Sure," Evelyn answered, anxiety crawling through her gut. She didn't like dropping the ball on her duties, but she was losing her grip. Couldn't anyone sense that?

As guilty as she felt, she had more important things to worry about. Evelyn went upstairs to change from her nightgown and robe, though she felt like she was stripping away important armor. Her robe, long nightgown, and thick socks were buffers, insulating her from the real world.

She tried to wear her nice black jeans, but they'd gotten loose, and she told herself she'd be happy about that later when she learned to be happy about things again. Her other pair of nice jeans didn't fit either, so she had to wear yoga pants. They were stretchy enough to still hug her body and not fall off. She added a long sweater, brushed her hair and teeth, and set out for Oakwood Elementary.

Out of curiosity, she took Old Highway 23 to get there. It wasn't the fastest way, but apparently it was the way Juliette took between their two towns. If Evelyn were being truthful, it was a beautiful drive. Most traffic around here was into or out of the city, so the space between the towns was quiet and dotted with farms.

She wondered, once she reached civilization again, what Juliette's life was like here. She really did seem to have it all, so why had she risked it for an affair with Gary? Was this something Juliette did often, just a normal part of her life? Or had she thought she'd loved Gary? Had she daydreamed about him as she ran errands, carting her children in and out of the grocery store? Had she jogged these streets while plotting their next rendezvous?

The school was on the far side of Juliette's town, tucked into a little neighborhood of new houses that looked like Evelyn's own. She drove around the school and found a parking space that faced the playground. There were two hours of school left. With a second-grade class, there must be an afternoon recess. The kids couldn't sit still long at that age.

As soon as she switched off the car and settled in to wait, Evelyn's phone rang from an unfamiliar number. She looked nervously around. Gary's mistress couldn't know what Evelyn looked like, could she? Frowning, she tried to remember if there was a picture of herself on Gary's desk, but she was almost sure there wasn't. Too personal. Too unprofessional.

She put the phone to her ear slowly. "Hello?"

"Evelyn? It's Jackie."

"Jackie?" One of the school doors opened, and tiny children spilled out like ants surging from an anthill.

"Jackie Arthur. The office gave me your number."

"Oh." She and Jackie had only ever communicated in person or through email. "Jackie, this isn't a great time."

A teacher followed the kids out, but it wasn't Juliette. Another group of kids followed. Evelyn craned her neck, trying to see past the doors.

"I know you're sick, but the book-fair boxes are coming in, and nobody knows what to do with them. And I think only two people have volunteered as cashiers, so . . ."

So. So what? "Maybe you could take care of that while I'm sick?"

"Oh, I don't know anything about the book fair. I've just been getting lots of questions from people, and I don't want this to become a disaster."

Suddenly she was there. Juliette. She followed a third wave of tiny children, crossing her arms tight across her chest as she stepped outside.

"If you could answer the questions I've emailed, then—"

"Jackie, I'm sorry, I need to run to the bathroom. I'll call you back."

She hung up and grabbed the small binoculars she'd taken from Gary's golf bag. Aware that watching a school with binoculars was a no-no, Evelyn hunched down before putting them to her eyes.

Strangely, she felt less wrong about this than anything else she'd done. Juliette had slept with Evelyn's husband. This kind of reconnaissance was just routine in this situation. Juliette should be happy Evelyn hadn't knocked on her front door.

She fiddled with the focus for a while, grunting when Juliette finally came through crystal clear. It felt as if Evelyn were standing right there with her as she leaned over and accepted a dandelion from a little boy. A *dandelion*. How adorable.

Evelyn really did feel like puking now.

Juliette smiled her wide smile, and the boy grinned back before running off. Did every male love her? Was it that petite, golden helplessness they couldn't resist? Maybe they'd all love her more if Evelyn ran up and punched her in her cute little nose. Maybe they'd all gather around to protect her from the big mean old lady.

Evelyn growled and rubbed her eyes before looking again. Juliette hung back close to the school, arms crossed over her chest again.

She wore sensible ballet flats and an innocent-looking blue dress that fell past her knees. She wasn't dressed like a man-stealing whore at all. In fact, she'd covered the dress with a thick black cardigan that washed out her face. Or maybe her face was just washed out. She did look pale as she watched the kids scramble up and over ladders and monkey bars.

This wasn't the girl Evelyn had come to know on Facebook. She didn't look angelic or bright or even particularly pretty. Mostly she looked tired.

A strand of hair came loose from her ponytail and blew across her face. She didn't seem to notice.

Was she genuinely sorry for what she'd done? Was she worried she'd lose her job, children, and marriage? Was she tortured over Kaylee's death?

Evelyn supposed that she could confront Juliette at some point. Demand answers to these questions. But she'd have to expose herself then. Right now she was safe. She held all the power. Juliette didn't even know she was being watched.

If she confronted her, Evelyn might learn things she didn't want to know. What if Juliette screamed that she and Gary were in love? That he'd wanted to leave Evelyn and now he couldn't? What if Juliette laughed in Evelyn's face and called her fat and old and disgusting?

Evelyn slouched down a little further and peered over the steering wheel. As she watched, Juliette drew her phone from her pocket and frowned as she read whatever was on the screen. A moment later, she typed out a text.

It didn't occur to Evelyn until that exact moment that Gary might still be in touch with Juliette. That the affair might still be going on. He could be texting her right now, asking to see her again.

He'd said it was over, but isn't that what men told their wives? What else was he going to say? "She's the best sex I've ever had, and I'm never giving her up, but I don't want a divorce." Probably not a good strategy.

Or maybe he had tried to end it and Juliette wouldn't let him go. Maybe *that* was why she looked so awful.

How the hell was Evelyn ever supposed to trust him? Why would she even want to? Her only comforting thought was that Gary hated texting. Whoever Juliette was texting, it likely wasn't him.

Her phone buzzed again, and Evelyn glanced at it in disgusted irritation. Why couldn't everyone just leave her alone? This time it was her sister asking how she was doing. Evelyn clicked off the screen.

She watched Juliette until the recess ended, though she wasn't sure what she learned. Juliette seemed subdued for most of the time, brightening only when a child approached. If she had to guess, Evelyn would say that maybe she wasn't an emotionless monster. But she wasn't ready to render that judgment quite yet.

After the last of the children were ushered inside and Juliette disappeared, Evelyn searched for the nearest grocery store on her phone and started her car. If she waited to do her shopping at home, someone might spot her and know she wasn't bedridden at all.

As she drove, she realized Juliette might take this route for her own grocery shopping. She pulled into the parking lot and wondered if it was Juliette's normal store. Was it possible she was just an average woman who did the same things Evelyn did?

"No," Evelyn said as she got out and retrieved a cart from the lot.

No, normal women didn't seduce their psychiatrists. Or drive away from victims of accidents.

Still, seeing Juliette in the flesh had brought Evelyn some calm, even if it had raised more questions. Tonight she'd spend some time with Gary after dinner. They could watch *Antiques Roadshow* or the news, and she'd keep an eye on his phone. That password would be easy enough to crack. Just four numbers, and she'd be able to watch the pattern without even seeing the screen.

Tomorrow she'd force herself to get up early and sneak a look at Gary's phone while he was in the shower, just in case. If he wasn't texting or calling Juliette, Evelyn could try to start making peace with this.

But as she walked the unfamiliar aisles of the grocery store, she found herself watching constantly for a blond ponytail, eager to push the limits of this spying game she'd started.

She walked at a snail's pace, slowly gathering the ingredients for meat sauce, then deciding she'd make garlic bread as well. Not that she'd be able to choke down much of anything, but Cameron would love it.

By the time she left the store, she'd been there for ninety minutes, and she felt oddly deflated as she got in her car and started for home. Juliette hadn't shown up.

But tomorrow Evelyn would get more information. Tomorrow maybe things would start to get better. The storm that had hit her life had to start easing soon or she'd never hold up.

CHAPTER 25

After

"I just want to know what's going on with you," Gary said, arms crossed as if to convey sincere concern.

Evelyn hunched over her coffee, hoping its heat would warm her. She felt cold all the time lately, but it was worse in the mornings. "Nothing is going on with me."

"You've stopped going into work—"

"I quit."

"You *what*?"

"I quit. I was tired of the office politics. I never planned on staying after Cameron graduated anyway."

"You never mentioned that to me."

"Well, now you know. As fulfilling as it was to take high-school attendance every day, I'm moving on." Granted, it hadn't been "I quit" so much as "I stopped going in or returning their calls," but there it was. She no longer worked at the school. Somehow the world kept turning. In fact, some days it felt like it was spinning faster and faster and Evelyn would just fly right off and float into space.

"You never called that therapist," he said.

Evelyn sighed, her breath steaming over the coffee. "No." No, and she wasn't going to. There was nothing she needed to say that she wanted Gary to hear. She had no desire to feel closer. Not to him.

"Evelyn, I have no idea what you're thinking lately. You won't talk to me at all."

"Why would I talk to you when you're just going to psychoanalyze me?"

"I'm not trying to be your doctor, for Christ's sake. I just want to know what's going on with my *wife*."

She could see it then. No wonder he'd turned to someone else. She'd left him years ago.

She'd pulled away to escape Gary's superior attitude. His superior intellect. His superiority complex. He'd made her feel small with the petty criticisms that had increased over the last ten years, but she would never care about that again. She was swollen up with feelings that had nothing to do with him.

"You didn't even want to go out for your birthday," Gary said. "You barely touched your cake. You just retreated to your *studio*." She didn't know if he'd meant to sneer the word, but it was there, clear as day.

"Aren't you going to be late for work?" she asked.

Gary sighed loudly, as if projecting his frustration to an entire audience instead of just her. She ignored it.

He finally walked out, slamming the garage door behind him like he thought she still cared about his moods. Did she have to write it on a piece of paper for him? *Please leave me alone. I don't care about you anymore.*

A few minutes later, Cameron breezed by, though he tossed a kiss somewhere near her cheek as he passed. "You didn't have breakfast," she said out of habit.

"I'll grab something at school. Bye, Mom."

And then she was alone. Thank God.

Yesterday had been her birthday. She'd waited for Noah to get in touch. Surely he would wish her a happy birthday. In Monterey, he'd said they'd go out to dinner. He would risk closing the gallery early and take her back to Ranbir's restaurant as a treat. That had been ten days ago. He couldn't have forgotten so quickly, yet he hadn't said a word. Her hand ached from clutching her phone too hard for too many hours.

Had he even thought about her? Had he at least struggled not to reach out? Or had he just decided to move on and that was that? They'd had a good time. That good time was over. The end.

That kind of callousness didn't seem possible. They had a connection. Something real and rare. Surely the particles of her constant pain must bombard him, even from this distance.

Every day she searched for signs of what he was feeling. She checked the gallery's Facebook page for clues. Then Juliette's. She reread every text Noah had ever sent her, trying to puzzle out whether she'd misinterpreted his words. She looked at the paintings she'd shown him and tried to remember his exact comments. What had he meant? What had he been trying to tell her? She replayed every act of sex in her mind, every motion, every word and whisper. Had he meant the sweet things he'd said? Did he even recall that he'd said them?

She'd typed out text messages to him a hundred times. Five hundred times. She wasn't sure anymore. Each day ran together. The memories of him began to fold into one long stretch, as if they'd spent whole weeks together.

Only one thing kept her steady enough to never hit the "Send" button: patience.

The truth was coming. It was a freight train barreling toward all their lives. No one could stop it.

Despite Noah's silence yesterday, one of Evelyn's birthday wishes had come true: there had been news from Dawn.

Thank you for coming forward, she'd written on her Facebook page at five in the morning. A cryptic message to some, perhaps, but not to Evelyn. The witness to Kaylee's death had been found.

How long would it be before the police came knocking with questions? Hours? Days?

It wouldn't be easy, but Evelyn could wait. As soon as the police showed any interest at all, she'd delete her fake account and lie low. She'd wait for the shock of it to shake through their lives; then she'd reach out to Noah and apologize for the stupid deception she'd perpetrated on him. He would understand. He would need to talk to someone, after all, and Evelyn was easy to talk to. He'd told her so.

He'd be confused by Evelyn's lies, yes, but she could explain them. She'd been in so much pain. He'd forgive her. He had to.

And the people who needed to pay for this—Juliette and Gary—would pay. Then Noah and Evelyn could rebuild their lives. Not that they'd get married. She wasn't delusional. He would want to protect his young children from more scandal. He'd want to be careful and quiet. But he and Evelyn would comfort each other. Start again. And eventually . . . eventually they'd find their way together.

Feeling reassured, she took her coffee to the desk and signed in. She checked the gallery's page, then Juliette's, just like normal. Then she pulled up Dawn Brigham's account to see what today's news was.

At first, Evelyn had no idea what she was seeing. Yesterday's message had been clear to Evelyn, but this one was opaque as paint. *I'm very disappointed in the authorities for obvious reasons. I will keep fighting for my baby.*

The replies expressed only standard sympathy and didn't offer more insight. Evelyn clicked around for a while before finally looking up her favorite local news site.

Girl's Hit-and-Run Death Ruled Accidental.

"What?" Evelyn gasped as the blood seemed to drain from her head in a wave that left her face tingling.

She clicked the headline and waited for the article to load. Hands clasped together, she rocked shallowly in her chair. "What, what, what?"

It couldn't be true. It couldn't be about Kaylee. But it was.

A witness confirmed that Kaylee Brigham was using heroin the night of her death and likely wandered onto Old Highway 23 from a shed in a nearby wooded area. There were no witnesses to the actual accident, but police confirmed that there are no streetlights on that stretch of the road and that Brigham, dressed in black, would have been difficult to see. "Toxicology reports indicate she had heroin, Xanax, and cocaine in her system," a police spokesperson said. The spokesperson also confirmed that brake marks on the road indicated the driver was well within the lane and had not swerved onto the shoulder when the collision occurred. The county coroner confirmed that the reason for death will be listed as an accident. "However," the police spokesperson added, "failure to report an accident, leaving the scene of an accident, and failure to call for assistance are all prosecutable crimes. If the driver is identified at some point in the future, there will be charges brought."

If the driver was identified? *If?*

Evelyn stared at the screen, her breath scraping in and out of her throat at a faster and faster rate.

The friend hadn't seen the accident, so the police were doing *nothing*?

No. No, this wasn't right. This wasn't okay. What about Noah? Who was going to tell him the truth about Juliette?

"Oh, God," she groaned. "Oh, God."

Nobody was going to do anything. Evelyn was the only one who knew the whole story. She was the only one who could tell it.

"Okay," she whispered, rocking in her chair again, trying to calm the muscles that were screaming with unreleased tension. "Okay." She had to stop being a coward about this. Because that was what she'd been. A coward. Waiting for someone else to do what she should have done the moment she'd walked into the Whitman Gallery.

New Evelyn wasn't a coward. Hadn't she already proven that to herself? She was brave and untamed and bold.

She could do this. She had to.

She got to her feet and paced across the kitchen, trying to burn off the adrenaline flooding her blood. Hands shaking, Evelyn opened a text box on her phone and typed in his name.

CHAPTER 26

BEFORE

Two weeks. Two weeks since Gary had called and tossed Evelyn from her bed into a nightmare. Two weeks since Kaylee's awful death. Two weeks, and it wasn't getting better yet.

But Evelyn was still trying.

This time she pulled into the parking lot of Oakwood Elementary just a few minutes before school let out. The pickup lane stretched on for nearly a quarter mile down the neighborhood street, but it was a new school that had been designed to keep traffic flowing even at the busiest times of day. Evelyn sailed right past all the waiting parents and found a spot in the lot. Few parents wanted to actually get *out* to retrieve their children. Not when they could idle in their giant SUVs and continue their important phone conversations.

The day had started off well. A promising beginning to today's reconnaissance. It had taken a couple of days to get Gary's phone code. And a couple more days to actually find his phone unattended. But this morning, she'd finally opened it and it had been clean. If he'd been in touch with Juliette, he'd been wiping the messages and calls as they were sent and received. That was certainly possible. After all, the two of them were covering up a crime together. But Evelyn definitely felt better to have found nothing. It meant she could hope, at least.

An hour after Evelyn's arrival at the school, Juliette finally emerged. She was typing on her phone again, and that pushed Evelyn's new hope higher. Gary might have exchanged an urgent text with his mistress once or twice a week, but not often.

Both of Juliette's children scampered out behind her, and Evelyn made a little bleating sound at the sight of them. Gary had been right about that, at least. She didn't want to hurt these children. They were so much smaller than Cameron or any of the other kids Evelyn saw every day. She'd forgotten how tiny they were in elementary school. Closer to being infants than teenagers.

Juliette slowed, and Stephanie and Connor ran to the flagpole like this was a normal stop for them. As they took turns trying to climb it—neither of them making it more than two feet from the ground—Juliette typed on her phone, frowning the whole time.

She was probably texting a friend. Or maybe even her own husband. Evelyn knew next to nothing about him. Maybe things were rough between them. Maybe they were on the verge of a breakup. After all, even if things were bad, Juliette might fight tooth and nail to stop him from finding out she'd cheated.

Evelyn watched intently as Juliette finally looked up. She flashed a brief smile at the sight of her daughter trying to slide her son higher on the flagpole, pushing both hands against his rear end. When she called out, they both ran back to her without complaint. On top of everything else, her kids were well behaved. Great.

Juliette put her phone away so she could hold hands with both kids as they headed for the lot. They walked within ten feet of Evelyn. She stared, mouth gaping, unable to pretend nonchalance. Luckily, Juliette didn't look over.

They got into a little red compact car and pulled out. Evelyn followed. She knew from TV that she couldn't follow too closely. These suburban streets weren't busy, so Evelyn could be easily spotted. Then again, there were so many turns and curves designed to keep everyone at twenty-five miles per hour that she couldn't hang back too far or she might lose Juliette altogether.

"Oh, what the hell," she muttered. If Juliette wasn't expecting to be followed, she wouldn't be watching for it. They headed out to the main road pretty quickly, then made a right turn two miles later into a nicer neighborhood than Evelyn expected for a teacher. They weren't McMansions, but they were close. Her husband must make more money than Juliette did. Maybe he was a doctor.

Evelyn snorted, then waited a beat before following Juliette into another right turn.

"Oh crap," she whispered. It was a cul-de-sac, and Juliette was pulling into one of the driveways. Before Evelyn could panic and screech into a U-turn or drive over a mailbox, Juliette pulled into a two-car garage, and the door closed behind her.

Evelyn, who'd very conspicuously braked right in the middle of the street, edged forward and rolled slowly past the house. Brick facade, front porch, cheerful spring flowers in pots on the railing. Just lovely. Just perfect.

Curling her lip, Evelyn swung the car around the end of the cul-de-sac and drove by again, but there wasn't much to see. No warning signs that a murderer lived inside. The children had seemed happy and well fed. The grass was still mostly brown from winter but looked as if it had been nicely trimmed in the fall. An Easter wreath hung on the door, and there were sun catchers in the front windows.

Maybe Juliette was just an average suburban mom with some mental health problems and boundary issues. Maybe she was selfish, but not psychotic. Evelyn was still missing some piece of this puzzle, but she realized what it was now. The mystery husband. Noah.

She'd have to rectify that as soon as possible.

CHAPTER 27
AFTER

Evelyn decided to play it casual, as if this were the first time she'd thought of him since Monterey. No big deal. Just dropping a line. `Hey, you missed my birthday! ☺`

She would have been a writhing mess if she'd had to wait long for a reply, but he responded right away. `Happy birthday. I wanted to say hi, but I didn't know if I should.`

`Why? Can't we call a truce?`

`There's no need for a truce. I surrender. I don't want to hurt you more, Evelyn. I know I was an asshole.`

`So can I talk you into a cup of coffee?` she wrote, her throat clicking dryly as she tried to swallow her nervousness.

`When?`

`Now.` She waited a few breaths before she sent another. `You can consider it a belated birthday gift to me.`

`Of course. Not much of a gift for you, but I'd love to catch up.`

`Meet you at the gallery?`

She raced upstairs to shower and get ready in record time, throwing on one of the flowy summer dresses she'd bought for California. When he saw it, maybe he'd remember. Maybe he'd feel *something*.

She wore flats to make herself seem harmless instead of trying to cultivate the intrigue she'd preferred before. After grabbing a sweater and her bag, she drove straight to his gallery, taking the quickest route, driving as fast as she dared, hoping all the local police officers had finished with the morning commute shift and were now taking a break.

The last few times she'd gone to Noah's gallery, she'd entered through the back, so she parked on a side street and walked through the alley, then knocked hard on the delivery door.

The latch clicked, the door slowly opened, and he was there. Noah. It felt as though all the organs in her body lurched toward him. Her skin went tight.

"Hi," she whispered as he opened the door to let her in. She slid past him.

"Hi," he replied. The door shut, cutting off most of the light in the back room. He stared down at her from only inches away. Neither of them moved.

"Did you miss me?" she asked.

His only reply was a groan, then his arms were around her and he kissed her.

She didn't know how they got from the door to the couch. It was a blur of hands and mouths and grunted needs. All she could think was *yes*.

They could have this again. She could be satisfied with this. She would belong to him again without having to be brave, and everything would be fine. She wouldn't ask for more. Only this.

He yanked off her dress and underwear in rough pulls that left her shaking with lust. And then she was on her back, the nubby fabric of the couch a comforting abrasion on her skin as she opened her legs for him. He pushed inside, filling a space that had been woundingly empty since that last time, and suddenly her world was right. She was whole.

Strange that something so animal could feel divine. His thrusts felt like worship.

She clutched his back, dug her nails in, desperate to keep him close or at least *mark* him. No matter what he'd meant to do in the name of fidelity or morality, he was hers again. Their connection was a vital need, too strong to deny. She couldn't live without him, so how could he possibly live without her?

"I couldn't stop thinking about this," he growled.

"I know," she whispered back, pulling him down for a kiss. But the kiss didn't last long. They were both breathing too hard, gasping for air. His back went slick under her hands, and she opened her mouth on his skin to taste the sweat. "Noah," she whimpered over and over. "Noah."

Afterward, they lay tangled up together for long minutes before he finally pulled away. She wanted to tug him back. "You didn't bring any coffee," he said with a smile.

"I didn't actually want coffee."

He laughed and left to use the bathroom. She wanted to lie there and wait for him, but after their farewell in Monterey, she felt too vulnerable to lounge around naked and dirty. She dressed, then went to use the bathroom herself, blushing a little at the feel of his gaze on her as they passed.

When she emerged, he was waiting with a steaming cup. "Thanks," she said a little shyly as she took the coffee.

"I guess we shouldn't have done that." He gestured toward the couch with his own mug, as if she might not know what he meant.

"Oh, I don't know. It felt pretty all right."

"That's one description."

They sat on stools at the table, and she realized every place in this room was a memory of their relationship. It must have been difficult for him to try to forget her here. At least in her home, Evelyn didn't have to picture Noah there and there and there, all the delicious, forbidden moments.

"Did you have a good birthday?" he asked.

"No. I missed you."

"I'm sorry."

"It's all right. That made up for it."

He stroked a lock of her hair off her cheek. "I'm glad."

"Me too." She smiled at him, but he dropped his gaze to his coffee. "So what did you want to talk about?"

No point in bringing that up now. "I just wanted to see you."

"Evelyn."

"Noah," she teased, dropping her voice to match his.

Sighing, he tipped his wrist to look at his watch. "It's ten. You'd better go. I need to open up."

"Have you picked a new piece for the front recently?"

"No, nothing new this month."

"Then let's look for something. I have time. We could have a little fun. I mean, a little *more* fun." She waggled her eyebrows, but her smile froze when he looked at her, his face twisted with discomfort. "What?"

"Evelyn, we can't hang out together."

"Why?"

"You know why. It's wrong."

"It's *wrong*?"

"Come on," he sighed. "You know this is wrong."

She barked a laugh. "Oh, really? It's *wrong*? Was it wrong to tear off my clothes and do me on the couch?"

He winced. "Yes. Obviously."

"But you did it."

"That doesn't mean we need to make it worse."

"Wow. You know, the sex strikes me as a little *more* wrong than looking at art together, if it's your wife you're worried about. But you somehow got through that before your spasm of conscience. The wrongness didn't hit you until just now. After the sex. Amazing."

Noah scrubbed both hands over his head. "I'm sorry. You're right. It's—"

"You're *unbelievable*. Aren't you embarrassed to be so damn typical?"

He growled, his hands fisting in his hair. "We're both married, Evelyn! What do you want from me?"

"How about a little damn intellectual honesty?"

"Okay, fine. I don't want to give you up. The sex is great. I have trouble resisting. The truth is I don't even want to resist. But I can't live like this. I can't!"

"Why?" she demanded.

"I just *can't*."

"You said we could do this forever! You're the one who changed *everything* after California!"

"I know, and I'm sorry. But I love my wife, and I can't hurt her. She's an amazing person. A wonderful wife and mother. She's just . . . amazing."

Evelyn felt the truth boil up in her. She couldn't stop it, and that was comforting because she didn't want to stop it. He needed to know and maybe, just maybe, she wanted to hurt him after the slap in the face he'd just given her.

"Your wife cheated on you." The words emerged from her mouth and left behind a little hollow filled with peace inside her. Yes. This felt right.

Noah tossed his hands in the air, then let them fall with a slap on his thighs. "Oh, for godssake, Evelyn. This is ridiculous."

"Her name is Juliette."

That froze his eye-rolling show of disbelief. He watched her warily for a moment. "I told you that."

"I can't remember if you did, but I first heard it from my husband. They had an affair. Him and your Juliette."

"Evelyn." He stood very straight, his body edging itself back, away from her. "I don't know what you're thinking, but this is over now. We both wanted it, and we both knew it had to end sometime. Please don't do anything stupid."

"What, like tell her about us? I'm not going to do that. I'm not some psycho, Noah."

"Okay. Yeah." He crossed his arms tight and tried to make his mouth form a pleasant smile.

He was scared of her already. Watching her as if she might be dangerous. She slumped a little with that defeat. "Noah, please. I'm not telling you this to hurt you. I don't want to hurt you! I just want you to know that you don't have to be careful with her. She isn't who you think. Not at all."

"What do you—?" His eyes went suddenly wide, and he took a step back. "I don't understand what you're saying. You're trying to tell me that you came in here and I just happened to be married to a woman who—"

"No. I lied to you, and I'm sorry about that. You have no idea how sorry."

He shook his head.

"It was wrong. I know that. If I'd even suspected that you and I would . . . But of course I didn't. When I came into the gallery, I just wanted to see who Juliette's husband was. That's all."

"Holy shit," Noah whispered. He looked from her to the back door several times. "Who *are* you?"

She held up her hands in surrender, trying to calm him. "Please, Noah. Just listen. I found out Juliette was sleeping with my husband, and I admit I got a little crazy. The circumstances were . . . Well, I'll tell you more about that later. But when I came in here, you were . . . God, I swear it wasn't about Juliette anymore. It was about *us*. The way you spoke about art. The way you spoke about me. We just . . . clicked."

She grimaced at the fear in his eyes. "I'm not telling you this as a threat; I just couldn't stand to see your loyalty to her anymore. She doesn't deserve it. What we're doing . . . It's okay. It's honestly okay. We don't have to give it up."

"I don't . . ." He swallowed so hard that the gulp was comically loud in the metal-raftered room. "I don't know why you think that, but it's not true. Juliette wouldn't cheat. She's been struggling with sex for years. She thinks it's because of her past. Her childhood. And I totally understand that. But you see, she couldn't be cheating."

"Noah. My husband is her psychiatrist."

His forehead tightened in a shocked frown. "What?"

"If they were working through her sexual issues, they were doing it with actual sex."

"You're insane," he whispered.

"I'm not," she pleaded. "I know this sounds crazy, but please listen. *Please.* I saw them together. My husband confessed. It's the truth." She'd tell Noah the circumstances later. Much, much later, judging by his current expression of horror.

"Your husband confessed," he repeated, "and then you stalked my wife and started an affair with me?"

"No! Noah, please. I just wanted to see who you were. But then I *liked* you. And you liked me. We really saw each other, remember? And all of this just *happened*."

He shook his head. His tanned face had turned a sickly gray. She wanted to reach out to him, but she didn't dare. She could hear how it must sound to him. He'd need time to adjust. "Jesus Christ," he muttered.

"This is shocking," she said, trying to keep her voice soothing. "And I know it must hurt, but your marriage isn't what you think it is. Neither was mine. Whatever rules or obligations might have kept us apart, Juliette and my husband forfeited those."

"Jesus," he repeated, scrubbing a hand through his hair again, setting the waves into wild angles.

"You can leave her, if you want."

His wild gaze swung back to Evelyn, and he watched her as if she might come at him with teeth bared at any moment.

"Or we can just keep doing this," she offered, "while you think about it. You'll need time to think about it. I see that."

"Think about what?" he rasped.

"How you want to live. What you want to do. When I found out, my first instinct was to try to hold on to my husband, but I deserve more than that. And you do too."

"I'm not leaving my wife." His voice was a dry husk of its former self. She wanted to touch him, hold him, comfort him.

"I'm sorry," she whispered.

"You need to leave."

"I know you're reeling—"

"Get out," he ordered.

Evelyn flinched at the hardness of his words. "Noah, you can have the life you want now. Dreams, adventure, sex. Remember when you said that? You can have it all. Your kids and your gallery and everything you want. Just—"

"This gallery belongs to my wife."

Now it was Evelyn's turn to play the sick, shocked victim. "What?" she gasped.

"It's Juliette's. Everything is."

"No. She's a teacher."

Noah laughed, and the awful sound cut through her. "Yes, she's a teacher. Who comes from money. Old money."

Evelyn shook her head.

"Her parents like me," he went on, his voice distracted now. "They love that I'm cultured but still outdoorsy enough to be a *real* man. But there are limits to their affection for me. They wouldn't let their daughter throw money at a man. There's a trust. It's all hers."

"Noah—"

"It's all right," he murmured, pacing across the concrete floor. "We both cheated. So we'll wipe the slate clean. We can get past that. We have a good life."

Evelyn watched as he reassured himself, nodding as if he'd solved a terrible problem. The terrible problem of *Evelyn*.

Her head buzzed. Her eyelids fluttered. When she turned her head, the room dragged sickly by. He was choosing his wife. He wanted her more. Juliette had won again.

"Okay," he said. "I'm going to open the gallery. Everything needs to look normal. Please leave, and don't ever come back."

"Please—" she tried, but he shook his head.

"You're sick. You need help."

"But Noah—" She raised a hand toward him when he breezed past, but she wasn't quick enough. He disappeared into the hallway, then reappeared on the monitor above, far away now. Gone.

Evelyn lurched forward. She made it to the wall and set her forehead to the cool steel of the doorjamb, resting it there until the buzzing in her skull stopped. Once she felt strong enough, she found the keys she'd dropped when she'd come in, but instead of slipping into the alley, she walked down the hall and into the gallery.

Noah sat at the desk.

"I love you," she told him.

He didn't look up no matter how long she stared. Eventually, Evelyn's feet somehow carried her out the front door and down the sidewalk toward her car. She had no idea how she got the rest of the way home.

CHAPTER 28

BEFORE

Evelyn shuffled through the living room, still dragging from the sleeping pills she'd taken the night before. Irritated by the continued ringing of the doorbell, she glanced at the clock on the fireplace mantel, ready to snap at her visitor that some people were still sleeping. Except no one was still sleeping. It was three thirty. Oops. Maybe she'd better cut back to one pill a night.

She smoothed down her hair, rubbed her eyes, and opened the door.

Her sister gasped. "Oh my God! Evelyn, you look terrible."

"Thanks a lot," she said, forcing herself not to pull away when her sister grabbed her in a hug. "What are you doing here?"

"I came to check on you, and thank God I did. How much weight have you lost?"

"I don't know."

"You look like you need to go to the hospital."

"I don't need to go to the hospital. My husband's a doctor, you know."

"Well, where is he?" Sharon pushed past her into the house. "Why are you the one answering the door when you're half dead?"

Evelyn shrugged. "Is it Saturday? He's probably golfing."

"And Cameron?"

That was more of a mystery. Frowning, she tried to remember. "Robotics?" she guessed. "No. Water polo."

"Well, come on. I'll make you some tea."

"I just woke up. I want coffee."

Sharon stopped and spun to aim a harder look at Evelyn. "You just woke up?"

"I was napping," she lied.

"And when was the last time you washed your hair, exactly?"

"Kiss my ass."

Sharon, like any good sister, ignored that and stormed into the kitchen. She opened half the cabinets until she found the coffee, then got it brewing in no time. Evelyn just slumped into a chair, feeling like a useless lump in her own kitchen. Sharon had always been the one to take charge. Evelyn had always been happy to let her.

"All right," Sharon said as she watched Evelyn inhale the coffee's aroma. "Tell me about this stomach flu that makes you lose twenty pounds in two weeks but still lets you drink coffee."

Evelyn paused midsip, her eyes rising to meet Sharon's through the steam. "Huh?"

"Coffee, Evelyn? That's pretty hard on even a healthy stomach."

"I've been feeling better today."

"You don't look like you're feeling better."

"Thanks for the support." Evelyn swallowed a large gulp of coffee, realizing that she needed to get some caffeine in her quickly to keep up with this.

"I'm your sister," Sharon said. "Please tell me the truth."

"Oh, you think I'm lying?"

"Evelyn." Sharon reached across the table and touched Evelyn's wrist. "The last time we talked you asked me about Jeff cheating."

"Did I?"

"You asked me how I knew. Then you disappeared, and when I show up at your door, you look like a woman in the middle of a crisis."

"No, I'm fine. I'm getting better."

Her sister's fingers tightened. "Did you catch Gary cheating?"

"No," she said automatically. "No, that's not it." But she could barely get the words out past her tight throat, and when she broke down into sobs, Sharon was already there, on her knees, holding her, telling her it was all right.

"It's okay. You'll be okay," she promised.

"Six months," Evelyn sobbed, needing to say it to somebody. "He was sleeping with her for six months."

"Oh, sweetie, I'm so sorry."

"There have probably been others. Hundreds of others!"

"There haven't been hundreds."

"How can I know?"

Sharon patted her back and rocked her gently. "Is he gone? Did he move out?"

"No. He's golfing. Nothing has changed for him. Nothing at all."

"That asshole," Sharon growled, startling Evelyn into a watery laugh.

"He is an asshole."

"Yes, he is. Get your things. You're coming to my place."

"Sharon! I can't move in with you!"

"No, but you're going to spend the night. The kids are with their dad, and we never had our girls' night."

She resisted for a moment. She'd left the house a few times in the past week for spying purposes, but she hadn't had to *be* with another person. Not really. Cameron didn't need her, Gary gave her space, but

Sharon . . . She couldn't hide from Sharon. "I don't want to go to a restaurant or anything. I don't want to see anyone."

"No problem. We'll pick up wine and pizza on the way there."

The wine part didn't sound bad anyway. Nodding, Evelyn went upstairs to brush her teeth and get dressed.

Two hours later, she was sprawled out on her sister's couch, stuffed from pizza and more than halfway drunk. When her phone rang, she saw Gary's name and groaned. "It's him."

"Give me that," Sharon ordered.

Grimacing, she handed the phone over.

"Hi, Gary. It's Sharon. Did you lose your wife?"

Evelyn snorted.

"Yes, she's with me. She's spending the night here. I'll bring her home after I've fed her a few more times. Someone needs to look out for her." She hung up and gave the phone the finger.

Evelyn's snort turned into a cackle. Once she'd quieted, Sharon nudged her foot. "So do you want to tell me what happened?"

Yes, she wanted to, but she couldn't. "You know what happened. The typical thing. He met some blond bimbo and wanted her. They did it, and did it, and did it some more! I found out. The end."

"Did he admit it?"

"Eventually. After he lied several times."

Sharon's voice dropped. "Did he love her?"

Evelyn swallowed hard. "He says it was just sex. He said . . . Well, he wasn't getting it at home."

Sharon sighed and topped off Evelyn's glass with a healthy amount of wine. "You know what my favorite thing about men is? They all love to joke about not getting enough sex. How wives lose interest after the wedding. But the truth is, their sole seduction technique becomes, 'Hey. Wanna go upstairs?'"

"Ha."

"I'm serious. Think about how hard they work for sex *before*. Oh my God, when you're first dating, it's like a full-time job for them. They dress nicely and use breath mints, and they shave. Hell, these days they even groom their pubic hair. And God, they're so fucking charming, aren't they?"

Evelyn laughed. "They are."

"Flowers. Gifts. So many jokes. So many phone calls. Do you remember when you used to talk to Gary for hours on the phone?"

"I'd forgotten that!" She'd also forgotten what it was like to be *charmed*. Just the word was delightful. The feeling itself? That was . . . lost. Gone. Extinct.

"Jeff used to ask me which book I was reading, and then he'd read the same book just so we could talk about it! He doesn't even like books."

Evelyn sipped her wine and sank into the cushions. "Gary once wrote a whole letter about my breasts."

"No, he didn't!"

"Yes, he definitely did. Two pages. It was beautiful and dumb and I loved it."

"And when was the last time he did that?" Sharon demanded.

"Please."

"You see what I mean? They never get enough at home, but they treat us like milk cows. 'Come on, Bessie, this won't take long at all.'"

Evelyn laughed, but her laughter faded quickly.

Sharon was right. The blame was always on the wife for losing interest. No one ever joked about how husbands seemed to think a clitoris was a reorder button at an office supply store. They pushed it for more of what they wanted, then got quickly back to more interesting things. Whatever sport was on TV, or golfing with friends, or just *work*. Even work was more fun than writing an ode to your wife's breasts.

She shook her head. When was the last time Gary had tried to charm her? When had he even tried his best to make her smile?

"What are you going to do?" Sharon asked.

"I don't know."

"Have you given up?"

Had she? No. She was fighting for her marriage, or that was what she'd been telling herself she was doing. Fighting the power of Juliette. "I've been stalking her on Facebook."

"What?" Sharon gasped. "Evelyn, no! Don't go down that hole. How did you even find out her name? Do you know her?"

"No. I made him tell me. I made him tell me everything."

"God, that was a terrible idea."

"I guess it was. It's all I can think about. I'm just . . . I'm losing my mind a little, Sharon."

"Well, stop it!" her sister demanded, and at least Evelyn was laughing again. "I'm serious," Sharon said. "Stop obsessing. No wonder you can't eat."

"But what am I going to do?" she wailed.

Sharon scooted over on the couch and wrapped an arm around Evelyn's shoulders. "What do you want to do? Do you want to get divorced?"

Evelyn looked around her sister's living room. There were pictures of her three kids everywhere, but the children themselves weren't here because they were with their father this weekend. It was his year for Christmas too, if Evelyn remembered correctly. Sharon would come for a quiet dinner at Evelyn's house.

"No," she answered.

"Does Gary want a divorce?"

"No." Not that she'd given him a choice.

"You still love him?"

"I think so. Yes. Maybe."

"Then I guess you'll both have to work your asses off. Fight for it."

"That's . . . That's what I planned, but I'm so damn tired now."

"I know. But not as tired as you'll be if you have to fight your way back from a divorce from a man you still love. Believe me."

Yes, she believed that was true. She'd seen the toll it had taken on her sister. All the years of plans and dreams with a spouse. It wasn't just the past you walked away from in a divorce; you walked away from your future as well. Everything you'd expected from life was changed.

She didn't want to start over. She couldn't. She wanted her marriage. She wanted Gary. He was all she'd known for so long. "We agreed to go to couples' therapy."

"Good. But first you need to start eating again. Stop trying to die."

She laid her head on her sister's shoulder. "How do I do that?"

"You get up in the morning. You shower. Put on makeup. Wear something that isn't fleece."

"That sounds awful."

"I know, but you do it anyway."

"Okay." Evelyn sighed.

"Promise me? Tomorrow?"

"Tomorrow's Sunday. Don't be ridiculous."

Sharon laughed and poked her shoulder. "Fine. On Monday you'll start living again. Okay?"

"Okay."

"And you'll stop being obsessed."

"Sure."

"Do you promise?" her sister pressed. "No more Facebook? No more stalking?"

"All right," Evelyn said. "I'll stop on Monday. I promise."

CHAPTER 29

AFTER

So perfect little Juliette was going to walk away with everything. Her career. Her friends. Her reputation. Her children. Her life. Her sanity. Her husband. And Evelyn's husband too. All of it.

Evelyn got nothing. Dawn Brigham got nothing. And Kaylee got worse than nothing. She got dead and forgotten and blamed for something that was Juliette's fault.

Rocking, Evelyn clutched the steering wheel of her car and watched the line of vehicles picking up schoolchildren, who screeched and laughed with freedom and joy as they waited. Had Evelyn ever been that happy? It was hard to imagine, but she supposed at some time, even walking home through cold, slushy streets to a dingy apartment, she and her sister must have chased and laughed and screamed like that. They'd had no idea what life would bring.

Neither had Kaylee. When she was tiny like Juliette Whitman's children, Kaylee must have bubbled over with happiness too. Now she was rotting in the ground, a worthless junkie. Even the messages of sympathy on Facebook had died off. Kaylee had officially done this to herself. No point in getting too worked up over it.

Evelyn had gone home after this morning's confrontation at the gallery. Shivering, she'd drawn a bath to warm herself, but she hadn't been able to soak any comfort into her skin. Because she didn't deserve any comfort. She hadn't yet done the right thing.

She'd been lied to her whole life by TV and the movies. The police didn't solve all the mysteries. With some cases, they didn't even try. Evelyn was still the only one who knew the real truth, and if she didn't tell it, it would die with her.

This wasn't right. It wasn't justice. She had to do this for Kaylee. The girl's family deserved to be left with more than guilt. If Juliette just went on with her life like normal, it would be Evelyn's fault.

If Juliette's parents were as rich as Noah had implied, maybe she wouldn't lose much at all, but at least everyone would *know*. She wouldn't be a beloved, adorable teacher anymore. She'd be called a heartless animal, just as she deserved. Everyone would look at her and see the real Juliette.

Evelyn rocked and waited. Her phone buzzed with a text message, but it wasn't from Noah, so she dropped the phone back in the passenger seat and watched the school doors.

An hour later Juliette emerged with her towheaded children. She was smiling today. Moving on. She was happy again, as if she'd somehow sensed that Evelyn had lost everything.

Evelyn got out and walked straight toward her.

She was talking to little Connor and didn't notice Evelyn until she was only a few feet away. "Hello!" Juliette said with a smile that quickly faded. "Are you okay?"

Evelyn swiped a tear impatiently from her cheek. "I'm Evelyn Tester. Do you know who I am?"

Juliette's expression of vague concern turned immediately to stark fear. Her nostrils flared, and Evelyn could see a pulse beating hard and fast in her throat. "Kids," she said, "I changed my mind. You can have ten minutes on the playground." The kids squealed and rocketed toward the swings at the far corner of the school.

Smart. Quick. She was good at this.

"Mrs. Tester . . ." Juliette paused and took a deep breath as her sweet little voice sank into Evelyn's brain. Standing this close to her, Evelyn was aware of just how delicate she was. Six inches shorter than Evelyn and probably fifty pounds lighter. Evelyn's hands shook.

Juliette seemed to have steadied herself. "I don't know what you think is—"

"I know exactly what happened. All of it."

"I doubt that's true," she countered.

"Her name was Kaylee Brigham," Evelyn said. "Did you know that?"

Juliette didn't panic. She just pressed a hand to her mouth and nodded. "Yes. I know that."

"She was seventeen years old. She didn't deserve any of this. And I want you to know I'm going to the police."

Juliette's eyes widened, and she dropped her hand. "You? Why?"

"Because you deserve to pay, that's why. Every man in the world might be a sucker for your helpless little act, but the moms at this school won't want their children around a monster who'd seduce their husbands and run over a child without even stopping."

That made her step back. Finally. "Is that what he told you?" she whispered.

The power was back, swelling inside Evelyn's veins and pushing out her heartache. Noah might have chosen Juliette, but Evelyn could stop all of this. "Kaylee deserves more than that. Her mother deserves more. They need justice, and I will give it to them."

"He said I was driving?"

"You were. He'd had too much to drink."

"He said I *seduced* him?"

Evelyn sneered. "Oh, you're going to pretend you didn't?"

Juliette laughed. She actually laughed while her whole adorable life was resting in Evelyn's hands. A gust of wind blew her blond hair across her face, and when she shoved it back her eyes had narrowed. "I can't believe you're threatening *me*."

"Did you think I wouldn't have the guts?" Evelyn demanded. "After you destroyed my life?"

"I've been protecting you!" Juliette's loud words rang across the schoolyard. "I'm the only one standing between you and *ruin*."

"What are you talking about?"

"I wasn't driving that night. Your precious husband was."

"No. He'd had too much to drink at dinner, so he asked you to drive. When you hit Kaylee, you kept driving, but you were hysterical. You went off the road. You—"

"The car went off the road because I grabbed the steering wheel and tried to make Gary turn around."

Gary. The sound of her saying his name distracted Evelyn for a moment, but only a moment. "No," she whispered. "He'd been drinking."

"Oh, yes. He'd definitely been drinking. He'd insisted on taking me to dinner, but all I wanted to tell him was that it was over. That I was going to turn him in if he didn't stop calling me."

"No."

"Yes," Juliette answered.

"He was trying to break it off with you. It wasn't healthy."

"It wasn't *healthy*?" Her voice had risen again. Evelyn glanced around, surprised Juliette would risk attracting attention.

But Juliette didn't seem to care. She raised her chin and stared straight at Evelyn. "I hope you came here for the truth, because here's the truth. I went to your husband because I couldn't enjoy sex anymore. I told him that I'd shut down in bed. I'd become unresponsive. Impassive."

Even in the midst of the horror of what Juliette was revealing, even in that awful moment, Evelyn felt proud of what she'd given Noah. That was why he'd been so hungry for her. Because his wife was impassive and Evelyn was insatiable. Even in this terrible conversation, that was what her mind grasped onto.

"*Doctor* Tester," Juliette sneered, "told me we'd need to explore my boundaries. It took time. It was months before he even touched me. But that first visit . . . that was when your husband decided he'd have me."

Evelyn shook her head. "That's not what happened."

"That," she spit out, "is exactly what happened. He knew I was so screwed up I wouldn't say no to him. Not to an authority figure. I mean, good God, even I thought it was mutual at first. I thought it was a love affair. And even then I wanted to kill myself for what I was doing. But it wasn't mutual. It wasn't love. It was *sick*. He was supposed to be *helping* me, and instead he used me as a sex doll."

"No," Evelyn insisted, her voice still sure and strong.

No. But wasn't that the more likely story? Hadn't it been happening just that way between doctors and patients for so long that there were strict rules against it? A psychiatrist was never allowed to sleep with a patient because the doctor was in a position of authority.

"I'd been trying to break it off for weeks. He kept saying that we had more work to do."

Evelyn shook her head, but Juliette wouldn't stop talking.

"He thought we were getting a room that night. He thought we'd go to dinner and then have sneaky, dirty sex afterward like normal. But I was there to tell him it was over. He was angry. He had a few drinks. He was pissed and drunk and driving too fast. And after he hit that girl, he drove away like she was nothing."

"He got out," Evelyn breathed. "He checked on her. She was too far gone. He couldn't help her."

"He never did any such thing. He stopped for a second, but then he took off again. Told me he'd lose his career, his wife, his house. He said it wasn't his fault. She'd been in the middle of our lane. That much was true. But I tried to make him turn around. I tried. I swear."

Juliette was crying, finally. Her face crumpling into sobs. "Maybe we could have helped her. Maybe she was still alive. But he said I'd lose everything too. My job and husband and kids. I didn't know what to do."

"No, it was you," Evelyn whispered, but even she didn't believe it now. She remembered the way Juliette had jerked away from Gary that night, snarling, "Don't touch me." She'd been furious. Horrified. Disgusted.

Juliette groaned. "I think about that poor girl every day. I think about what I did, what I didn't do, and I wish I could go back and change everything. So if you want to go to the police, just go. I'll tell them everything."

One of her kids squealed. Juliette's reddened eyes moved to the swings as more tears spilled over. "I'm sorry," she whispered. "My poor babies. I'm so sorry."

Evelyn reached out, not sure what her hand was doing. She might have hit Juliette then. Slapped her. Grabbed her silky blond hair and thrown her to the ground. But her fingers only wrapped around Juliette's arm. "Are you telling me the truth?"

"Yes."

Evelyn gave her a hard shake, and Juliette just let herself be shaken. "Do you swear? *Do you swear?*"

"It's the truth. I swear. I'm sorry. It's the truth. Go to the police. Maybe it will be better for all of us. Maybe I'll be able to live with it. Finally."

Yes. It was true. Even Evelyn knew. It all made so much more sense than what Gary had told her. He was the bad guy here. The predator. The heartless monster. This woman looked as if she might dissolve into nothing very soon.

And Evelyn, who'd been so self-righteously invested in doing the *right* thing, wasn't the least bit interested in justice for Kaylee. Because she wasn't going to do anything at all.

She turned and left Juliette standing there. Broken, blameless Juliette. Gary had used her in the sickest, most immoral way. He'd traumatized her. And Evelyn had further degraded the woman by sleeping with her husband. And still, Evelyn just left her there, crying.

She walked to her car, drove home, stumbled into her house. She crawled up the stairs on hands and knees, but when she got to the second floor, she managed to stand and walk into her room. After locking the door, she slipped into her bathroom and dropped to sit on the cool tile.

She had a dozen nearly empty prescription bottles in the bottom drawer on her side of the bathroom. When she emptied them all out, she laid the pills on the floor and counted them. Twenty-two. Twenty-two plus a few more in the bottle in her nightstand if she needed them. But twenty-two sleeping pills would do it, surely. The nightstand was very far away. She didn't think she'd make it there and back.

Staring at the pills, she thought idly that she couldn't put anything in her mouth that had been on the bathroom floor. But that was silly, wasn't it? Was she worried about germs? Worried about putting germs in her mouth right before she killed herself?

Laughing, she wiped snot and tears from her face. All these weeks of seeing herself as the victim, but she wasn't the victim at all. She was the villain in this story. The one who should have known better. Gary's infidelity had freed a demon inside her, as if she'd been waiting her whole life to lie and cheat and steal and ruin lives. She'd become a stalker, a cheater, a liar, and an accessory to more than one crime.

And if Evelyn needed further proof that she was a worthless excuse for a human being, the only thing she truly cared about was that she could never have Noah. He was lost to her. He would never love her now. Never.

How was she supposed to live without him? What had she even thought about before him? He was in her bones now. In her womb and her mouth and her mind. Even when she'd imagined she only had to wait a little while longer, it had felt impossible to not be near him. And now? Now he was gone forever, and she couldn't go on.

She loved him. She needed him. Or was it just more sickness in her? More obsession, and evil, and dirtiness?

"Oh, God," she groaned as the pain welled up and spilled out of her mouth in a wail. *"Oh, God!"*

Curling onto the floor, she screamed out her pain. She screamed and screamed until her voice cracked and faded and she could only weep, her arms wrapped tight around her body as if the touch of her own awful hands could help anything. But she had to hold on. She had to hold tight or she'd explode. This would all be over. Done.

But wasn't that what she wanted? To be done?

"Yes," she whispered, pressing her face into the tile. Her lips spread over the hard, slick surface. "Yes," she grunted out. She wanted to be dead. There'd be no living with this pain. It was impossible to imagine.

She sat up and tried to gather the pills her body had swept around the floor. When she could only find nineteen, she panicked a little, but soon enough she found that three had scooted under the rug near her feet.

She lined them up again and stared at them. Would she vomit if she took them all at once? Maybe she could take them with an antacid to soothe her stomach, but might that keep her body from absorbing the pills? Much worse than dying would be almost dying and then having to face it all again with everyone watching.

She didn't want attention. She just wanted blankness. Forever. She picked up the first pill. Put it on her tongue. Swallowed it past her aching throat. She was good at taking pills. She did it every night. That was something people could say about her when they sat around gossiping at her funeral. "You know, she always was good at taking pills."

She swallowed a second pill and a third. Her throat closed a little on the fourth one, like a body would strain for air even when you didn't want to rise from the bottom of a pool. She forced the capsule down.

The fifth pill was still stuck in her throat when a bang from outside startled her. Coughing, she looked toward the window, worried that Cameron was home. But the sound of a diesel engine shook through the windowpane, and she realized it was only the garbage truck working its way through the neighborhood.

Not Cameron. Not her husband. Not the police. Just a garbage truck, as if everything were normal and fine. As if life could just go on.

She looked back to the pills, but it had taken only that one moment to break her concentration, and now she was shaking. Her entire body trembled with horror.

What had she done? Cameron would come home. He'd come home and find a dead mother waiting for him. He'd live his whole life with it. Wondering why. Why she'd done it, why she'd left him. She couldn't do that to her baby.

Shaking her head, she spit the fifth pill in her hand and cried again, her swollen eyes burning from the salt now. "No, no, no. I can't. I can't."

She wanted to be dead. She deserved it. But Cameron didn't. He was a good boy. He'd be a fine man. He deserved a happy life and a mother who at least pretended to be decent.

The remaining pills glowed in pretty colors against the dark tile.

New Evelyn had had so many dreams. She'd been strong, independent, and proud. She'd been sure of herself. Sure of what was right in the world. Sure of her body and her heart. New Evelyn had meant to embrace life and be something better.

But had she been real? Or had she only been the horrid imaginings of Evelyn's twisted mind?

Maybe she'd been old Evelyn the whole time. Old, stupid, worthless Evelyn, who'd built a life around a husband and son and didn't want more than that because other lives were so complicated, weren't they?

People had affairs and got divorced and made stupid, selfish decisions that ruined families and sent their kids to therapy. Not Evelyn. Never Evelyn.

People had dreams and took risks, and those risks destroyed lives. Evelyn didn't destroy lives for the sake of her dreams. That was reckless. Rude. Selfish.

Maybe she could just go back to that. Have her old life. Calm down and carry on, pretend Gary was a man she could love, keep Cameron safe and happy.

Her stomach rolled. Evelyn pushed to her knees and crawled quickly toward the toilet. The edges of the tiles dug into her kneecaps, but she kept moving.

Crouched over the toilet, she stuck all her fingers into her mouth, pushing until she gagged. It wasn't difficult. Her body knew it had been betrayed. As she vomited, her vision went blurry with tears, but everything was suddenly clear to her.

She couldn't let Gary win. She couldn't. She wasn't nothing. She wasn't old and worthless and stupid. And if she'd lost her mind, she could get it back. It was somewhere waiting. She'd find it. She'd make this right. For herself. For Juliette. For Kaylee.

She coughed and spit out the last of the vomit. When she opened her eyes, she carefully counted each pill shimmering beneath the water and the liquid remnants of the day's stomach acid. Four pills. Plus the one clutched in her fist.

Laying her forehead against the toilet seat, she sobbed out a mixture of relief and fear. The pills had been the simpler solution. But now . . . God. Now.

It had been so much easier to imagine being brave when she'd thought Noah might love her. The idea of being brave alone seemed nearly impossible. It was all up to her. Just her. It always had been.

She swiped toilet paper over her mouth and rose to her feet. Then she picked up each pill from the floor and carried them to the toilet to flush away. They swirled and bobbed and disappeared. Two of them clung stubbornly to the bottom of the bowl, so she flushed again. She didn't toss the ones in her nightstand, though. She'd need them to sleep. She'd need them for a very long time.

Watching herself in the mirror, she stripped out of her creased and rumpled clothing. She stared at her breasts and belly and pubic hair. This body had loved him. Noah. This body had loved Gary too. It had betrayed her and misled her, but someday she'd forgive it. Maybe someday she could even forgive herself.

It was five thirty when she emerged from the shower, her skin raw and red from scrubbing. Evelyn put her wet hair in a bun and pulled on yoga pants and a sweatshirt. She piled the empty pill bottles back in the drawer, tidied up the bathroom, and walked slowly downstairs.

When she saw the mess left in the kitchen from this morning's breakfast, she pushed up the oversize sleeves of her shirt and washed the dishes. When her sister texted her, Evelyn texted right back with a funny smiley face, its tongue sticking out sideways.

She took out the recycling, set the table, and finally, called to order Chinese food. They hadn't had it in months. Cameron would be over the moon. He loved chicken lo mein so much.

Grabbing a glass and a bottle of white wine from the fridge, Evelyn nodded at the pretty scene she'd set. The kitchen looked better than it had in weeks. Homey and warm.

Cameron and Gary came home at almost the same time, Cameron's hair still wet from practice. The Chinese food arrived minutes later. Evelyn poured another glass of wine, and she and Cameron discussed the team's chances in the state meet this weekend. They didn't expect to place, but Cameron still seemed cheerful about it. He was competitive, but he'd never been a sore loser. More evidence that maybe Evelyn had done something right in her life.

As for Gary, he made a meal out of fried rice and a few steamed vegetables, but he didn't complain as he usually did when she ordered Chinese. Maybe he could sense the tension in the air. Maybe he could feel the force of something coming.

The pain was waiting for her. Evelyn knew that. It was upstairs in her room, in her bed, lying in the faint outline of Evelyn's body in the mattress. It would live there with her for years. Maybe for decades. But she somehow managed to laugh with Cameron over the awful pun war he and his friends had waged with each other in English class. She even met Gary's smile once, accidentally. A last, lovely family dinner.

When Cameron finally excused himself to do homework, Gary packed up the leftovers and took the dirty dishes to the sink.

She almost felt sorry for him in that moment. He looked so unsuspecting. She could feel the weakness in his ignorance. It came off him in waves. He believed the worst had passed. He thought he'd gotten away with it.

He was wrong.

CHAPTER 30
BEFORE

Mr. Noah Whitman. An elusive man, but she'd finally found him.

She'd checked for a Noah Whitman or any Noah who followed Juliette, of course, but he hadn't existed. Either he didn't follow his wife on Facebook (interesting) or he wasn't signed up.

But this morning she got off Facebook and tried a new search. It yielded the typical hundreds of hits to online phone directories all across the country. But when she added the name of Juliette's suburb to the search, she found something likely. A Noah Whitman in the area. Triumph crawled up her spine and tightened her scalp. This was him.

And then she stumbled across an honest-to-goodness surprise. Noah Whitman was the owner and manager of an art gallery. The Whitman Gallery. And not only did the Whitman Gallery have a Facebook page that Juliette followed, but there was a whole website there for Evelyn to explore. Noah Whitman's picture was on the front page, and he was the same man from Juliette's family photos. Bingo.

So . . . Juliette was married to a man who loved art. How horrifically ironic. Evelyn had been a painter once, long ago. Their lives were a disgusting spiderweb of connections.

The Saturday night with her sister had managed to tame some of Evelyn's sick interest in Juliette's life, but it came roaring back as she paged through the Whitman Gallery's collection. If he hadn't fallen prey to Juliette Whitman's perfect-damsel routine, Evelyn might have respected this man. He had good taste in art, if nothing else. How had he loved a woman like Juliette enough to marry her?

Evelyn could find out. His gallery was just a short drive away. It was closer than Juliette's school. And Evelyn didn't have to worry that he'd recognize her. Surely he knew little about his wife's psychiatrist and even less about her affair. Evelyn could go browse through his gallery and get a feel for him.

Then again, Sharon was right. Evelyn needed to pull herself up by her bootstraps and move on with her life. If she wanted to stay with Gary, she needed to work at it. Make herself happy again. She couldn't keep indulging this obsession.

And she wouldn't. After today. She'd promised her sister she'd give all this up on Monday, but she hadn't said what *time* on Monday.

Still, she wouldn't put off all of Sharon's advice.

She showered, shaved, put on makeup and perfume. She even took the time to blow out her long brown hair, pleased that even though she hadn't gotten it colored since February, there wasn't too much gray. She was lucky in that, at least.

Instead of putting on the sweats she'd been living in, Evelyn dressed in real clothes, and she felt better, just as promised. She really did.

It didn't hurt that the only nice clothes that fit right now were a black pencil skirt and a red blouse. The skirt had been one of those ill-advised, surely-I'll-fit-into-this-soon purchases she'd made years ago. Her hope was realized at long last. It fit perfectly.

Unwilling to pair her new power outfit with flats or sandals, she dug her nicest pair of black pumps out of her shoe pile and slipped them on.

Her stomach rumbled, and Evelyn was shocked to realize she was hungry. Starving, actually. The twisting of her stomach felt foreign after so long with no appetite. The cream cheese and bagels she'd bought for Cameron a few days ago suddenly sounded like manna. After adding a swingy little set of earrings to her outfit, she rushed downstairs to eat.

She felt excited. Excited about this one last little bout of spying, yes, but more excited about moving forward. She didn't have to be a victim forever. She could choose to be happy. Choose to let go of some of this awful fury.

Taking her toasted bagel to the desk, she wrote an email to Gary.

> *Please take another look at these therapists so we can choose one. I don't think we should put it off. In fact, I'll move your stuff back into the bedroom today. I love you.*

She would never forget what he'd done. She'd never feel good about this secret. In fact, just typing *I love you* made her gut burn. But maybe, with time, she could learn to forgive.

She'd worked on the puzzle of his affair for far too long, trying to solve it, sure that she could. But the truth was, even if she never truly solved it, she had a clearer picture now. A hint of an understanding. Just one more piece, and surely she'd be satisfied.

The mysterious Noah Whitman awaited.

NOW

Strange that it was possible to regret something so completely and yet miss it every day. But she did miss it. Desperately. She missed the anticipation of seeing him. The possibility of pleasure. The yearning. The sweet ache.

She missed Noah's scent and taste. Missed his words. The need in his eyes. Even the smell of paint was enough to send her spiraling sometimes, and she'd stumble for the shower to weep and weep beneath the hot spray of water.

It hurt to not be with him. Her organs and skin and bones protested. They wanted to reshape themselves into the woman she'd been with Noah, and now they had nowhere to go. Evelyn was just starting to settle them down.

Out of everything she'd been able to set right in the past eleven months, her affair with Noah was the one transgression she could never correct. All she could do was leave him. Every day. Walk away and leave him behind.

Each morning she'd woken and told herself she would not check Facebook. She would not text. She would not call or drive past or even fantasize about what could have been.

She had no idea if he and Juliette had confessed to each other or if they'd managed to find happiness again in their marital deception. After everything, she owed them privacy now. So she left Noah behind just as she'd left Gary.

At long last it was finally getting easier, if only because she'd put them both a thousand miles behind her.

Letting go of the steering wheel, she tipped her head back against the headrest and took a deep breath. This was a new day. A new start.

After locking up the Range Rover, she threaded her way through the other vehicles to a stairway. Once she reached the second level, she leaned against the metal railing that overlooked the sea.

Waves glinted in the afternoon glare, flashing light and dark and light again. She raised her face to the spring air, still cool despite the bright sun. Closing her eyes, she let it soak into her. She'd worn no sunscreen, hat, or glasses. She didn't want anything between her and the light. The wind tossed her hair with wild, whipping hands, and it was all she could feel for a long while.

When a seabird screamed overhead, two others screamed back, and she opened her eyes to watch them hover on the air above her. They looked nothing like blackbirds, and she felt thankful for that. Maybe out here she'd never see a blackbird again.

A ship's horn blew. The metal deck dipped and rose. Evelyn needed to call her lawyer before they got too far from shore.

Gary had finally confessed to the authorities.

Not willingly, of course. Evelyn had left him no choice. She'd told him if he didn't confess, she'd tell the whole truth and he'd go to jail and lose everything. If he went to the authorities himself, she'd simply file for divorce, and he would lose half. He'd wisely chosen to lose half. Well, half plus a little more. The settlement with the Brighams was to be signed today.

Evelyn dialed her lawyer. "Is it done?" she asked, skipping all the niceties.

"His attorney called five minutes ago. It's done."

Evelyn slumped against the railing in relief. "They agreed to two hundred thousand dollars?"

"Yes. Both your husband and the Brighams have signed."

"It's over," she whispered into the wind.

"Not quite. The divorce will take a few more days to finalize, but aside from that, yes, it's over."

Evelyn wasn't worried about the divorce. She'd finalized that in her mind months ago. She'd asked for a lot, but not as much as she could have. And she'd let Gary take what he needed: his reputation, his work, his freedom.

She hadn't done that for him. She'd done that for Cameron, for Juliette, for Noah, though none of them would ever know.

That day on the floor of her bathroom, she'd given up completely, but somehow that was when the answer had become so clear. She'd dropped every defense, every lie she'd told herself about being strong, and that had freed her mind.

Because she hadn't been strong. Not then. She'd been an animal willing to chew off limbs to escape the trap that had snapped around her. She'd been eager to destroy lives just to avoid making a choice that scared her. She could still feel that last pill stuck in her throat, the dig of its edges lifting the veil from her thinking.

She hadn't been strong, but she could be.

She'd told Gary in no uncertain terms that as soon as Cameron graduated, they'd begin divorce proceedings. And as soon as Cameron left for college, Gary would go to the police.

He'd balked, of course. Panicked. Begged. Raged. But Evelyn had leverage that couldn't be dislodged: she had the truth.

It had been a difficult needle to thread, protecting Juliette Whitman from further pain while bringing the Brigham family some peace, but Evelyn had managed it. She'd agreed not to reveal that Gary had been sleeping with a patient if he would take sole responsibility for the accident.

Responsibility, of course, was too strong a word. It was Gary, after all. There had been hours and hours of meetings with a criminal defense attorney before Gary had even agreed. His lawyer had negotiated a plea deal with the district attorney's office. That part had been surprisingly easy. A rich white man with no criminal record willing to plead guilty to not reporting an accident? The police had already stopped investigating the case. Gary's confession was an unexpected gift dropped in their laps.

He'd been too resentful of Evelyn to tell her the details, but she'd gleaned enough to know that Gary had admitted only to hitting someone or something. He'd claimed he thought it was a deer until weeks later when he'd heard about Kaylee's death. He'd been scared to go to the police, his attorney had said, but he'd finally worked up to it out of the goodness of his heart.

In the end, his driver's license had been suspended for six months, and he'd attended a four-hour class on defensive driving.

During civil settlement discussions with yet more attorneys, Evelyn had said she knew nothing about any of it. She didn't remember that night. They'd never discussed it. A lie, yes, but the last lie she meant to tell for a good, long while.

It wasn't a perfect solution. She'd made Gary promise he'd never victimize another patient, but she couldn't be sure. Still, she couldn't turn him in. That was Juliette's story to tell . . . or to never tell.

Evelyn shook off the memories. "You've got my new address," she told her attorney. "When everything is finalized with the divorce, send the documents there. The money can be wired to my account."

Cash was a little tight, but even that felt good, because she'd used all her savings for a down payment on a new house. An investment. A beginning.

She was finally starting to find bits of herself she'd lost years ago. Most of those pieces had nothing to do with men or lust or marriage.

They were hers and hers alone. And in finding them, she discovered she was no longer angry. Not at Gary. Not at Juliette or Noah. Not even at herself. Whatever she thought had been taken from her, those were parts she'd given away willingly. She'd offered love or caring or sacrifice, and if she'd wanted more in return from Gary or Noah or family or friends, it had been her job to ask.

But she'd never asked, because she'd been the easy path. For everyone. She supported Gary through his residency and early career. She cooked his meals, cleaned his house, raised his child. She surprised him with little treats or trips when he was stressed. She put his clothes highest in the dresser so he wouldn't have to bend down to get his socks in the morning. She made holidays special for their family and friends. She smiled at strangers to brighten their days and apologized to people when they bumped into *her*. She took on the volunteer work that no one wanted to do, filled gaps that needed filling, tried to make sure everyone had fun at parties when she wasn't even hosting.

And who had ever done that for her? Who made her life easier while she was busy being easy for everyone else?

No one. There'd been no need. She'd never asked.

She even knew why. It was right there, so obvious to her and probably to everyone else. She'd chosen a life she felt she didn't belong to. A neat, wealthy world of country clubs and nuclear families. A life she'd only known from TV shows and movies. She'd thought she needed to earn her way in. So she'd worked hard at it.

It had been no different with Noah. She'd believed he was too handsome for her. Too cool. Too exciting and forbidden and sexy. So she'd made herself easy to love.

And boy, had she been easy. The path of least resistance for a brief moment in Noah's life. And when that path had gotten sticky and complicated, it had been time for a new one. She hadn't been worth the work.

He hadn't claimed to love her. He'd never even called her beautiful. Not once. Not when he'd eased off her dress or kissed her neck or slid inside her. He'd never breathed, "You're so beautiful, Evelyn," not even when she'd stretched out on the bed and bravely offered him her whole body.

Because even she hadn't believed she was beautiful. She'd only been easy to talk to, easy to get, easy to please.

But she could forgive herself all of that now. She'd made those choices out of fear, and she wasn't afraid anymore. From now on, if something was important to her, she would demand it. Because the truth was that she belonged anywhere she wanted to be, and she was beautiful just for being brave.

The sun shifted around her as the ferry turned. The roar of the engines dropped to a lower pitch. Evelyn returned to her vehicle, and a few minutes later she was nervously easing it off the ferry and back onto dry land. That had been the most stressful part of the trip so far, guiding her SUV and rented trailer onto the bobbing ferry. But she'd have to get used to it. At the very least, there'd be a big trip to the mainland for groceries once or twice a month.

That was why she'd kept the Range Rover, but she had fantasies of zipping around in a little electric car someday. Maybe in a year or two, when she was more sure of what she'd need.

The cars made a slow procession down the ferry road, then Evelyn turned left and was free. A new place. A new start.

She'd read online that all the cells in a person's body replaced themselves over time. Taste buds once a week, skin cells every month, blood cells every six weeks or so.

If that was true, then no one had ever touched this body. No one had run a hand over this waist, or stroked this skin, or slid a touch down this spine. No one had been inside her, and these hands had never caressed a man. Even her child was a separate person now. No part of the womb that had held him was still within her.

She was her own person now. Her own being. Old and new selves together, all her strengths and weaknesses combined into someone she couldn't wait to know.

Following the directions sent by her Realtor, she turned onto a narrow, pitted road and eased her vehicle up a hill. At the top were rows of little cottages. She spotted hers right away.

She'd bought it sight unseen, though she wasn't sure that saying applied in the modern age. There'd been dozens of pictures, after all, and a detailed inspection report. But the gray wood and white trim were instantly recognizable, even among the other similar structures. Evelyn pulled into the gravel driveway and jumped out to race up the front steps.

The key was under a little flower pot, just where the Realtor had promised. The flowers were dead, but she would fix that soon enough.

Opening the door, Evelyn found that the house was exactly as represented. Nothing fancy or new, just a tiny cottage with only a sliver of a view of the sea. But it was hers. And the living room and kitchen were exactly as described. *Homey* if she was being generous, *run-down* if she wasn't. But there were two bedrooms, so Cameron could visit from college anytime. Or Sharon could come for a week with her kids every summer. There was a table for six, more than she needed. And there was the deck.

Evelyn walked outside to take in her new backyard.

The stained wood of the deck needed scraping and painting. The one tree on her property was half dead and would require trimming at the least, and the sliver of view of the water was just that: a sliver. But she could hear the ocean and smell the sea, and the sandy path at the bottom of her stairs led right to a trail to a rocky beach.

She breathed in. Let it fill her. New lungs. New air. She closed her eyes, but the promise of it all made her dizzy, and she had to open them again.

Another seabird floated above her. A tern, she thought, and suddenly she needed to see the ocean. *Her* ocean. The one she planned to walk to every morning. The one she planned to paint. It would be her companion here, and she should meet it right away.

She was halfway down the stairs when a voice called out. Looking around in confusion, Evelyn finally spotted an older couple coming up the trail with a tiny dog.

"Hello!" the woman called. "Hello!"

"Hi!" she yelled back, jogging down the rest of the steps to meet them.

"You must be the new neighbor."

"I am!"

"Oh, we're so excited. Outside of summer we hardly see anyone new, as you can imagine. And there are only a thousand of us here year-round. Are you going to live here year-round?"

"Yes—"

"Oh, that's lovely. So lovely. We're the Harleys, and we're only three houses down. Are you moving in today?"

"Yes, I just got off the ferry, and—"

"Well, I'm Win, and this is Bob. Are you retired? Most of us are retired, but the—"

"For godssake, Win," the man finally interrupted. "Let the woman speak. I'm Bob Harley." He offered a hand, his gray mustache trembling in the breeze. "Welcome to Block Island."

She took his hand, feeling as if she were shaking on a very important deal. "It's nice to meet you," she said. "I'm Evie Farrington. I'm an artist."

And maybe she really was.

About the Author

Victoria Helen Stone is the nom de plume for *USA Today* bestselling author Victoria Dahl. After publishing more than twenty-five novels, she is now taking a turn toward the darker side of genre fiction. Born and educated in the Midwest, she finished her first manuscript just after college. In 2016, the American Library Association awarded her the prestigious Reading List Award for outstanding genre fiction. Having escaped the plains of her youth, she now resides with her family in a small town high in the Rocky Mountains, where she enjoys hiking, snowshoeing, and not skiing (too dangerous).